BROKEN DOVE

C. Lymari

TO: Victoria

BROKEN DOVE

DANCE OF THE DEAD
BOOK 2

C. LYMARI

C. Lymari

Editing: Rumi Khan

Proofing: Proofing: One Love Editing

Cover: TRC Designs

ALSO BY C. LYMARI

(Dark age gap/daddy romance)

Broken Dove

(Dark Romance/Age gap)

Standalones

For Three Seconds

(Forbidden/ Sports Romance)

Falcon's Prey

(A Dark bodyguard Romance)

In The Midst Of Chaos

(MC dark romance)

Gilded Cage

(Dark Fairytale Retelling)

Press Play

(Romantic Suspense/Thriller)

Boneyard Kings Series (with Becca Steele)

Merciless Kings

Vicious Queen

Ruthless Kingdom

(*Reverse Harem*)

Bonus Stories

Hollow Vow

(Halloween special)

Home Sweet Home

(Homecoming prequel)

Clymaribooks.com/bonus

AUTHOR'S NOTE

Broken Dove is a dark romance. If you have read my books
before, you know they can be triggering. Although it is in
dual POV, it is told mainly from Summer's perspective, so it
might seem a little confusing at first.
For more information on triggers, you can go to my website:
clymaribooks.com/triggerwarnings

Enjoy the crazy ride.
Love,
Claudia.

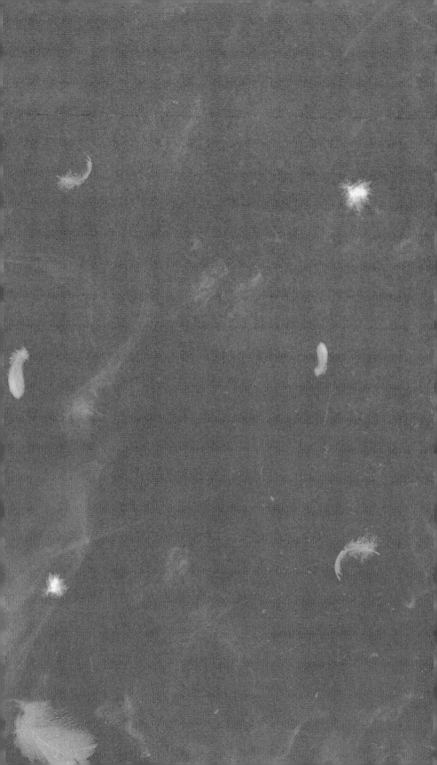

BROKEN DOVE

Welcome to The House of Silence

I lived my life with darkness all around me.
Everywhere I went, I needed constant guidance.
I listened.
And obeyed.
I learned to dance so I could be freed from my gilded cage.
A dove who could not find its way home.
Then one day, I met Luke.
He made me feel happy—safe. Mending my wings so I
could soar once again.
All the while biding his time to rip me to shreds.
Because, at one time, I belonged to *La Casa Del Silenzio*.
If their whores weren't blind, they were mute.
Too bad for everyone, I could still speak the truth.
With him at my side, I could conquer my past.
But I don't think either of us expected my wings to finally
snap...

Here's to finding beauty in our scars.

FOREWORD

"Believe nothing you hear, and only half that you see."—
Edgar Allan Poe

PART 1

Winter

PREFACE

Summer

My heart once ached to see the wonders of the world. To scour the earth until I couldn't go on anymore. I was young with dreams and a full life ahead of me. Now I was scared to go out alone, with nothing but my shadow keeping me whole.

But I guess that was what growing up did to you, right? That fearlessness we were born with, the one that made us climb trees and ride our bikes at top speeds, diminished with each passing year. The price of growing up was not aging but losing ourselves to the fear of living.

When I was young, things were so simple. Right and wrong were as clear as night and day, but the older I got, the more I realized that the world had shades of gray.

If I could describe the man next to me, it would be just that. He wasn't nice, and he wasn't kind; *he just was.* The kind of man that existed for himself and no one else. The kind that was selfish and rude but would do anything in his power to protect those who were brave enough to withstand the trials of his affection.

Like salt to the sea, flowers to spring, he was a part of me. Even now, as he held my hand, I could tell he was holding back. Every time I took one step forward, he took three steps back, and at this rate, I wasn't sure if I would ever be on the same page. It was like he was fighting a war on all ends.

"You look beautiful," he said, and I had no doubt he was beginning to notice my discomfort.

My smile was weak, but I believed him.

It was in the way he stopped breathing when I walked into the room earlier. The way his hands touched the tiny tendrils of hair that framed my face. The delicate way his finger traced the hollow of my throat and then dipped down to my collarbone with a barely there graze of my chest.

Even though I had spent the last few years prancing around in tights and a tutu, I had not felt as exposed as I did now because being naked didn't count. I spent the better part of my childhood catering to old men and women who liked to have pretty little things to look at, touch, or feel. You could say I had been desensitized to my sexuality.

It was a weapon. Something to be exploited.

I knew my body, but I wasn't in love with it. I thought I would never feel desire, yet being here with him made me feel like a woman for the first time in forever.

The dress I wore was off the shoulder, formfitting lace that flared out mid-thigh.

It was long enough to hide the fact that I was not wearing heels. There was only so much trust I could give out; all of it was now on the man next to me. For the next few hours, he would be my crutch, and I didn't think he realized just how much I was giving in by allowing him that position.

He squeezed my hand as if to assure me that he would be my strength.

"What's wrong, my dove?" He shifted, getting closer to me.

"Nothing," I lied. "So, where are we going?"

Luke used the opportunity to lift me and sit me on his lap.

My stupid heart started to beat faster. The intimacy we shared had not been like this. It was felt but not seen. It touched your heart without needing anything physical or more concrete.

This time, it was me sucking in a breath as he wrapped an arm around my waist. I tipped my chin toward him, wondering how he looked at me. I rested my head on his shoulder and bit my lip when I felt the evidence I had been hoping for.

He was hard for me.

He wanted me.

And that proposal I had made in the beginning was now haunting me. I ached to lean up and touch him.

I wanted to push past his boundaries and obliterate every wall he had set up in my wake. My fingers came to his throat and lightly grazed the way his artery throbbed. Moving them, I traced his Adam's apple and felt his long swallow.

Daring to be bold, I moved my fingers higher, and he went still beneath me. That arm that was wrapped around me was like a steel band, cautioning me without words. His fingers dug into my hips as a final warning.

I ignored this.

I knew pain and what he would dish out would not hurt

me. A thin line existed between pain and pleasure, love and hate, because they were the same side of a coin. All I knew was the negatives, and I didn't care what I had to do to get the positives.

My heart was now beating fast. It was like a tune of drums spurring me on as my fingers glided to his jaw.

It was sharp—strong. The skin was smooth in some areas, with a hint of prickliness in others. Before overthinking it, I leaned in and kissed the underside of his jaw.

Dull pain bloomed in my hip from where he now dug his fingers in deeper, as if trying to steady himself, prepare to pull me away, or brand his hand there so I wouldn't go anywhere.

"What are you doing?" he hissed.

When I pulled back, he relaxed a bit. I ached to see all of him, but I didn't want to push him. Things lost beauty when they were not freely given. And I knew better than anyone what kind of scars the things you were forced to do left on you. They were not only physical, but they went skin-deep. I could feel them with every breath I took. With every trip down memory lane, they were there, always with their arms wide open, ready to grab me in their clutches and sink me back in.

I didn't reply, for he knew and remembered from our past conversation what my intentions were. All I wanted was a small part of him. Even if he didn't realize it, he had stolen a part of me already, so it was only fair I got something in return as well.

With my thumb, I traced his lips. They were smooth, the bottom one a tad bit bigger than the top one, with a wide and defined Cupid's bow. I liked the feel of them on my lips, and I couldn't help but remember the way they felt moving between my legs.

I shifted in his lap, trying to find some relief from the feelings he had awoken in me.

He parted his lips, and I was prepared for him to tell me it was enough, but instead, he took my thumb into the cavern of his mouth. He waited until it was all the way in, then wrapped his teeth around it and began pulling back.

"Luke," I moaned as the feeling between my legs intensified.

He swirled his tongue against the tip of my thumb before wrapping his mouth around the digit and letting it out with an audible pop.

"We are here," he groaned with regret.

The door opened, and he sat me astride him while he wrapped the coat over my shoulders.

Luke got out of the car first, then took my hand and guided me out. As soon as my foot touched the ground, he had a possessive hold on me.

"I won't let you fall," he promised.

I nodded as he began to lead the way.

"Will you tell me where we are now?"

"Soon," he told me as he led us over a threshold.

The first thing that hit me was the smell. It was a mix of perfume, alcohol, and cigarettes.

My mouth went dry.

It couldn't be, right?

This should have smelled like a bar, but it was far too classy for that. The cigars were only the best, alcohol top-shelf, and the perfume and cologne designer.

Although I said I felt nothing and nothing mattered, that was because I thought I had escaped my first cage and the flames that had branded me would never touch me again.

The murmur of people stopped the moment Luke and I

stepped fully into the room, their soft gasps enough to let me know we had been unexpected visitors.

"Lucas," a familiar voice drawled, and it came from directly next to me.

I jolted with fear, trying to wrap my brain around it so I could pinpoint the place and time I had once heard the voice, although I already knew the answer all too well. I almost made myself believe that the last time I'd heard it had been a fluke.

"Run!"

My mother's chilling voice rang, sinking into every pore of me, and instead of spurring me into action, it made me immobile with fear.

"Mamma," I screamed as I ran toward her. The man who had her stopped and looked at me, and I sucked in a breath when I recognized his face.

Tears welled in my eyes as I really took in and saw the way he was holding on to my mom. He wasn't helping her. He was the reason why she was in pain. His hands were on her neck, and my mom pleaded for me, but I didn't know what to do.

They were my world, but I was beginning to realize that perhaps it wasn't big enough for both of them.

Without thinking, I grabbed the first thing I could find. It was a container from the lab, a tray with tubes on it, and maybe I should have wondered why it was home and heeded my papà's caution never to touch it, but I just wanted to help in any way I could.

I threw it up, the contents spilling as it went. Screams echoed all around, and it wasn't until I gasped for air that I realized that the haunting sounds were coming from me.

My hands came to my face, and I couldn't even open my eyes from the pain. Someone rushed to me, and they tried to pick me up. They said words I did not care to hear. I needed to open my eyes. More than anything, I needed to get away. Since my eyes were closed, I couldn't see what I touched, but I pushed away from the arms trying to hold on to me.

"Fuck," the person roared.

"Mamma!" I yelled, but her answer never came.

With my eyes closed, I made my way through the house, knowing where everything was from memory.

I got knocked back when my body collided with someone.

"Where's your mom, little one?" I instantly recognized my padrino's voice.

As I gasped for air, I tried to beg him to help, but instead, he carried me away.

"We have to get out of here now," he rushed out. "He will kill you next."

As my heart broke, I could feel the pain of every jagged end that was currently shattering before me.

The chaos and the pain had lulled me to sleep. When I woke, everything was now black. A thundering voice echoed through every corner of where I was currently lying. If the devil had a voice, his would be it.

"Benvenuto nella Casa del Silenzio."

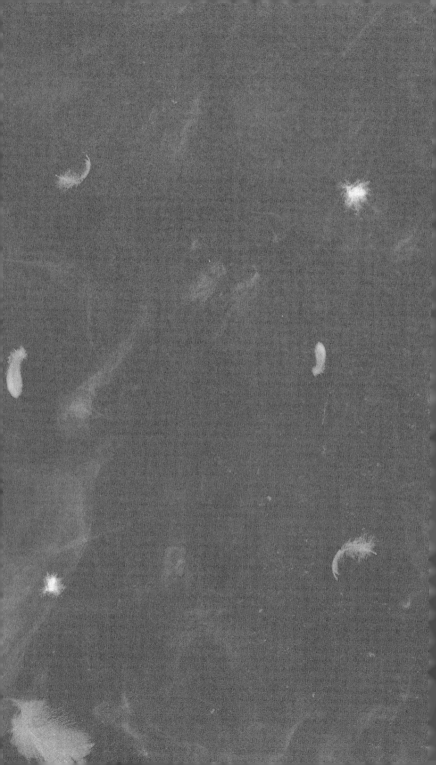

CLOSED EYES

You close your eyes so you won't see,
but those demons don't come out in the dark.
They exist, even if you don't blink.

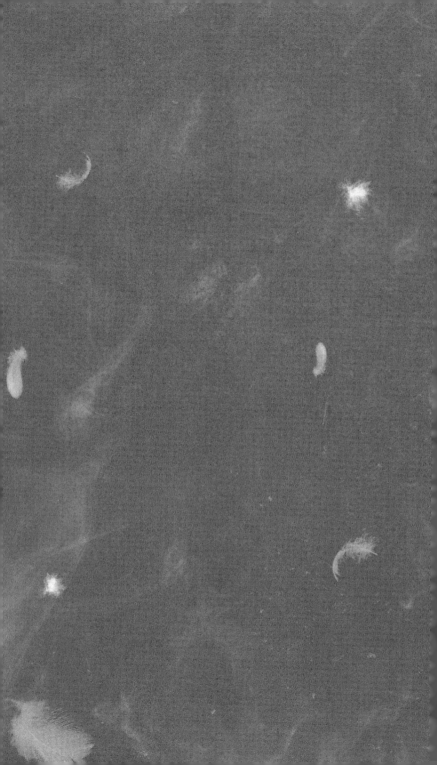

CHAPTER ONE

SUMMER

I USED TO BE A DANCER—NOT A VERY TALENTED ONE, but we all paid our dues somehow.

The only thing I remembered was the pain in my feet and the last flash of color as my sight evaded me. Those were the things that fueled me, that kept me going. For peace was just an illusion, and dreaming was for those who still saw life in all its vibrancy, no matter the good or the bad.

I was part of the *Danza dei Morti*, a renowned, hauntingly beautiful ballet act, or so I've heard. You didn't have to be talented for them to hire you—the main requirement was to be broken. Although the company did have talent, the prima ballerina was said to be death with the face of an angel. For you could mimic pain, sorrow, and anger, but unless you lived in horrors, you couldn't duplicate it.

And that was my life now—I was the chaos after the storm.

In this world, there needed to be a balance, and some people had to be at the end of that spectrum. You see, when I was young, I did a bad thing, but karma didn't wait a single second to claim me. She was fast and served her justice upon me.

Blood was thicker than water, and I let it slip through my fingers just as quickly.

"We have arrived," Nico Dos Santos announced.

Nico was the man who saved me from paying my dues on my back. He got broken girls and gave them a purpose. He took our broken wings and showed us how to soar. I guess I should be thankful because when he set us free, he made sure he found a place for me.

His last show ended with a bang—literally. To the world, he was dead. He and his prima ballerina were never to be heard from again. Except all of us knew the truth. After all, you couldn't kill the things that escaped hell, and Nico had been wandering this world with a purpose, so now I assumed he had found it.

The plane ride had been mostly silent. There wasn't much for us to talk about. Besides, his so-called daughter had come with us. I didn't mind her, but at times, she scared me. Since I was one of the last dancers to always clear out, I'd had more interaction with her throughout the years. She could be sweet one second, the next a total bitch.

Nico left her at the hotel while he dropped me off. I assumed this was for protection. You couldn't have two "dead" people prancing around.

I didn't ask questions. I did not care because, honestly, there wasn't much more left of the person I used to be. As long as I had a place at night to lay my head, some warmth, and food to fill my belly, that was more than enough for me. I could be in China, Buenos Aires, or New York, and it would all be the same to me. The days would drag on, and night would be all that remained.

We couldn't have it all in life. At one point, I had, and

look at how well that turned out. I took it as a lesson learned and stopped asking the world for things. Maybe someone had to pay for the sins of their fathers, and that was why life fucked us over extra hard.

"What time is it?" I asked as I stepped out of the car. As I figured out the terrain, my cane moved from side to side.

"Just after five," Nico let me know.

Okay, good. With the time difference and the jet lag, it wouldn't be rude to disappear to whatever room they gave me and just sleep it all away. With winter here, it meant the nights were longer. I might not be able to see, but I enjoyed the cold and the snow, even if I wasn't a fan of the ice.

People pitied those who couldn't see, but I pitied everyone who could—people with eyesight were often the blind ones. They relied on their vision for everything. They could smell something foul, yet they didn't believe it until they saw the evidence. They could hear screams and chaos erupting, yet they wouldn't start running until they saw the danger.

It wasn't that blind people had their other four senses heightened. It was that we learned to rely on all of them and didn't dull them like everyone else.

I walked side by side with my old ward so I could meet my new one. The place had to be huge, judging by the number of steps we had taken, and we had yet to reach the entrance.

My nose was cold when we reached the front door, and I smiled at the thought. If we had more time, I would have touched the tip. It was things like this I found joy in—the evidence of winter. The seasons didn't have to be seen to appreciate them—you had to feel them.

Like standing outside the first shower of spring, lying under the hot summer sun until it burned your skin, the wind and leaves of autumn, and the snowflakes in the winter.

I was so distracted that I didn't notice when the door opened.

"Luke, you look well," Nico greeted as he took a step forward. He knew I didn't like to be touched. He led, so it would be easier for me to follow him.

The first thing that hit me was the smell of cologne. My nose twitched as I took it in. It was strong, spicy, and masculine, masking the scent of menthol, but it wasn't all that bad.

I knew the person was next to me because I felt his presence. It was tall and imposing, like a force field. The verdict was still out if it were to pull me in or tell me to run, not that I could get very far anyway.

The other girls thought I was lucky because even when I landed in hell, I was already blind. I couldn't see any of the horrors that happened around us, but I sure as fuck could feel them.

With their eyes closed or wide open, they still had an advantage over me. They could see life in all its vibrancy: flowers, odd-shaped clouds, blue and gray skies, and that already was more than most of us had at one point. They could see their freedom, while I would always be stuck in a cage.

It was the same if my eyes were wide open or shut closed. It wasn't that I saw in black; everything was just *numb*. Like white noise that never went away—everything was blank. There were no colors, just pain.

I might not have seen my monsters, but I felt them. I smelled the alcohol on their breath as they whispered dirty words on my nape, the sharpness of their nails as they scratched my hips, and their violent thrusts as they let go of their demons between my legs. For you didn't have to see to feel pain. You didn't have to see to feel every part of you being broken as time passed.

"Luke, this is Summer. Summer, that is Luke to your left."

I turned my head to face him, and the moment I did, I heard the softest gasp leave the man's lips. I might not be able to see him, but the air in the room changed. The presence I felt earlier was near suffocating now.

"Interesting name," Luke murmured.

And God, his voice, it was smooth yet held a coarse hoarseness to it that made my skin shiver. It was unlike anything I had ever heard, but I stopped myself from telling him to speak some more.

My chin lifted defiantly at his words. Summer wasn't my real name; it was just the one I had chosen for myself.

My life was like summer once. It was bright and warm, I had everything, and then one mistake took it away. It might be fucked-up of me, but I liked to have that reminder follow me everywhere so I would never forget all the things that had to happen to get me where I was today.

Our choices defined us.

My choice had blinded me, but it had also woken me up.

"Cecilia," the man called out. "*Portala nella sua stanza.*"

My brow furrowed a bit. I mean, it shouldn't be all that surprising that the man was Italian; after all, Nico was as well. The place he had rescued me from had been in Italy. I didn't know if it was funny or cruel the way life worked.

When Cecilia approached, the first thing I noticed was the smell. She smelled like lilies, and there was something soothing about it.

After she collected my things, I guess she made a move

to grab me when Nico spoke. "She doesn't like to be touched," he told her in English, for my sake.

I could feel their stares coming from all sides, but I ignored it and instead turned to face Nico, the man who had taken me out of the hellhole I had been in. I was aware that this would be the last time I would feel his presence near me, and I waited to see if the pang of sadness would hit me, but just like always, it never did. Forming bonds had been a struggle for me, even before everything—something had been broken in me long before the devil found me.

"*Grazie.*" It was one word and the first time I had spoken in my native tongue for as long as I could remember. If he was surprised that I had kept this from him, I had no way of knowing.

This was the third time I had changed cages, and as long as it wasn't as bad as the first one I had ever had, I could live the rest of my days this way.

If you didn't have expectations, then there wouldn't be a chance for disappointment. Besides, I already knew that freedom always comes at a price.

As we walked, a scent caught my attention. The smell was fresh and sweet, and a melancholy feeling ran through me. I knew the word *flower*, but I couldn't recall them. Not the shapes, not the sizes—they were something that were long lost and forgotten, yet here I found myself reminiscing about them.

Being in a traveling ballet company didn't leave much room for exploring, just running around the globe but never far enough from your own demons.

"Welcome home," the maid said as she opened the door to what I assumed was my room.

I smiled bitterly at her.

Home was something I had destroyed all on my own.

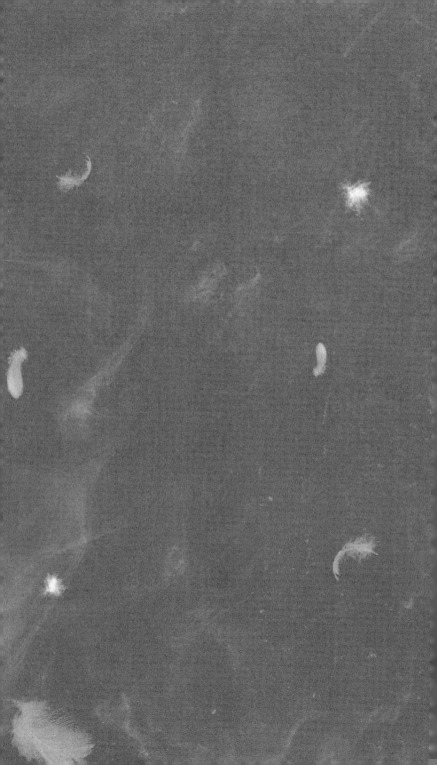

RUNNING

You run from the desires of your heart.
You run from the demons that haunt you at night.
Yet you feed them at every single chance you get.

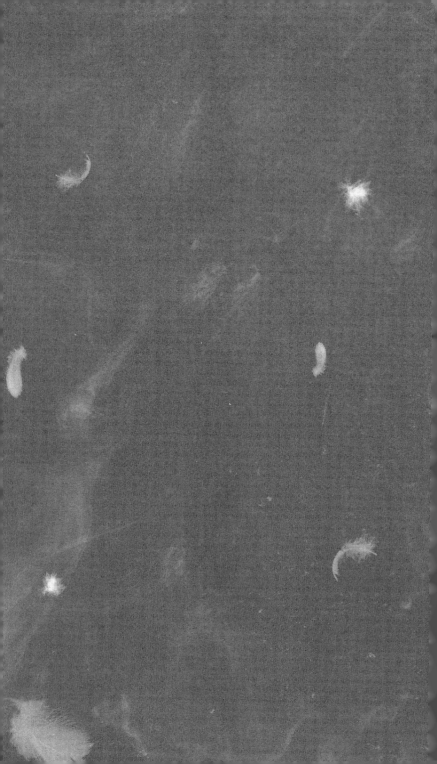

CHAPTER TWO

SUMMER

Blind people can dream; we don't dream in colors or shapes like others, or maybe we dream in colors that have yet to exist. So, there's no way to explain to a person who still has their vision how our dreams are as valid as theirs.

It wasn't often that I dreamed, but when it did happen, it left me feeling frightened and my hands sweaty, like I needed to wash them immediately. I could feel a sting in my eyes, but there was never anything there.

My heart was pounding as I woke up. I sat up immediately, a bit disorientated, and the first thing I did was touch my eyes. Like always, they felt wet. The only thing that was there was the scarring. Slowly, I put my hands down, moving them around my sides.

I was used to sleeping in beds where I could stretch my arms and touch the wall with one hand and the edge of the bed with another. This was maybe twice that size, and I felt like I was drowning in it.

It was by far the nicest bed I had ever lain in. The silks

were soft, the pillows fluffy, the covers warm. It was elevated, so getting on had been a bit of a struggle.

With the other girls, I was grateful to have a bedmate. It made cleaning more manageable, and if that wasn't possible, I was always glad to take the smallest room or the one they said had a shitty view.

The room was silent, but I knew a light must be on. Not because I could see it but because I could hear that faint murmur of electricity humming.

"Hello?" I asked, but no one answered.

I moved my hand until it made contact with my cane. My feet touched the cold floor, and then I got up so I could get a sense of the room. It never happened with the dance company, but before, men liked to play tricks on me. They wanted to know if I really couldn't see, to ensure their secrets would be safe with me.

Slowly, I made my way to the other end of the room, where Cecilia showed me where the bathroom was located. My cane moved around as my heart pounded heavily with each step I took.

Fear was a pattern of something that manifested over an unpleasant action or a single event that terrorized you. I didn't fear the dark, for you couldn't fear things you couldn't see, but I did fear the actions of men.

I told myself that Nico wouldn't have sold me off to someone who would harm me, and that gave me a sense of peace. When I got to the bathroom, I opened the faucet and splashed my face. The cold water felt divine on my hot skin. I might not have remembered my dreams, but the voices I heard lingered.

"*Zio.*"

The screams of my younger self followed me around. I couldn't remember him, but I knew he was my uncle, my hero, and the person I was terrified of. It was in these moments of weakness that my past tried to catch up to me. Prancing around the world did me no good when my demons decided to give chase.

When I woke up again, footsteps were coming toward me. I sat up immediately, my hand reaching for my cane, but as soon as the smell of lilies engulfed me, I relaxed a bit.

"Morning," I greeted as I stood up before the maid could come and help me.

She was quiet for a second before speaking, but I could feel her gaze on me, and I knew she had to be looking at my face. I quickly reached for the nightstand and put on my sunglasses.

"It's not safe to go wandering around at night," she told me softly, and the pity that always followed when people saw my face was evident in her tone—it beat the disgust.

"I didn't go anywhere," I replied, my mind immediately racing to what I had felt when I woke up.

Had someone been in here with me? I had stayed up, and not even a stir or a creak could be heard. Only the silence remained. Surely it wasn't the door, right? I made myself believe that whatever electricity was on had to be that way since the afternoon. I had just not picked up on it.

"Oh, the wind must have opened it," she muttered to herself before telling me it was time for breakfast.

The smell of lilies became stronger, and her presence was in front of me. Then, I jumped back when she touched me.

This seemed to make her hesitant if her sharp intake of breath was any indication.

"Would you like me to pick out your clothes?" she asked, her voice drifting toward the other end of the room, where I had remembered leaving my luggage.

She was trying to pick out my clothes as if I had not been doing it all on my own for years. What was next? Would she want to change me like a toddler? I gritted my teeth, trying to remain calm since I was a guest in this house, and I wasn't sure if I was also considered an intruder.

I lifted my chin in defiance and turned to where I assumed she was located.

"I can pick my own clothing."

She didn't say anything more. I thrived in awkward silence. People often started to fidget, their body language betraying them. I bet their eyes wandered around aimlessly, trying to find somewhere to focus and still their thoughts.

Cecilia put my luggage on the bed and hovered as my hands touched every piece of fabric I owned so I could figure out what I wanted to wear. It wasn't like it would be hard. All of my belongings fit into this bag. Some dancers had more. They had their own places when we were in the off-season, while others like me had been wandering. We were more than ready to run when the time came.

As soon as I had my selection, Cecilia touched my arm.

"Please don't touch me," I snapped. "You can guide me just fine with words."

"Of course." Her voice was lower, and the giddiness that had been there before was now gone.

A lump formed in my throat, and I couldn't explain why or how, but I figured I had a cotton mouth. There was no way feelings were coming to me after being stuck in an eternal winter. When I emerged from the bathroom, I thought she had left me, but with her words, she let me know she was by the door.

I used her steps as a guide to know where we were heading. The fresh smell was back, and I couldn't help but stop so I could keep inhaling.

"There's a greenhouse to the left," she told me.

"Can we go in there?"

My throat constricted as I realized the longing that came out with my question. When was the last time I asked for something? Longing and wanting things was something I had stopped myself from doing.

"After breakfast," she assured me.

The rest of the walk was silent as she guided me to the dining room. This time, she stayed a few steps behind me. I knew he was there before I took my seat. I could smell his cologne in the air, and the menthol smell was more pungent.

"Good morning," I told him without turning my profile to him. I wasn't about to bite off the hand that would feed me, but I wasn't going to be at its mercy either.

Something was off about this, and I could almost guess what this man wanted from me. It was the same reason Nico Dos Santos had taken me in the first place. I was the keeper of secrets.

My previous owners didn't think I could unravel what I could not see.

I was blind, but I wasn't mute.

"Leave us, Cecilia," he said instead of greeting me, and the rushing of retreating footsteps followed.

He had to be older than me, or I could be wrong, and his voice was naturally deep despite his age, but I was going with the latter, judging by Nico's age. Not that I ever got a chance to see him the way I wanted to. He just gave me a small part of himself; my guess was to form some sort of trust between us.

If this man wanted me for what I thought he did, older would be the correct answer from what I was told; that horrible place had ceased to exist. So, his search must have started a while ago.

"Does it make you feel powerful to have people cower at your feet?" I bit out.

"What makes you say that?" he asked. I could feel his gaze, hot and penetrating, on my cheek. "For all you know, she could have been smiling."

"Was she?"

My hands started to move around the table. I could smell food, and I didn't think the asshole next to me was going to help me.

"No, but that is not because of me," he replied.

He didn't say more, but I heard a few things being dragged across the table and positioned in front of me.

"Here," he told me as he took hold of my right hand. The moment he did, I felt a zing of electricity run through me. I pulled my hand back as if he had burned me.

I could hear his intake of breath, and I wondered if he had felt it too.

"Don't touch me," I hissed.

"So if you're going to fall, just let it happen? Noted," he mocked darkly.

This time, my hand wrapped around a warm cup. With both hands, I brought it close to my nose. I could smell the caffeine goodness, and my mouth watered. I didn't have anything I particularly wanted, but the smell of coffee had always reminded me of happier times. And happier times always made my heart ache.

"I wouldn't be any use for you dead now, would I?" I

countered after that first sip. "You did not ask for me out of the goodness of your heart. You asked for me because you are looking for someone or something…"

I let my words trail off into the air.

He didn't speak, but I could hear him shifting his weight.

"You would be no use to me dead at all. After all, I've been waiting a long time."

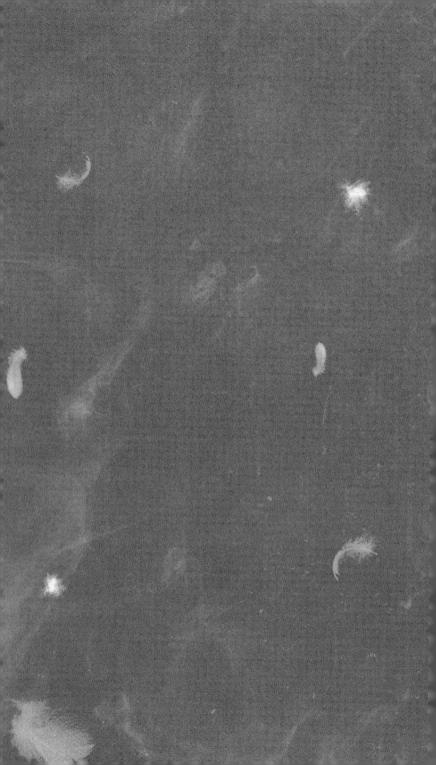

CHAPTER THREE

LUKE

SOME PEOPLE WERE QUICK TO SHED THEIR SINS LIKE A snake. It came quicker for some than others, but at the end of the day, they left them behind, forgetting all about them. Some knelt and prayed every day, lying to themselves that they had come to the point where they were finally free of their sins. As if they had not already tainted their souls. Too bad for me, my sins never left me alone. They stared at me from every single mirror I came in contact with—silent but always judging.

Life had a funny way of working itself out. I was looking for answers, and now they were sitting right in front of me in the most interesting packaging.

I never saw the point in attending *la Danza dei Morti*. I tried to avoid large crowds unless absolutely necessary, but now I was regretting that decision. This game I had started would have come to an end a lot sooner if I had been to just one dance. In my circles, no one had any secrets, so it was no surprise when Nico reached out to me, asking me for help.

The Shipper, as he had been known to some of us, had seen his last days in his traveling act, and now he was trying to get rid of all his dancers, except this one didn't know where to run. Of course, at first, I had said no, but then he had said the magic words that had me opening my doors.

Casa del Silenzio.

It was a brothel—well, that would be too nice a word to call what that place had been. House of Silence was the more tactful name those who frequented the place liked to call it. Calling it a sex trafficking ring was too distasteful for the bastards.

All these men liked to bed girls or boys, and I said that because everyone in that house was prepubescent or barely developing. Wealthy men and women would travel from all over the world to visit the House of Silence without any worry that their secrets would be revealed. If their whores weren't blind, then they were mute.

Nico knew what I had been seeking all along, and he dangled it in front of me, knowing I was not strong enough to resist.

I looked at Summer and took her profile in. She was right; I did need her, and more than anything, I needed the information she might carry.

There was something innocent about her, but that innocence wasn't soft. It was shaped by darkness and ready to strike. It was alluring to watch someone who on paper should have been fucking broken come at you with sharp teeth and claws.

It was enticing to see someone's survival instincts. The way they lost themselves in the will to live in this fucked-up world.

Her hair was long and fell down in loose waves. The color was a light brown with blonde highlights that I imagined shone brighter in the summer. Her skin was pale, but some freckles marred it, making a bridge above her nose. Her eyes, I had yet to see them since she kept them covered with dark shades.

"You must be a patient man," she muttered.

I didn't answer at first. Like most men, patience wasn't something that had come easy to me. Patience came in the form of a hard fucking lesson that had fucked me in the ass. Since then, I'd learned to take my time. There was a reason it was said that revenge was a dish best served cold.

You have no idea," I told her as I watched her hands try to find the syrup.

Taking pity on her, I handed her the syrup for the waffles.

"Thanks." Her voice was soft but not grateful.

My lip twitched in amusement as I watched her. I let myself take in the moment and the implications of what it meant to have her in my home. Even if this was something I had waited for and wanted, I didn't stop to think about the person who would be sharing the information. To me, they were just a source to be exploited, but now that source had a face, had a voice, and I couldn't help but feel *some* remorse.

We sat in comfortable silence while she ate, and I watched. If she noticed, she didn't comment right away.

"So my information in exchange...in exchange for me to be your—whore?"

I choked on my drink.

"I will not touch you," I hissed.

To this, she raised an amused eyebrow and turned toward me. She couldn't see me, could she? No, she would have gone out running already if she had, but I still felt the weight of her stare through every pore.

"And after I give you the information, what happens to

me then? You'll just let me stay here with no sort of payment?"

She was wary of me. I wondered how it was that Nico came in possession of her. How did he gain her trust? She certainly had good instincts, but then again, I bet after everything she's been through, she would have been crazy to trust her own shadow.

"The information you will provide me with will be more than enough." My tone came out harsher than I intended when she cocked her head, and a seductive smile spread across her lips.

I didn't know what shape or form she would be. Since it had to be a few years since she had been with Nico, I assumed she wouldn't be a complete mess. But I did not expect this—then again, people dealt with trauma in different ways. Some wanted to regain their sexuality, while others wanted nothing to do with it.

"Were there men on the road with you guys?" I found myself asking.

"Yes," she replied immediately. "But Nico's men weren't allowed to touch us."

She didn't speak fondly of Nico, but she did say his name with too much familiarity.

"And Nico?" I leaned back, waiting to see if her face would reveal things she didn't wish to speak of. Nico wasn't someone I would say was good, but he did seem to live by his own moral compass. Although I didn't think he would touch his *workers*, I wanted to be sure.

"He refused my sexual services." She shrugged it off, and my throat constricted. There was an ache and regret that should not be there.

"Do you go offering to spread your legs to whoever puts a roof over your head?"

She smiled at me, but it held no warmth. It was a cruel smile that might as well have been dripping with venom, but God, if it wasn't beautiful.

"Trust me, no one wishes they could die more than me, but a part of me refuses to do so. So, in order to survive, we adapt and use the skills we have. Unfortunately, the only ones I have involve sucking or taking cock."

For a moment, I was glad she could not see me. She would not see the sorrow and pity on my face. This should have never been her fate, and she had adapted to it the best way she knew how. If I had to guess, she put the offer on the table before the choice got taken from her. This way, she felt like she was the one in control, when the sad reality was that she never had any.

"If you need anything, let Cecilia know," I told her once I was sure my voice was strong enough not to crack.

"Do more people live here?"

"My driver, and there's a cleaning staff that comes in once a week."

When she didn't say anything, I kept going, but I wished I could know what was going on inside that head of hers.

"You can roam freely. Just don't go to the left wing, and I wouldn't suggest trying to run away. There's nothing for miles."

She snorted.

"I'm not stupid."

"And maybe try to find new skills you could hone. You have nothing but time now," I told her as I stood up.

Her face turned toward me, her brows scrunched in confusion.

"You're not going to ask me questions?"

"Not today."

It was more for my sanity than hers. I left the room before she could say more because I had a feeling she was the kind of girl who liked to have the last word.

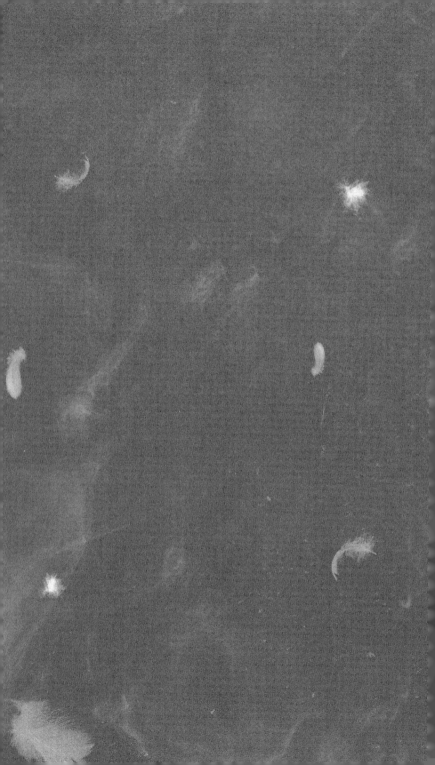

TRUTHS & LIES

He was a monster in my eyes.
I was a traitor in his mind.
All we had was half-truths and an ocean of lies.

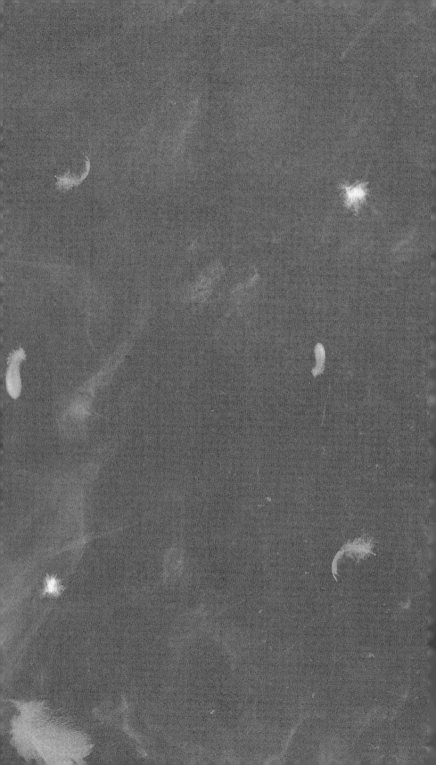

CHAPTER FOUR

SUMMER

THE MOST MAGICAL THING WAS A BEAUTIFUL PLACE TO call home. This house was like a maze, but I loved it. It was filled with lush flowers as soon as spring arrived. The moment fall came, the leaves crunched everywhere you went, and in the winter, it was the best. The place looked like a snow globe—miles of snow everywhere. There was no place to go, so if a snowstorm came, my parents would evade work. We were stuck in our own little world. I wished it had been snowing on that day. Then maybe things would still be the same.

"Principessa." My uncle's voice boomed through the other side of the garden.

Picking up a rose, I yelped when a thorn pricked my finger. It wasn't the first time it happened, and I knew it wouldn't be the last. With the rose in my hand, I ran back inside to where my mamma was with my zio.

I hoped my flower perked my mamma up. She had been sad lately, mostly because she and my zio would argue a lot.

They were in the ballroom, and my mamma looked like she had been crying. She wiped her tears when she saw me. I *ran up to her and gave her the rose. She smiled as she took it, but I knew it was forced. It didn't reach her eyes. My mamma was beautiful. She had gorgeous blonde hair that fell in waves and bright aqua eyes that were now covered in tears.*

My uncle looked as tense as she did. His face, however, morphed as I came into view. He was always happy to see me. Since Papà passed away, he had been coming here more often—well, him and his son.

I gasped for air as soon as I woke up. Tears welled in my eyes, and I found it odd. When had been the last time I'd cried? I couldn't remember when that had been. I couldn't remember their faces, but the feeling it brought to my heart was like no other. The past gave me glimpses of my old life, and then when they were gone, there was just eternal darkness and an ache that wouldn't go away.

I was about to lie down again when I heard a sweet melody drifting to my room. Without thinking, I sat up and reached for my cane. Then I grabbed my robe so I wouldn't go prancing around in just a silk nightgown. I didn't have much to my name, but the necessities were more than enough for me. As soon as I got to the door, I remembered that I had forgotten to put my glasses on. I quickly went back to get them, praying the music didn't stop.

My slippers made no noise against the marble floor. The time I had spent here was already making me feel secure. I was adapting to this place quite well. It had been a week since I had been here, and I was quite comfortable. It was a little bit scary.

As soon as I made it out of what I now considered my hallway, the melody that was being played was louder. My heart sped up a bit because I knew who was the one playing. It had been one week since I last had been in his presence, and for some reason, I did not wish to stay away.

There was something about him that was drawing me in, and I couldn't explain what it was. It certainly wasn't his winning personality or his looks, since I obviously couldn't see those.

Or maybe I was used to someone around. My codependency wanted to latch onto somebody, anyone other than my demons.

Even in *that* house, there was always someone around, and being with the dance company never really left you room to feel lonely. I was either bunking with another dancer, having practices, or it was showtime.

My steps slowed the closer I got to the sound of the music. When I was younger, my father had gifted me a piano, but I was terrible at it, or more like, I never bothered to sit still long enough to learn how to play it.

When the keys stopped abruptly, I knew he was aware of my presence, yet he said nothing.

"I pass by every day, and I had no idea there was a piano here."

Loneliness—that's why I was trying to have a conversation with him.

"You play?" he asked in a muffled tone.

The reason for the muffledness soon hit my nostrils.

"No, but now I do wish I had learned."

"You have time. You can learn now," he pointed out.

I smiled, even though this part killed me, but I hoped he couldn't see the fakeness.

"I don't know how to read." I shrugged it off like it was no big deal. People sometimes tended to overlook my illiteracy because of my disability. I called it neglect, but then what could I have expected? Keeping me ignorant was what kept that vile place running.

There was no noise, just pure silence. I began to think Luke had left me alone.

"Come sit," he instructed after a while.

I should have been scared, but fear was nowhere near my mind. I had been alone in this house with this man from the beginning, and I believed those words he had told me a week ago. He would not touch me, and that made me feel safe. If he had wanted, he could have had me by now, whether I was willing or not.

Time would tell if this would be a mistake, but for now, I was going to hold on to his word.

I was a little disappointed when I sat down and didn't feel his heat anywhere near me.

"Go ahead." His harsh tone washed over the skin on my back. A shiver spread down my spine. "Touch the keys...feel them."

My hands shook as I extended both my arms. The piano was smooth, perhaps recently polished. I couldn't feel a speck of dust on it. It was obviously well taken care of, and that thought warmed me, much like the rest of the house. I knew the place was old based on the creaks of the pipes I often heard, but every surface was clean and smooth. Food was served every day, and it wasn't just a quick bite but a full spread, three- or five-meal courses.

"Is it big?" I asked as I spread my arms, trying to figure out the length.

He chuckled darkly, and I was enticed by it.

"A grand piano."

My hand made contact with a round object. I tentatively touched it since I didn't know if this was a part of the instrument or not. I was surprised when it moved a bit. My brows scrunched as I picked it up. It was hollow, and I dipped one of my fingers and made contact with what seemed like little padded stumps.

I could smell the smoke coming from behind me, but I could also smell the ash in front of me.

"You must come here a lot," I said as I put the ashtray back in the place I had grabbed it from.

"Are you going to touch the keys or what?" he said, somewhat annoyed.

My lips quivered. I usually was able to brush things off like this easier, but being here was making me soft. The icy walls I had built were beginning to thaw.

"What kind of car do you drive?" I asked, and if my question confused him, he didn't say.

"A black Valhalla."

"That means nothing to me." I shrugged off as my fingertips grazed the keys carefully, not to play them. "I can't picture things I don't know. Taking my time to feel them is how *I* see."

His arm lightly grazed my shoulder. I heard the small tray move, knowing he was putting his cigarette out.

"The piano is huge," he began to say. "It's positioned by the windows at the edge of the room. You can oversee the entrance, the hall, kitchen from here."

I cocked my head, deep in thought at what he was describing.

"Stop stalling and touch the keys."

I shook my head from the imagery I was trying to put together and instead focused on the task at hand. I didn't know where to start, aware that whatever I played would be horrible, but when I let my fingers press down, I couldn't help but smile.

I did it again and again, playing the world's most horrible tune.

When I finally stopped playing, the whole place was deafening. Without any noise, it felt cold and lonely.

"Luke?" I wondered if, this time, he really left me alone.

"Sorry, did you say something?" he questioned, his tone coming across from me. "I'm trying to regain my hearing after that atrocity."

There was no malice in his voice. Dare I say, he sounded amused, causing my smile to widen.

"Thank you." The words slipped out before I could think better of it.

I wasn't sure what exactly I was thanking him for, but I knew something in me was beginning to change. Dancing *la Danza dei Morti* had given me an outlet. Something to do, but it was never for my own gain. This was different. It was like time was standing still, and I needed to figure out who I was all over again.

"Luke." I tentatively said his name. Tasting the way it came out of my mouth. I could hear his sharp intake of breath, and that triggered heat to spread across my cheeks.

"Summer," he countered.

"Are you going to ask me about that place?"

"Yeah," he said softly, his voice closer this time. "But not now."

I opened my mouth to ask why not when he spoke again.

"Why do you always wear black?"

His question caught me off guard but, at the same time, made me sit straighter. A warmness spread through my cheeks. I had not "seen" him for the last week, but he had seen me. He had paid enough attention to me, and instead of feeling repulsed, I liked it. Being disabled sometimes made you feel invisible, and even if I couldn't see those around me, that didn't mean I didn't want them not to see me.

"It's just easier," I told him as my hands found the cover on the piano. "That way, I can always match. It avoids awkward situations."

"Have there been many situations?" His tone had a bite to it.

I shook my head. "Not really."

"Have you always been like...this?" His question hung in the air.

"No, I lost my sight young."

"Do you remember much?"

"Not really."

He didn't say anything, but I got the feeling he wasn't happy with my nonanswers.

"Why won't you ask me about that place? You said you have been waiting a long time. Why stall?"

"And I can keep waiting some more."

"But you—"

"Are you so eager to revisit your past?" he snapped.

I licked my lips and shook my head.

"I thought it would be easier to get the information I needed, not caring about the price I would be paying to get it."

Did he mean hurting me?

"What does that mean?" My tone was laced with hope.

"Go to bed, Summer," he demanded, leaving no room for argument.

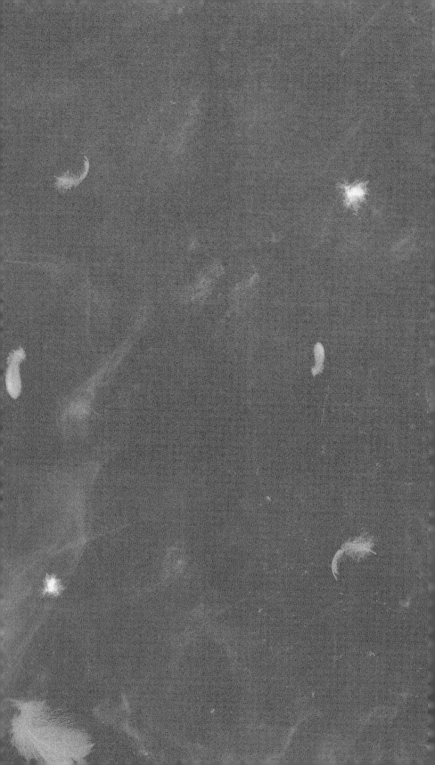

BROKEN PIECES

The saddest thing would have to be
when we make ourselves believe
that two broken pieces
might just perfectly fit.

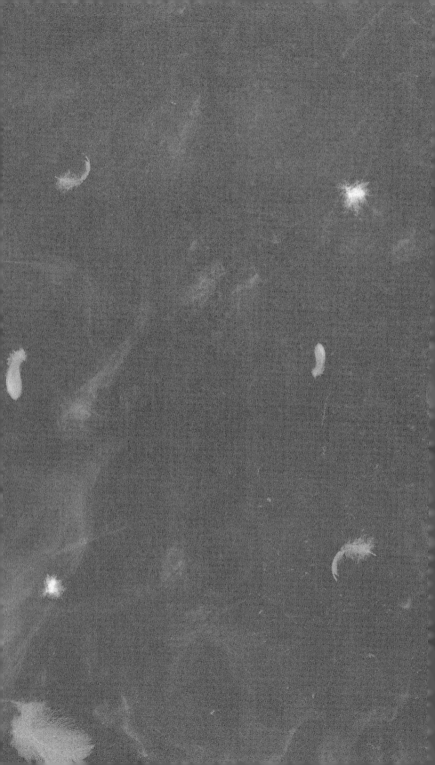

CHAPTER FIVE

SUMMER

IN THE MIDST OF WINTER, I WAS SURROUNDED BY spring. I let my lungs fill with fresh air as I breathed in everything the greenhouse had to offer.

If I thought that last night's events had made a difference, Luke made it perfectly clear when he didn't show up for breakfast this morning that last night didn't change anything.

The more time I spent here, the more I could feel the loneliness in the air. It clung to this house like an omen. As lonely as it felt, there was something beautiful about it. There was also peace in this house. Like a bird with broken wings, I had finally found my perfect sanctuary.

I wanted to explore the house, but something kept stopping me. I was too afraid to get attached. A part of me was holding back because if I ended up leaving or got sent away, then I wouldn't have anything to miss. If I didn't have anything to call my own or to miss when I lay awake at night, I could continue feeding the numbness that lived inside of me.

The smell of lilies warned me that Cecilia was near, so when she spoke, I didn't get spooked.

"Would you like to water the flowers?" I could hear the warmness in her tone. Would it be too awkward if I asked to touch her? I wanted to feel what she was like. All my interactions besides that first morning with her had been pleasant, and they had left me wanting more.

"Can I?" I turned toward her and hated that my smile gave away the joy she had brought me.

"I'm going to reach for your hand," she told me, and I gave her a nod.

After my outburst, she quickly learned to ask for permission before touching me.

She took my hand and then pressed a hose with a garden nozzle attached to it.

"Have fun," she told me as her footsteps began to retreat.

As far as I knew, there was nothing poisonous here, nor had they warned me about any particular plant, so I touched away as I watered them. Every flower had a distinct smell, and although I recognized many of them, there were a few I didn't know by name, but once I touched them, I could imagine their beauty.

The smell of wet soil reminded me of warmer days filled with sunlight. What I wouldn't give to go back in time and rewrite my life.

When I got to the middle, a slow smile spread through me at the distinctive smell. I leaned in when I made it to the roses. My hand reached out carefully so I could touch the petals.

My finger went lower carefully, trying to see if I could cut a flower for myself. Nothing moved, but I turned my head anyway. My heart accelerated a bit, and I waited to see if it did it again. I got the feeling that I was being observed.

"Cecilia?" I asked, but no answer.

Shaking my head, I went back to the task I had at hand.

"Fuck," I hissed as my finger got pricked with a thorn.

Why do you always grab the roses if you don't know how to cut them?" My uncle's son broke the tension that had filled my body. Instead, now I was apprehensive for different reasons.

He wasn't mean, per se, but he also didn't go out of his way to be kind and loving like my zio did.

"If you want to smell the roses, then you must face a few thorns." I shrugged off the words my papà had said to me the first time I had cried after pricking myself. Beautiful things sometimes came at a price, for nothing worth having ever came easy, and if I shed a few drops of blood, that would be no big deal.

He took my hand and wiped the blood with his shirt, then led me away.

"Come on. The grown-ups need to talk."

That made me sad. Since my papà died, all the grown-ups ever did was talk.

"You're bleeding." Luke's smoky tone filtered through my unwanted memories.

I turned, trying to figure out where he was positioned, but he didn't give me a hint.

Asshole.

"A few drops of blood won't kill me," I told him.

I had lived through much worse. A cut from a rose wasn't on my list of traumas. I didn't feel him come in. He was being quiet and stealthy on purpose.

"Then what will?" His voice made me jump.

How had he gotten behind me? Was he the one who

had been there earlier? Was he cautioning his steps so I wouldn't be able to follow along? I took a deep breath and noticed the menthol smell was missing.

I didn't want to jump to conclusions and think he was doing it to mess with me. I licked my lips, trying to gather my wits and keep my cool, but no words were formulated. My mind was still on *that* memory. Telltale signs that my world was about to change; I just chose to ignore them.

"So far, nothing has." The words escaped me before I could think better of them.

"Why are you trying to live if you're just hoping to die?" His voice was harsh.

Now that I knew he was behind me, I could feel his presence taunting me, toying with me to see what my next move would be. I'd always wondered if the grim reaper followed me around, but it didn't feel like this—not like him. He was testing me, but not in the way the people in that house did, yet I didn't like this either.

Maybe it was the earlier memory that left me feeling melancholy and in need of sharing with him a piece of my past. Or maybe I had not talked about it in a long time, and I needed a reminder of who I had once been.

"My father died when I was young. He was my best friend, my whole world, and I continue to live because he could no longer do so."

"And your mother?" That harsh tone was still there.

Whenever I went back to those last weeks, the memories kept changing. Those blinders I had put up because I looked up to her with love kept disengaging, and I felt like she could have done more.

"She's also dead." There was no need to go into detail, especially when he didn't ask for any.

"Hmmm," he hummed, and I felt him walk around me.

I suddenly felt like prey in a game I didn't know we were supposed to play.

Was I being paranoid?

He took hold of my hands, and I instinctively pulled them back to me, but he didn't let go. Instead, he forced my hand toward him and then elevated it. I held my breath, waiting for what he would do. I didn't like crying over spilled milk. My sight was there, and then it was gone, and feeling sorry about it wasn't going to make me feel any better, but right now, I wished like hell I could see what he was doing.

More than that, I wanted to see his face. To know his expressions. It wasn't even to see if he was what others considered handsome because the social norms of the world didn't apply here. I'd been next to beautiful people whom others praised when I was the only one who saw their real faces. A beautiful face could hide an ugly soul. But a beautiful soul overshadowed everything else. I wanted to learn the face of the man who couldn't bring himself to hurt me over the information he desired.

A shiver ran down my spine the moment I felt his wet tongue on the pad of my finger. My mouth parted in shock.

"Why do you bother coming in here...?"

If I couldn't see a thing.

He didn't finish his sentence, but it hung in the air.

"Because beauty doesn't have to be seen. It can be felt."

"Maybe the whole place is ugly and torn down, and you're just deluding yourself."

He was still holding on to me, and I made no move to pull away. Instead, I leaned forward until the tip of my nose touched the rose.

I made a show of taking a deep breath, letting the sweet fragrance fill my nostrils.

"Rotten isn't something you see. It's something you inhale."

What did I say? People relied on their vision for every little thing, even when that wasn't the primary sense.

"Why do you live alone?" I questioned him instead.

He quickly let go of my hand, and the loss I felt from it was imminent. Still, I didn't regret my question.

"I've answered your questions," I reminded him.

"Ah, but I'm the one with the power here."

I faced away from him at his response. One must never forget the precarious line they walk or who is the master of their leash. He might not pull at it, but he was still holding on to it.

"I have no family."

His tone left no room for argument, so I dropped it. Instead, I moved away, continuing to water the plants, pretending like he wasn't with me. I knew he had not left because I could hear his steps next to me as I moved. My hands trembled because I knew his gaze was on me or on what I was doing, but either way, I was his sole focus.

This was a new feeling.

I was used to people looking at me, but that was always temporary. I had never been anyone's center of attention. I was a memory, just something to pass the time. They would always leave me, and then shame would sweep to my every pore. Right now, there was no shame, and I didn't feel like I was something that would fade.

"We have one thing in common, little dove," he finally spoke.

"Dove?"

Luke took the hose from me, and then I felt him walk to

the other side of me. He took hold of my hand and began to lead me away. My reaction was to pull my hand from his grasp, but he immediately gripped it tighter, his fingers digging into my palm.

Was it supposed to be soothing or a warning?

"Doves are smart. It doesn't matter the distance. They always find their way back home."

Did he mean I was now home?

"Yet you are lost, wandering from one cage to another."

Okay, ouch.

"So you mock me?" I bit out.

"I'm stating a fact."

Perhaps he was, but it felt like more than that. It felt like he was trying to get under my skin. He didn't want to give me anything but wanted to bare all of me.

"Can you describe this place to me?" I asked him as we kept walking.

"No."

My throat constricted at his response. I didn't know why I expected him to answer any differently. None of his past actions screamed warm and fuzzy.

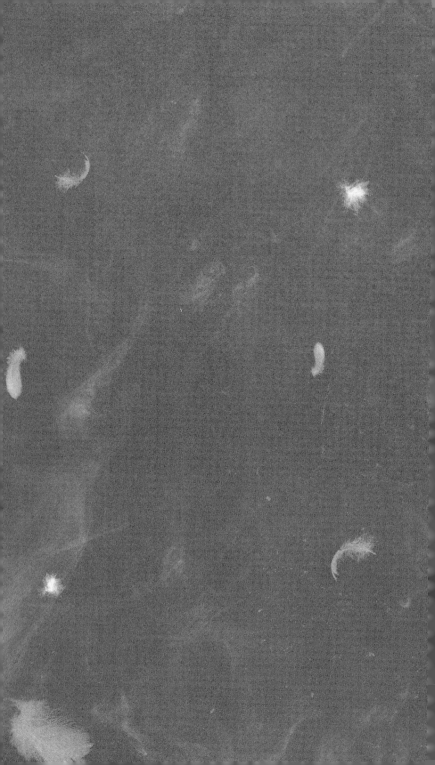

CHAPTER SIX

LUKE

Keeping my distance was crucial, but like a moth to a flame, I kept coming back. There was something intriguing about the way Summer saw—no, that wasn't it—how she *felt* the world. I'd never met anyone like her, and I knew this fascination was dangerous—wrong, even.

At the same time, I kept coming up with a thousand excuses as to why I should check up on her. When Nico contacted me, he made me swear she would be taken care of. I was many things, but I never went back on my word. If a man didn't have honor, he didn't have anything.

"What was that look for?" Nico said as soon as Summer was out of view.

I turned to look back at him. He had been one of my father's associates, so it was no surprise he knew why I wanted revenge. He was dangling the key to my answers all on his own.

"I didn't realize she would be so...fragile."

It wasn't entirely the truth, but it wasn't something I could say aloud. He didn't look like he believed me. His brows were scrunched, and his blue eyes pierced me with intensity.

"If I find out you hurt her, I'll come back for her."

Yeah, that wasn't going to happen. Summer was not his to keep—not anymore.

Summer was hurt by my lack of answer, and knowing I put that look on her face didn't feel good, but I couldn't describe this place to her. The way I saw the world was all black, and she needed some beauty in it, and I had never seen the beauty in things.

Even as a child, all I saw was the fucked-up. I was stuck on it. Even when my life started to get better, I kept going back to the past. It had a fucking choke hold on me that wouldn't let me prosper.

I cleared my throat once we arrived at the window. Her hand was still clasped in mine, and this time, she made no move to take it away. The more I wanted to leave, the more my mind dared me to defy the odds. I turned sideways and then used my other hand to guide the small of her back in front of me. Her breath hitched, and I wished I could unsee all the reactions she had to me. I was supposed to be her protector, but everyone who had ever been close to me had found death. I brought our joint hands to the thick rope and then had her wrap her palms around it.

"What is it?" she asked in a breathy tone, then licked her red lips.

My eyes zeroed in on the action. The way they moved, the fullness of them, how they would feel—shaking my head, I cut that thought off fast.

Instead of answering her, I removed my hand that had been on her back, sliding it down slowly as I did it.

Her body trembled, and I closed my eyes and inhaled, but it did nothing to calm me down. While I was still doing stupid shit, I grabbed her free hand, put it on the other rope, and then took a step forward so she would be forced to do so as well, except this was a fucking bad idea.

I could feel her heat, and it was fucking calling to me. It wanted to melt the glacier I had surrounded myself with.

"Turn around." My voice came out thick, and I hoped she didn't make a comment about it.

She did as I asked and then tipped her head up. I knew she couldn't see me physically, but it felt as if she could see things that everyone else missed. The façade I put on for the world kept fading when I was near her.

"What is it?" I could hear a small tremble in her voice.

"Sit." My command was nothing but a whisper.

Maybe that was why she did it because I could see apprehension all over her face, and she didn't think it was a good idea. Unless it was her intuition telling her to get as far away from me as she could possibly get. In that case, she should heed the caution.

The swing swayed as she sat down, which caused her to shriek. One of her hands left the rope and instead was on my thigh. I gritted my teeth when I looked down to see where she had the material of my slacks bunched in a small fist. Right next to it was the imprint of my hard dick.

Trying to make myself believe that I had it under control was more believable when I didn't see the evidence of my arousal. Now all she had to do was move her hand a bit to the left, and she would undoubtedly know as well.

"What are you doing?" I managed to say between gritted teeth.

"I want to get up." She was about to take off her other hand from the rope, but I stopped her.

"Why?"

I removed the hand that was on my thigh. She clasped her fingers with mine in a viselike grip.

"The moment my feet stop touching the floor, there's nothing tethering me. I don't know the layout. It makes me feel like I'm drowning."

"You don't trust me."

It wasn't a question but a statement. Her lips pursed, but she didn't speak.

"Good," I told her as I took another step forward.

Her legs pressed against my own. I bent down, took a loose tendril, and put it behind her ear.

"If you let me, I'll teach you to fly," I whispered, my breath fanning her forehead.

The words came out before I could stop them, but I knew I meant every word.

It took her a second, and I was half expecting her to demand me to move so that she could get up, but when she nodded, I felt the tension leave my body.

The swing was white and made with thick ropes. Back in the day, it used to be covered in fake vines and flowers at the top. It was perfect for rainy days to just sit down on and watch the rain fall in the backyard. Or on those scorching days to soak the sun's rays while still being in the shade. In the winter, you could watch as the snow fell all around, all while being in your own paradise.

Things she would never get to see again.

"I'll be right behind you, okay?"

She waited. Her body was rigid, and her shoulders were tense.

"There's a curved window right in front that overlooks the backyard," I began to say as I gently pushed. "To the other side, there's a small firepit to add some warmth on those cold days."

"I bet it looks beautiful," she whooshed as she began to relax. "Can you push me a bit higher?"

A small smile tugged at my lips as I did what she asked. This time, she let out a small giggle filled with excitement that almost took me back to much happier times.

Wasn't it funny how the world took from you, but it also gave back? There was no denying that there was a familiarity with Summer that I had never had with anyone else. Not that I bothered. I went to board meetings when it was necessary for me, but other than that, I stayed here. I didn't know if I was hiding or punishing myself. Maybe a little bit of both.

Even though the house was huge, it still felt like I couldn't outrun her.

Had I been so starved for human connection that I now clung to the only person who made me feel a spark of heat? Or maybe the connection that bound us was making me feel and see things that were never there to begin with?

Either way, I knew I had crossed a line, and there was no going back now.

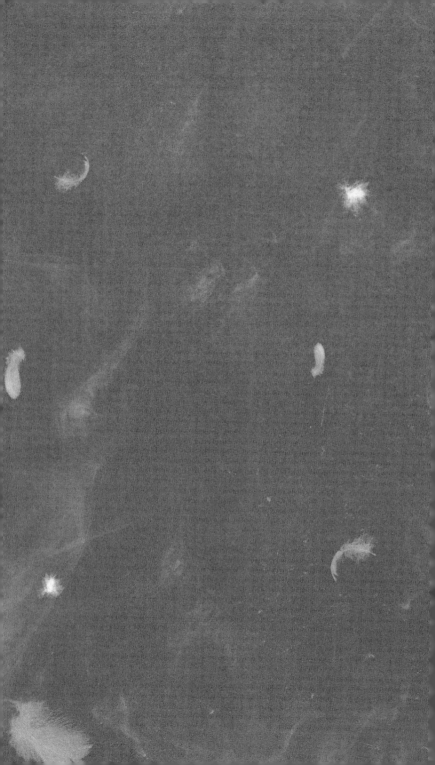

SCARS

We were cut from the same cloth.
Proud that we bore matching scars.
Not realizing the damage the knife had done.

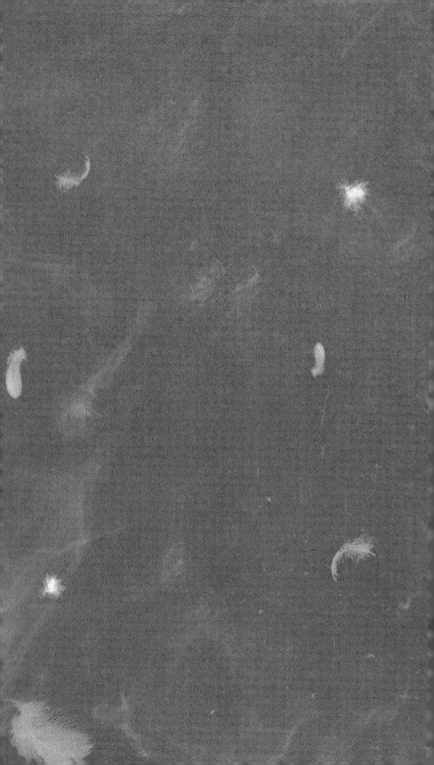

CHAPTER SEVEN

SUMMER

PARTS OF ME WERE ACHING. I FELT THEM AS SOON AS I became conscious. I wasn't in pain per se, but the feeling that engulfed me wasn't a pleasant one. My eyes were closed, and they wouldn't budge. It was like having a nightmare you couldn't wake up from. Was I dreaming? I didn't think so. I could feel the coldness of the room grazing my exposed skin. I could feel the sheets beneath me. They were coarse. At least, they felt that way since I was used to my soft ones. My fingers began to move when I willed them to, even though my eyes refused to do so. I also felt the stillness of my feet, and when I wiggled my toes, they moved instantly. All of this pointed to me being awake. I brought my hand to my face, and it was covered in some type of bandage. I traced the material, and it went all around my head. Fear spread through me in an instant.

"Mamma," I yelled.

Panic set in when I couldn't remember how I had fallen asleep. I sat up, trying to remove the wraps that hindered me from seeing.

Suddenly, my hand stopped at the last wrap when my memory came back to me. My mamma had been gasping for air as her eyes begged me for help.

Once again, I was the one who felt like a fish out of water. My hands immediately went to the back of my head, where I half expected to find it covered in wraps, but nothing was there, just my hair. This was the second time I was taken back to the past.

It wasn't that I was avoiding it, but I just saw no sense in thinking about things that I could not fix. Maybe that's how I was able to survive this long. I let everything just stay in the past, becoming numb because if I let myself, I would never recover from all the grief I refused to acknowledge.

It took a minute to catch my breath. I knew I would not be able to go back to bed, so I searched for my slippers and got up. I made my way to the door but stopped as soon as my cane didn't bump into the spot I knew the door would be. I moved my hand to the left, and sure enough, there was a wall, but the space next to it was gone.

The door was open.

My skin became cold, and I instantly felt a shiver make its way down my spine. Before I could make my next move, I stood still and made sure that there was no noise like the current flow I had heard last time.

"Hello?" I whispered because I knew that door had been closed when I went to bed.

Could it have been the wind?

How could one place make me feel safe and protected one day to want to run as far away as I could possibly get the next?

I stepped through the threshold, disappointed that the sound of music wasn't playing today. Still, I didn't let that deter me. This path, I had learned it by memory, so I went with ease to the place where the piano was set up.

Being in the greenhouse with the plants was relaxing during the day, but the night was already too silent. I didn't want to be there when my mind was already at war. Silence would not drown these unwanted thoughts.

Perhaps tomorrow I should ask Cecilia to show me more of the house so I could have more places to explore—or escape to.

I moved my hands around when I made it to the seat to make sure that Luke was not there. I tried to pretend like I wasn't disappointed when I didn't smell the burn of a cigarette.

What made him lonely? What were the things he was running from? I never really bothered to know much about anyone, not even Nico.

Nico got me for his personal gain. He was looking for someone he thought might have been taken to the House of Silence, but after he found out I knew nothing, he left me alone. I figured I had to pay my dues somehow, but he shot down my proposal and assured me I did not need to pay him with sexual services. We had a mutual understanding, so there was no need for me to know more about him. He saved me, he gave me a job I could somewhat do, and I got to live without being raped on the daily. At the time, it was all I needed.

There was something about Luke that called to me. Maybe it was the loneliness that clung to him, that begged me to free him. Or maybe my loneliness and cynicism were a match made for him.

Either way, there was no denying that there was something, and I couldn't be the only one who was feeling it. If there was one thing I knew better than most, it was that chemistry was not logical. My memories of my father were few and far between, but him naming fragrances and explaining chemistry in a way I could understand was engraved in me.

Since I was alone, I figured I might as well take advantage of the fact and explore the grand piano. I moved around it, my hands tracing the edges of it so I wouldn't leave fingerprints on the countertop. Once I had gone around it, I took a seat on the bench. My hands rested on top of where the keyboards would be if they weren't covered.

Without thinking, I began to mumble the words to a song my mamma would love to sing. *"Non posso più dividermi tra te e il mare..."*

"A thousand seas, huh?" Luke's voice caused me to jump.

I lifted my head to the other side of the piano, and I wished I knew what was over there. Had he been there all along? Again, I could not hear his footsteps. That didn't matter for now. All I could feel was the line we had drawn, and I was ready to go over it. My gut instinct told me to prod, and well, it had never spoken up before.

"It's a song," I told him.

"I know," he added. "Do you know where you are, Summer?"

His question caught me off guard.

"Italia?" my response sounded more like a question.

"Nico did not tell you where he was taking you?" There was a bite to his tone.

I sat straighter.

"He told me I would be safe, and that was more than enough for me."

His displeased snort was audible. I didn't have to know him to know he was not happy with my answer.

"Do you want to know where you are?"

"Does it matter?"

"You're not in Europe," he offered, but nothing more.

I bit my lip.

"I kind of figured that. Cecilia speaks to me in English, and so do you."

The smell of menthol soon filled my senses.

"You're up late," he said, changing the conversation. I didn't know if I was relieved or upset about it yet.

"So are you."

"I don't sleep much," he admitted.

"Why is that?" I leaned into the keys, and the piano played off-tune notes. He had opened the lid at some point in our conversation.

His voice sounded closer as he spoke.

"Don't worry your pretty little head about it."

My saliva thickened. I'd been called pet names before, but having him call me pretty made me feel something. I longed to hear more. The more time I spent in this house, the more I stopped recognizing myself. Maybe I wasn't losing myself, but I was becoming someone whom I was supposed to be all along.

"There's nothing pretty about the things that go on in my head."

Why I confessed that to him, I wasn't sure, but this time, I did hear his footsteps as he got even closer.

"Is it about that place?" he asked, his tone trying to appear calm and controlled, but I heard the hint of urgency that followed them.

"It's everything."

"Go to bed, Summer," he said, and he sounded like he was now next to me.

"No." I tipped my chin defiantly.

"I could always make you." There was something in his voice that made me shiver. It wasn't a threat, but it had an edge, and it begged to be defied.

"You could try," I whooshed.

A dark chuckle escaped him.

"Don't test me, little dove. I've never been a good man."

"That's fine with me. Good men tend to have the worst secrets anyways."

My thoughts went to my zio. How had I been so blind?

"What was that look for?" he asked.

My brow furrowed, and that's when I noticed that I wasn't wearing my glasses. My stomach sank, and my hands immediately went to my face.

There was nothing separating my bare face from his gaze. My fingers met the scarred skin surrounding my eyes. Was this why he wanted me to leave? Had he seen what lay beneath and was disgusted by it?

The heat of his thigh pressed against me. He sat next to me but didn't say a word. He didn't try to soothe me with words nor try to pry my hands away from my face.

Instead, he began to play the piano.

The tune was familiar and macabre, one I had not heard in quite a while. It was the haunting melody that had saved me. Up until now, I didn't realize how much I'd missed it.

One of the girls had been nice enough to describe the main act to me once. The way the lead ballerina would run around from side to side, paired with her change in costume, it almost made you think it was two different girls playing the same role.

Luke's hand grazed my arm as he reached for another key.

"Did you ever go see us play?" My voice was loud enough for him to hear me but quiet so as not to disturb the melody.

"No," he clipped immediately. "I got the music sheet from the internet."

"This is my favorite part," I told him as the melody started dying. It was the part where the swan changed and transformed. Once the notes picked up again, it was more intense than before. Like they now had a point to prove.

"Do you miss it?" His question was soft, as if he didn't want to interrupt the notes he was playing.

"I wasn't very good at it."

"That's not what I asked." His voice was louder.

"Dancing was okay. I was not a very good dancer... I've never been good at anything."

He abruptly stopped, and I could feel the heat of his gaze. I should have been uncomfortable to be so bare to him, but the fact that he had ignored the scars that marred me was liberating.

There had been no change in his tone. It lacked pity, and for that, I was beyond grateful. It was the accumulation of the scraps of kindness that he threw at me that were fogging up my judgment.

"Dance," he commanded.

My face turned toward his. My fingers itched to trace his skin. To see what the man beneath my touch looked like, but that wasn't going to happen. Luke made no move to keep playing, and I knew he wouldn't until he got what he wanted.

"I'm warning you, I suck."

He didn't give me any encouragement. He just waited

patiently until I took off my slippers. Then I got up and left my cane propped against the side of the piano. I moved a few feet away from him, feeling the coldness of the floor beneath my feet.

He started to play from the beginning as soon as I got into position. I wondered how he would watch me if he was looking at the keys but quickly shook that thought away. Instead, I danced as I had never danced before.

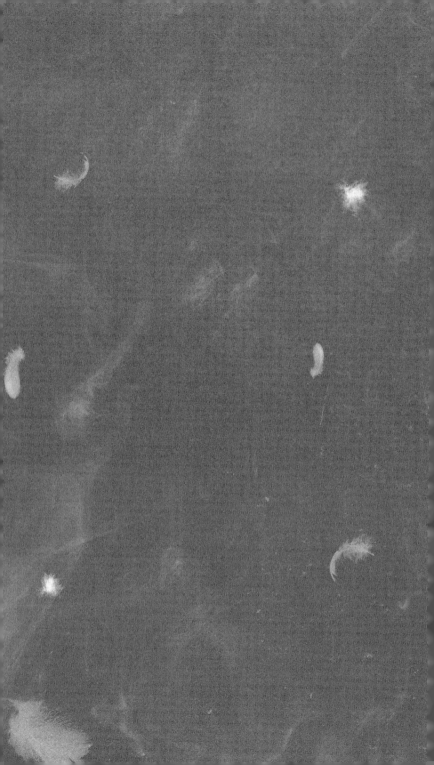

CHAPTER EIGHT

LUKE

I WAS FRUSTRATED. MY SMOKING HABITS COULD ATTEST to that because lately, I felt like a fucking chimney. Between work and this, it was safe to say I was on edge. Summer was as captivating as she was infuriating.

Did she care where she was, or at the end of the day, was it all the same?

Instead of getting more aggravated by this, I played the piano. It was one easy way to clear my mind. As I began to speed up the tempo, my eyes drifted to Summer when she began to move.

She didn't suck—far from it.

Her body was lithe and moved gracefully. The sash of her nightgown came undone, and it was hypnotizing to watch the way her nightgown molded to her soft curves as she moved. Summer rose on her tiptoes, and I shifted my weight in case I needed to get up and catch her if she fell. She lifted herself up and down a few times, stretching her body. Her pirouette was quick and clean. Once she successfully completed it, she gained more confidence and began to move around the room with more ease.

The cage that held her back had not been the one she had been locked in but the self-imposed one she imprisoned herself to. She lived just enough to be able to breathe but numb enough not to feel all the things that had damaged her.

My plan was to leave her alone, but the moment she realized she wasn't wearing her sunglasses, I could see the horror on her face, and I felt like I had to do something about it. The shield she had between herself and the world was nowhere in sight tonight.

My stomach churned, not in disgust but because I could imagine the pain she had been in. The terror she must have felt, and then to go through it alone, I admired her.

In all honesty, as the days went on, I was in awe.

The more I should have pulled away, the closer her essence kept me bound. I ignored these feelings and instead kept playing the piano as if nothing was wrong. If she insisted on keeping herself caged, then the least I could do was make sure it was a gilded one.

Today had been a fucking long day. I had a board meeting, and they had royally pissed me off. They were beginning to be swayed to *his* side, not knowing that if he won, they would be jumping into bed with the devil.

They feared me because I'd shown them my true colors early on. What I tolerated and what I did not. They also knew they could count on my word. But that was the weakness of men, wasn't it? They got blinded by greed and pussy, and nine times out of ten, that was their downfall.

This game I was playing would soon come to an end, and all the lies would be revealed. Even the ones I wished I could keep hidden and have them never see the light of day would surface, and they would change everything.

Summer was now moving all over the room. Her

rhythm was perfectly in sync with the chords I was playing. It was tragic to watch her like this, something that was broken and scarred, learning to fly again.

But it was also fucking beautiful.

My cock ached the more I looked at her, and I hated the reaction more than anything else. I was her guardian, her protector, and yet I wanted her as I had never wanted any woman before.

The years that should have separated us didn't matter. Not when those same years were the very reason she was made for me.

Fuck.

My fingers stopped moving when I realized I was stalling by not getting the information she may or may not have. Summer and I were a train wreck waiting to happen.

"I told you I wasn't very good," Summer divulged, sounding frustrated.

She had been perfect, but I wasn't going to tell her that. Instead, I turned my body to face her.

"You have nothing but time to get better."

This seemed to perk her up. Summer waltzed up to me. As she got closer, I could finally see her eyes. There wasn't much light, but it was enough to let me get a better look. It was like looking at an empty windowpane. Sure, they were a beautiful turquoise color, but there was an eerie vacancy that could not be explained. I saw the scarring around her eyes, but I didn't want to focus too much on it. The skin around them was puckered and burned, and I swallowed so my voice wouldn't betray the anger I felt every time I saw them.

"Can you hand me my cane?" she asked as she made her way over to me. I was about to reach for it when I realized she had gotten way too close.

My arms went to her small waist so I could steady her. Her intake of breath was audible, and the fact that I had an effect on her fucked with me, but I ignored it for now.

"You have to be careful," I told her, my voice coming out thicker. My fingers instinctively dug in to stop myself from pulling her closer or maybe imagining how it would feel to touch her naked skin as I sank deep inside her.

"Sorry." Her voice was a low whimper.

Shit.

We stayed like that for a second. I needed to let her go so I could get her cane. She was the first one to move, but instead of moving away, she came closer.

"What are you doing?" I asked, even though it was obvious.

Her hands came to my shoulders, and I held my breath.

"Summer," I warned, and she fucking smirked at me.

With another step, she lifted one leg and put it to the side of me until she was straddling me.

What the hell were we doing, and how had I allowed it to get like this?

"Get off me," I groaned.

Instead of doing as I asked, her hands came to my cheeks. My chest rose and fell as her breathing picked up, and I knew what she was trying to do. She was trying to see me in the only way she knew how.

My hands wrapped around her wrists before she could go any further. I pulled her body toward me, which was my first mistake because I could feel her chest pressed against me. The cut of her nightgown allowed me to peek down at her ample breasts, which I had no doubt would fit perfectly in my mouth.

"Why? I can feel that you want me," she stated as she subtly ground her pussy against my erection.

My vision blurred with need, and my nose flared. I abruptly stood up, letting go of her wrists and instead holding to her waist so she wouldn't fall, but that was another mistake. She immediately wrapped her arms around my neck and her legs around my waist.

"Summer," I warned.

She ignored me and instead ran her fingers across my nape. Fuck, that felt good.

"Luke," she replied in a breathy moan.

My already hard cock was fucking throbbing.

Every excuse I gave myself that what I was feeling was human nature, a simple reaction because I'd been void of human emotion, felt like bullshit.

"You don't have to feel lonely anymore," she whispered, her breath fanning my cheeks as she attempted to kiss me.

I averted my face just in time. I turned us around and laid her on top of the piano. The moment I did that, she spread her legs, and even if I wanted to look away, I couldn't.

Her skin was sun-kissed, her legs long—and *fuck me*.

"Summer," I hissed.

Her back arched as her legs spread wider, allowing me a perfect view of her bare pussy. She was right there for the taking. Needy, aching, and glistening.

"Luke," she moaned. "Please don't turn me away."

There was a vulnerability in her tone that made me snap.

I held on to her thighs as I dragged her to the edge of the piano. My thumbs rubbed circles on the inside of her thighs, working their way higher. Summer's breathing was jagged, her chest rose and fell rapidly, and her body kept squirming under me.

I was fucking livid.

I was mad at her for pushing me and at myself for being weak.

I leaned down and put one of my hands on her throat. She sucked in a surprised breath. It was gentle, with enough pressure to make her aware that I had the power here. She opened her mouth to say something, but I cut her off as my other hand moved higher. The warmness between her legs was like a magnetic force trying to pull me in.

"Is this what you want?" I spat as my fingers finally made it to her wet heat.

Her hips arched, trying to seek more pressure.

She was trying to speak, but my hold on her throat was stronger now, only allowing her enough air to breathe.

With my index and middle fingers, I teased her entrance.

My sharp inhale was audible.

Summer was fucking soaked for me. If I thought too hard about it, I knew it would make me sick, so I ignored it for now and instead slowly pushed my two fingers inside her.

Her mouth parted, her eyes fluttered, her pussy constricted around my fingers. She was warm and tight, and the deeper I pushed, the more she lifted her hips because she couldn't get enough of this—enough of me.

Beautiful.

"Are you that fucking horny that anyone will do..." I slid my fingers out and traced them up to her swollen clit. "...or just me?"

She groaned, her legs spreading more, allowing me more room. I pinched her clit, and her body arched.

"You want to be my little slut, is that it?" My words were intended to be harsh, but her blush and the wetness between her legs said otherwise. I could smell her pussy, and my mouth watered.

Would one taste be so bad?

Fuck, what I was doing was already more than enough to get me a one-way ticket to hell. I circled her clit slowly, and because I liked to torture myself, I let go of the hold I had on her neck just so I could hear her moan for me, and Summer didn't disappoint.

"Luke," she whimpered as I played with her clit. She was so swollen for me already it wouldn't take much. The noises she was making—fuck. My cock was aching and begging me to just sink in already.

Just when she was close to coming, I pulled away.

"Trust me, little dove, you don't want me." My words echoed in the air as I left her alone in the room.

The house somehow felt emptier than it did before as I walked away from her.

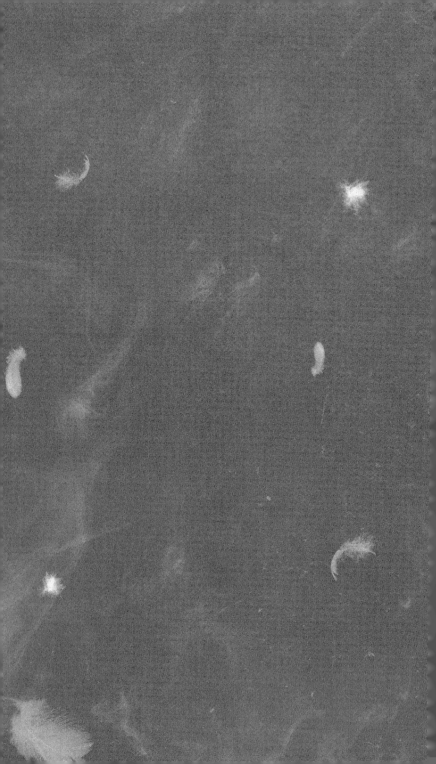

SHADOWS

The dark is not a scary place when all the shadows are your
friends.
All demons are the same when you can't see their faces.
For numbness and darkness are one and the same.

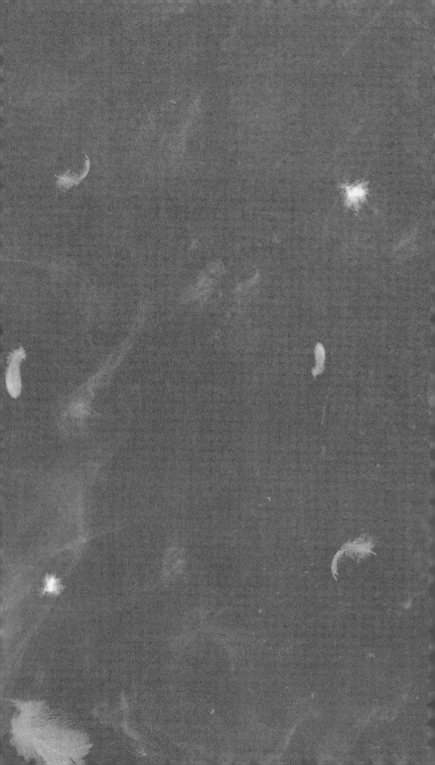

CHAPTER NINE

SUMMER

THIS MORNING, I WOKE UP WITH AN ACHE THAT I HAD never felt before—not like this. My phantom memory could recall the way Luke's fingers stretched me out. The way my body responded to him. How I had been right on the edge and I would have come harder than ever before, and then he was gone.

You see, not all the men and women who had me had been cruel. I had my first orgasm before I even knew what a period was. It wasn't until I was much older that one of the ballerinas decided to educate me. How sad was it to know what you were doing but not have the education on how it all worked?

There was no pity to be felt in the ballet company about our sexual exploitations. We may have traveled different roads, but our walks had been the same.

If I thought too hard about all the tragedies that happened to me, it was bound to make me sick, so I brushed it off. Sex was neither good nor bad at that point; it was something I did so I could live for another day. Except last night, it wasn't for survival. It was for me...something I wanted—no, something I needed. For the first time in my short life, my body was acting appropriately.

My needs and wants were not being controlled by anyone else.

Or was it the fact that he kept rejecting me that had me begging him for more? I had begged before, but it was all part of a game. I did what my masters wanted so I could be over and done with it. I played my role so I could find some peace afterward.

"Cecilia," I called the maid as she brushed my hair.

"Yes, Miss Summer," she replied as she gently combed.

I opened my mouth to pry more about Luke but thought better of it at the last minute. I wanted to know all his secrets, but not like this. As someone who had everything pried from them, I didn't feel right doing it to him.

"How is the weather outside?" I asked instead.

If my calculations were correct, Christmas Eve would be tomorrow. Not that it mattered much. It was usually just another holiday, although Nico did buy us a nice meal on the day. No one made a big deal about it, though. Holidays tended to be depressing when you had no family to celebrate them with. It was the number one reason why people got depressed during these times of the year. Nothing like a big reminder of the things you no longer have.

But now it was a bit different. It wasn't like I had found myself these things. I just thought it would be nice to spend it with someone else. Not that it mattered, right? No one here even mentioned anything about the holiday. I wouldn't even be surprised if Luke was against it.

"It's cold. Looks like it might snow later."

"Really?" I sat straighter.

When was the last time I played in the snow? Not that I wanted to go and build snowmen, but I was always embarrassed with the other girls around. So going out and just touching snow to throw it up in the air and then letting the flakes hit my face was something I had been dying to do for quite some time.

"Yes, we might actually have a white Christmas this year."

I couldn't help but smile at that.

"You love the snow." It was a statement, not a question.

"Yes," I told her. "It reminds me of home."

The last part was added involuntarily.

Her fingers froze on my hair.

"How was your home?" she gently asked.

My throat was clogged. What could I say? There were a thousand and one ways I could describe that place, and it still wouldn't do it justice.

"Is Luke here today?"

Cecilia didn't say anything about my abrupt change of subject.

"He had to go to work, but he will be here later."

I wondered what he did for work. What even was his last name? These were all questions I wanted answers to, but I was too scared to ask them in case they would be reciprocated.

"Have you been with him long?"

Getting her to trust me to divulge all his secrets seemed like a bad idea, but there was no denying that the more time I spent in this house with Cecilia, the more I felt like I had finally found a place I could belong. I had my routine here. I ate, I watered the plants, sometimes I ventured into the swing, and then I would soak in the bathtub.

"I've been here since before Master came to the house."

Well, that didn't tell me much, and I decided not to press more where Luke was concerned. Her evasive answers were enough of a clue that although she seemed to like me, she was loyal to him.

I had a set routine, and it was best not to mess with it for now. I liked it here, and out of all the places I had been, I would miss it if I were to be shipped away.

"Cecilia, what's the house like?"

She didn't answer me right away. In moments like these, I wished I could see a person's reaction. The downfall of my disability was that everyone had one hell of a poker face.

"It's beautiful. The structures are high, with big, accented windows and dark wooden floors. The details are what make this place gorgeous."

"I wish I could see it," I whispered.

My throat constricted because there was so much beauty in the world, and people often took it for granted. The little things mattered more than everything that was materialistic. The little things were what you carried with you when all the worldly pleasures faded.

Nothing good ever lasted—at least in my case. I didn't know why the thought of even getting attached was a possibility for me at this point. Everything I had once owned got ripped away from me. All I had was a bunch of scars to prove the damage that got left behind.

The scarring around my eyes was just the ones you could see and feel. The rest of my scars were invisible. I carried them within me, and with every jagged breath I took, it felt like I was being ripped in two.

Once I was sure Cecilia had left me alone, I walked to where my bag had rested since the moment I got here. All the way at the bottom were my ballet slippers. I told myself I was done with ballet when everything went up in flames. I told myself that what I had done to survive was all past me, but when I was told I was being moved, I stuffed my ballet slippers in my bag.

The dress I had on today was long but not enough that I would trip on it. I sat at the edge of the bed and put on my flats. Once that was done, I grabbed my cane, made my way to the hallway, and explored.

I went to the room where the piano was located and ventured. Two sets of stairs were on either end. I left the second floor alone for now. I knew the kitchens were on the other end, but since that hallway on that side was off-limits, I left it alone. Was that where he slept? I shook my head, ridding those thoughts away. In the middle, on the opposite side, was a door. Since it wasn't locked, I let myself inside.

The first thing I noticed was the smell of dust. After closing the door, I rested my cane against the wall and began to feel the walls. On the sides were bookshelves covered in dust. There were some books but not many. The room wasn't very big, but it was abandoned. If I had to guess, I would say it used to be an office.

There was no desk in sight, but on the far wall on the right was a set of spiral stairs. I made my way back to where I had left my cane, mapping the room and smiling to myself when there were no objects in the way.

Once I was in the middle of the room, I sat down on the cold floor and began to stretch.

It had been a month since I had been rescued. And I used that term lightly because I wasn't sure this alternative was better. This was my third day attempting to dance. My feet were killing me. I could feel the blisters when I went to bed a night and the dried blood as soon as I took my slippers off.

According to Nico, anything could be learned. I was in

the background and had to pay my dues in this twisted act he called a lifeline.

I bitterly thought that paying my dues on my back didn't hurt as much as this.

My sigh echoed in the studio. Everyone had left, but I stayed behind, trying to get the steps the choreographer had guided me with. For five days, she had been teaching me a dance I could not see.

I felt like a puppet. I wasn't sure my price for freedom was worth this much.

My only saving grace was that I wasn't completely blindsided by ballet. In my previous life, I practiced ballet not for sport but for fun. I wasn't committed, but I knew enough that I picked up on certain moves quicker. It also didn't help that I didn't like to be touched. When the other girl got frustrated, she moved me, and all I could do was grit my teeth and flinch.

"So this is why you wanted Nico to sleep with you," a voice on the other end of the room said. "You're so pathetic you can't dance."

Annoyance and shame spread through me. "It's easy to do something you can see."

She huffed, and I heard the soft thumping as she sat in front of me.

"Dancing isn't something you have to see. You just have to feel it."

I heard the sound of something snapping, and I jumped.

"Relax," the girl bit out. "It's just my new slippers. Nico thought that since we were the same size, I should give you mine...now I have to break a new pair in."

She spoke of Nico in a possessive way. I knew the tone all too well; I'd been on the receiving end of it for years. When a client got too attached, they would no longer be allowed to see us. I had my own room with a bathroom attached to it. My interaction with others was kept to a minimum. It was just me, my clients, and whoever brought in my meals.

The day all hell broke loose in la Casa del Silenzio, *I had been prepared to die. I stayed in my bed as the shots rang out. I didn't cower or attempt to run; I was sitting down, waiting for death to finally finish what it had started.*

But it had not been death who rescued me. Nico had stood in that room, and I felt him watch me for a few seconds before he even spoke.

"You're free now," he spoke.

He cautiously walked over to me and then began to take away the blindfold that covered my eyes. The clients didn't like to look at my scarred face.

The moment he noticed why it was covered, he hissed.

"Touch me."

I shook my head as the other girl spoke.

"W-what?" I stammered, not knowing in what way she meant it.

"Gently touch my feet, and keep up with me," she spat.

Tentatively, I reached out until I could feel her smooth legs beneath my fingertips. I slid my hands down until I felt the top of her feet. She began to bend her legs until they were crossed opposite each other. Then she rose on her tiptoes.

"Échappé," she stated.

Then she walked me through a glissade step by step. Her legs moved delicately despite the pressure my hands added. Then she counted all the steps of a pirouette enchaînement. She told me which positions I needed to land in after my sautés and walked me through my choreography.

"That's basically what you're required to do. Now, stand up, and I'll show you what to do with your hands."

I instantly did what she asked of me. Now that I wasn't on her feet, she moved faster as I kept up with her, my hands gliding up and down her arms as she moved. My guidance was her voice telling me where she would go next. The only times I let go of her was when she did pirouettes.

"That's it?" I asked once she told me to back off.

"No one will make you do a grand jeté. We aren't cruel."

When she put it like that, it made sense. Relief washed through me once I realized that I could do it, and it had not been as hard as I made myself believe.

"Thank you," I told her. "You make a great teacher."

"My show is only as good as all of my dancers."

Now it all made sense.

"I didn't know Nico was married."

She stepped closer. So close I could feel her breath on my skin. "I'm the prima ballerina. This is my *show, but make no mistake. Nico belongs to me."*

After that, she didn't really talk to me again. But thanks to her, I was able to be more than mediocre at dancing. She let me *see* and feel all my moves so I wouldn't be as blind as I already was.

I moved through the room for hours until I could feel those blisters form once more. Until blood soaked my toes. But this time, when I stopped, I did so with a smile on my face.

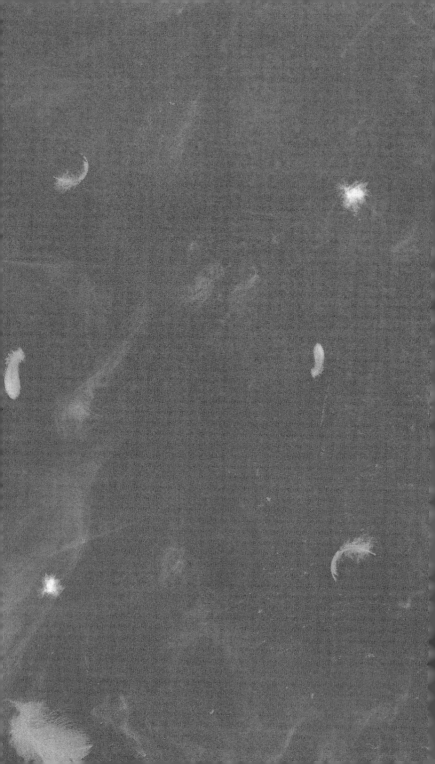

GRIEF

You wander the world with no place to go.
Your compass is broken, you can't find your north.
Dying from grief, numbing your pain so you won't feel a
thing.
Because you know that once you let it—rage will decimate
everything.

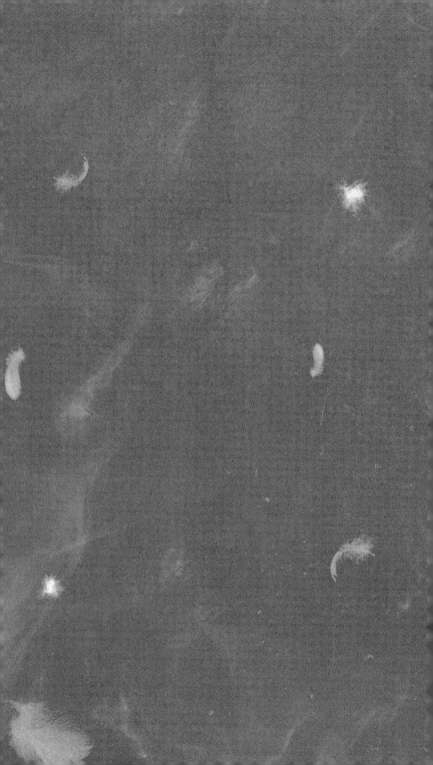

CHAPTER TEN

SUMMER

If you had asked me a year ago, I would have said I wasn't a fan of pain. Why would I make myself bleed when I could remain safe? A year ago, I was still wandering with no purpose. I was free but with no compass pointing me where to go. For most of my life, I had been at a standstill, fighting a silent war.

I told myself that I did not cry over spilled milk when I ended up the way I did because after crying, I knew what would come next. Rage would follow, and I think at some point, I convinced myself that feeling hollow was better than being angry. Numbness was easy, but everything else was exhausting.

Now, as the days went by, and for the first time in years, I could breathe. I could learn to be me, and I was scared of what it would unleash.

Cracks.

They were taking a hold of me. Pieces of the armor I wore were beginning to fade away, and it was terrifying.

When I heard footsteps coming my way, I began to stretch my body, but everything was tender.

"Ow," I mumbled as I stretched.

The way my body ached reminded me of my first week of practice. Then my thoughts took a much darker tone and went back to how much pain I was in after that first day in *that* place.

To say it was brutal was an understatement.

I gripped the sheets and took a deep breath to try and tame the anger that began to spread. My throat constricted, and my jaw was beginning to get sore from how hard I was clenching my teeth as if that would swallow back the vile things that were done to me.

I was usually good at ignoring what had happened in that place. It was a part of me, but I was okay with never revisiting that part of my life. Sure, I put on a brave face and acted like I was ready to talk about the secrets that I knew. But the reason those secrets still remained that way was because I had not spoken about them.

Nico quickly figured out that I was not going to be able to help him out in his endeavors, and he put me to work.

The door opened, and I hastily sat up, putting on my sunglasses.

"Cecilia?" I asked as I tried to place if there were any footsteps.

My heart began to beat faster. My skin got covered in goose bumps. Quickly, I reached for my cane.

"H-hello?" My voice croaked.

There was no noise that I could hear. No steps that I could trace or sharp inhales. Suddenly, it felt hard to breathe. It was just like being back there. The cruel customers liked to slam the door and then proceed not to say a word. They would taunt me, scare me, and then they would take me.

You never forgot the way a predator's eyes felt on your

skin. I didn't have to see them to feel the mark they left on my skin.

My chest was rising and falling faster now.

"Ce-celia?" I tried again.

For a second, I thought I heard thumps, but it was just my heart trying to get out of its confines. The sound echoed everywhere, impairing the one sense I relied on the most.

Every hair on my body rose when I felt like something grazed my skin. My hand gripped the cane even tighter. I was not a scared little girl anymore—but I couldn't move.

It was like being stuck in a nightmare.

My mouth opened, and I began to scream, but it got cut off instantly. All the air got cut out, and all I could do was wheeze. There was a weight on my chest holding me down. Everything in me was at war. A part of me was telling me to fight, but another part was telling me to give in, and I hated to admit that there was something seductive about it.

My body bucked because my will to fight was still somewhere in there.

Air—I needed air.

My arms finally decided to work. Now that I focused on them, I could feel them gripping the bedding. It felt like my brain was submerged in water; everything was fuzzy. Something was gripping my neck.

I brought my hands up, and I felt arms, long and thin, trying to choke me.

My wheezing got louder, and I didn't know if I was sobbing or trying to ask for help.

Suddenly, it felt like I'd come up for air, and my gasp echoed through the room. It burned to breathe. Something that was vital shouldn't hurt so much.

"Come on, deep breaths."

I did it again.

And again.

With each breath, I could focus more on the sounds coming from the room.

There were several footsteps, and that did not help my aching heart settle.

My hands came up again, and when I felt hands on me this time, I began to scratch. It took a second to realize I was screaming. There was no pressure in my chest this time, but instead, I found myself wrapped in it.

"Summer, calm down."

My body was shaking.

"Keep breathing."

Something stroked my head.

"You're doing so good."

It kept going like that until I felt nothing.

WHEN I CAME INTO CONSCIOUSNESS AGAIN, THE FIRST thing I noticed was that I was wrapped in someone's arms. They cradled me like a baby, which made the sorrow that was spreading through my body all that much worse.

I was too scared to speak. Had it all been a ruse? Was this what really had been awaiting me? Much of the same as what I already knew?

"Are you feeling better, Miss Summer?"

A part of me calmed with the sound of that voice. Before I answered, I took a deep breath, and sure enough, the smell of lilac was present.

My body became languid as I tried to recall what had happened. I was not too proud to admit I was scared to ask. Ignorance was my best friend.

It took about three minutes for me to notice that I was

being touched and another to realize I didn't mind it. My lips quivered, and this time, it wasn't from fear but nostalgia.

I couldn't recall the last time anyone had consoled me like this. My day-to-day life with my family might not have stood the test of time, and fragments were all I had left, but deep down in my heart, I knew I was loved.

Just as I had made my mind up to speak up, I heard footsteps coming down the hall. They were heavier and seemed rushed.

"How is she—" Luke's voice was cut off when he noticed I was facing him.

No one said a word.

I bit my lip.

My thoughts were racing, and the sad thing was I believed in the worst outcome. Nine times out of ten, that seemed to be my life.

"Do you remember what happened?" Luke asked in a soft tone he hadn't used with me before. His voice was much closer now; I'd bet he was almost next to me.

Two things happened at once: the weight on my back vanished, and then next to me, the bed dipped, and I felt the heat he was emitting.

I shook my head so my words wouldn't betray what I was feeling.

"You had some sort of panic attack," he told me.

He was waiting for me to tell him more, but I found I couldn't find my voice. I had no sight, so I couldn't see what had happened, and when I needed my hearing the most, it failed me.

"I'm so sorry, dove...it was my fault," he sighed.

Suddenly, I felt like I had a ball stuck in my throat.

"H-how so?"

I began to fist my hands, but he took hold of them, and I jolted at his touch. I had been a fool to think that his touch would bring me comfort. The joke was on me for being so desperate to want to feel something that I would accept the scraps someone else was willing to feed me.

"You're usually out of your room when the cleaning service comes. I never thought to mention that you were not to be disturbed. The cleaning lady got near you to ask you a question...she didn't think much when she touched you."

My mind was trying to piece it all together. I replayed his words, and as much as I didn't want to, I replayed my earlier feelings, trying to complete the invisible puzzle.

"Is that why you don't like to be touched? You have panic attacks?"

"Not always," I admitted after a while.

He cursed softly, and if he wasn't so close to me, I wouldn't have been able to hear it. And I wished that I hadn't because it pierced a part of me. My armor wasn't as impenetrable as his. Mine didn't need force to shatter but softness that eased its way in.

"You let me touch you," he stated as he rubbed his thumbs over my fisted hands.

If I wasn't still reeling, I would have said there was something different about him. I would have even thought his darkness called to me.

Luke began to move my hands, and I stilled. He put my closed fist over my arm until I was pressing down skin to skin so I could feel the scratches that covered me.

"You started to call out for your mother and begged her for help," he whispered, almost like he was in pain.

Blood drained from my face, and coldness stepped in. My eyes got heavy, and when I blinked, I felt two tears shed.

"I'll have Cecilia bring you some food," he told me, and I simply nodded.

He walked away but did not go toward my door. Instead, he went to the bathroom. I heard the water begin to run, and before I could question it, his footsteps could be heard, but this time going out of the room.

I sat there, too scared to move, but the water was still running. Was he running a bath? I allowed myself one deep breath and willed myself with faux strength. The soreness I had forgotten all about was front and center as I turned my body so I could get out of bed.

Something dropped to the floor that startled me. As soon as I heard footsteps, my head whipped toward the door.

"It's just me," Luke assured.

My nod was response enough for him because I heard him go back to the bathroom. As soon as my foot made contact with the floor, I realized it was my cane, the thing that had dropped.

It was right next to me, like always. Had I even reached for it? This time, instead of just wrapping my hand around it, I put on the safety band.

The water turned off, and then Luke's steps followed. We both stopped walking once we were a few inches away from each other.

I wished I could see how he was looking at me. Instead, I let myself taste the tension that was rolling off him. It gave me something else to focus on, and I could almost pretend that it was all for me. For a second there, I thought he was going to comfort me too. Even if I wasn't sure if I wanted him to, I would have liked the option of having him try.

"Take a bath while the water is still warm." It was a soft command.

I stepped forward but was met with no blockage. He had moved away so I could pass. I didn't know if I was testing him or myself.

He didn't move until I made it to the bathroom, and when I got in, I shut the door before turning back to my bath.

It wasn't until I dipped my foot into the bathtub that I realized what it was he had gone to go get. There were small petals everywhere. Lavender and eucalyptus, if I wasn't mistaken.

My heart skipped a beat, and I almost hated myself for the way I was starving for his affection.

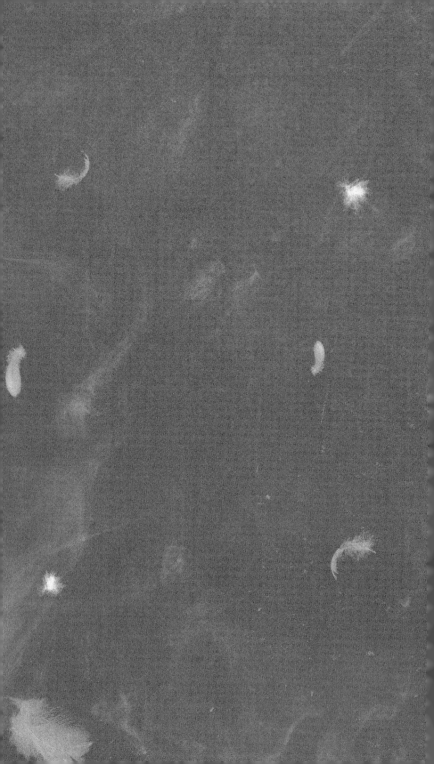

STARLIGHT

Sometimes we are born in sunlight but soon find ourselves in an abyss of darkness. From there, we learn to live with the fragments of starlight.

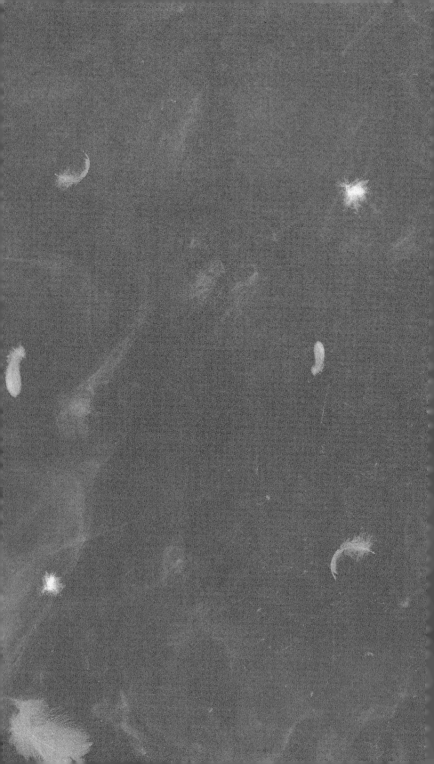

CHAPTER ELEVEN

SUMMER

GETTING COMFORTABLE WAS THE WORST THING YOU could do. I'd learned this from experience because whenever I found comfort in mundane things, hell's fire licked my skin, reminding me that all it took was one spark for my little world to go up in flames.

I was surprised that I had made it one year as a ballerina. One whole year spent prancing my way around the world. I couldn't see the sights before me, but as long as I never stopped running, it was fine by me.

At one point, I stopped asking where we were because, at the end of the day, it was all the same to me. So instead, I took a moment to appreciate the things I could feel. This time, it was a flicker of excitement.

Nico had a house on an island, and every year before the company would tour, he would give select guests a preview of what was to come. Instead of wearing tutus, we were dressed in light, flowy dresses that came down to our knees.

According to one of the girls, everyone was in whites and beiges, and the prima ballerina was in black.

I wouldn't say that dancing was now an extension of

myself, but it was almost like gliding. The way my feet moved me from side to side gracefully and with the rhythm, it was flying blind at its finest. One wrong move, and I knew I could mess it all up.

Trust was a human bond I didn't think I'd get to feel again, at least not one where I would be on the giving end. Who would want to trust their life in my hands? Yet as this year passed, the other dancers trusted me. It might not be much for some, but for me, it was everything.

"Summer," Nico's voice called for me.

It was more of a warning that he was coming to talk to me since the room was bustling with activity, and I wouldn't be startled by his presence.

"Yes?" I twiddled my thumbs.

I had been in his dance company for one year, and I already knew I didn't want to leave because compared to the last place I had been, this was heaven.

"I know you practiced the layout of the place, and the others told you how things are done somewhat differently here."

When he stopped talking, I nodded in confirmation that I was following along.

"For tonight, break rank and stay toward the back. Don't go past the first half of the tables, capiche?"

"I understand," I let him know.

I didn't need my sight to know he had retreated without a backward glance. That was the kind of man he was. Always on the go, always searching for something, but nothing seemed to fill the void.

This dance was different from the rest. It was intimate to the point that it felt frightening. I couldn't speak for my fellow dancers, but something about it all gave me chills. Just as Nico said, I broke formation and lingered in the back half, *just dancing around the room, giving people the show they came for.*

We were at the part where everyone was dancing around the tables, and the only one in the center was Ofelia—the prima ballerina.

As soon as she finished, cheers erupted. Jealousy burned through me at the sound of it. I wondered what it felt like to be adored. To be the reason someone would bend and almost break. The kind of adoration that was selfish because it was borderline insane.

I must have stood there for longer than necessary because the clapping had subsided. Quickly, I began to make my way to the back now that my part in the show was over, but before I could, someone stopped me.

It had been so long since I'd been touched that I felt like I was slapped. It was the reason why I stopped moving, and instead, I remained frozen. I would have gotten over the touch, but the voice destroyed a part of me I didn't think was worth destroying anymore.

"You are even more beautiful now."

Sure, it sounded like a compliment, but it was a mask for the humiliation those words brought.

I would never be able to recognize faces, but I never forgot voices. Especially not those of the abusers who called me their favorite girl. And unfortunately for me, I had been this man's favorite toy since I woke up in that hellish place.

The man who took my virginity never showed up again— at least not in my room. It might be fucked-up of me, but I sought him out in everyone else. What would make a man do such a thing to a child?

I could taste the bile in my mouth. My body felt like jelly, and my hands began to shake.

"Mon amour," *he sighed.*

A part of me was telling me to move, but another part of me knew that it would be better if I played along.

I didn't know his name. But I knew that he was thin and tall. His face was all sharp angles and a pointy nose. He would sometimes speak loving French words to me, while other times, he cut me down with his tongue.

I hated him the most because he found joy in bringing me pleasure.

Sweat marred my brow line when I woke from my nap. Funny how that memory was the one that came to me. Triggers were a funny thing, weren't they? A bunch of *pick me*s that wanted nothing more than to fuck you over.

It would be a lie if I said my days went back to normal, but after three days, I could finally breathe without thinking I would crack.

You'd think I would be out of my room trying to get away from the place that had triggered me, but I stayed, trying to conquer a demon, even if I was selfish in doing so.

My body no longer ached, and I was sure I would regret that decision later. When I went back to dancing, I would have to start from zero and get used to the soreness.

Had that been what triggered me?

Shaking my head and taking my own advice not to cry over spilled milk, I reached for my cane, and before I thought too much about it, I grabbed my coat.

I had access to the whole house, minus the left wing, yet I stuck to the same three places. My cage was small because I made it so. I got my wings back a long time ago, but I was still too scared to fly.

This time as I went to the greenhouse, I got close to the wall and began to feel everything that was near me. The material was cold, filled with a post every few steps. I reached as far as I could, even jumped a bit, but I couldn't touch the end.

Slowly, I parted my lips and whistled. Not surprisingly, it echoed, which made sense since I could hear the piano when Luke played.

The architecture reminded me of something, but I couldn't put my finger on what yet.

When I walked into the greenhouse, I went straight to the swing. It had been a frightening experience, and it took more than Luke knew for me to actually trust him.

Instead of going for the ropes, I went to the window in front. Judging by the way Luke had described this swing, I assumed there had to be an exit to go outside somewhere around here. It made sense, right? What better than to have a garden right outside these doors?

In no time, I found a latch. Taking a deep breath, I pulled it open. My eyebrows crunched when no rush of cold air hit me.

Weird.

I let my cane take the lead. There were no steps, so I tentatively followed.

Now that I was fully in this new room, I did notice that the temperature here was a lot colder, but there was no wind on my face.

A few steps later, my cane hit something else. I extended my hand and noticed that it was another door. I pulled the lever, but it didn't open. My hand moved up, and sure enough, I found a lock. Upon touching the knob to unlock it, I could feel the coldness that stuck to the metal. This time, once I opened it, the cold air immediately fanned my cheeks.

How did I forget how freeing it was to have the wind caressing you? The way it felt to breathe fresh air. That slight burn that came with the first inhale of the winter air. Little things reminded me that I was alive.

Without thinking of any consequences, I rushed outside.

The cold air tasted like freedom.

I had the urge to run, not away from this place but for fun. It was a dumb idea, I'll admit, but one I had never had before. My thoughts were all about survival and trying to stay with my head above water.

This was totally ridiculous, and it made me chuckle.

I walked a bit, my cane coming in contact with some sort of border. It was wide enough to fit three people side by side but perfect for two to take a stroll. When I got to the edge, I could feel some shrubs taller than my hand could reach. On other parts, it felt like it was made out of cobblestone. After my first few turns, I started to get an idea of the layout.

Some sort of maze, maybe?

My nose was starting to get cold the more I walked, but I couldn't stop. This path had to go somewhere, and I was determined to find out exactly where.

There was another turn, this one too close, and it didn't make sense with the pacing of the others. Mazes weren't scary or confusing when you realized that simple math was involved. I might not be able to see, but everything had a pattern. It was how I knew shapes.

Math might not be important to some, but it was to me.

My cane made contact with an object. I moved it around, but it seemed to go in a circle. I stretched my hand out, but nothing was there, so I moved it lower until I grabbed something made of stone. It went down, and it hollowed. I moved around it, my hand firmly on the edge of it, following its curve. It was some sort of circle.

"Summer!"

I immediately let go of what I was sure was a fountain when I could have sworn I heard my name being called.

The way back wasn't hard to figure out. Just needed to remember where I had taken all the various twists and turns.

"Summer!" My name was yelled again, and I stopped walking.

It was Luke, and my heart sped up while my stomach sank at the anger in his voice. Was this because of what had happened the other day?

With slower steps, I kept going, taking the last turn with caution.

My hands trembled, and it was part fear, and now that the excitement had faded, I began to feel the cold.

"Summer!"

It was a hoarse cry this time.

My mouth opened of its own accord, and I licked my lips, but that was a mistake because the air instantly cooled them.

"I'm here," I said, but it wasn't loud enough.

"Luke!" This time, my yell echoed around me.

I heard rushed footsteps coming toward me rapidly. Instinctively, I took a step back when they got closer.

"What the fuck were you thinking?" he roared once he was in front of me. My body instinctively took a step away from him, and my lower lip quivered. My body was shaking. This feeling was new. It wasn't just fear, but something else that made my stomach sick with dread.

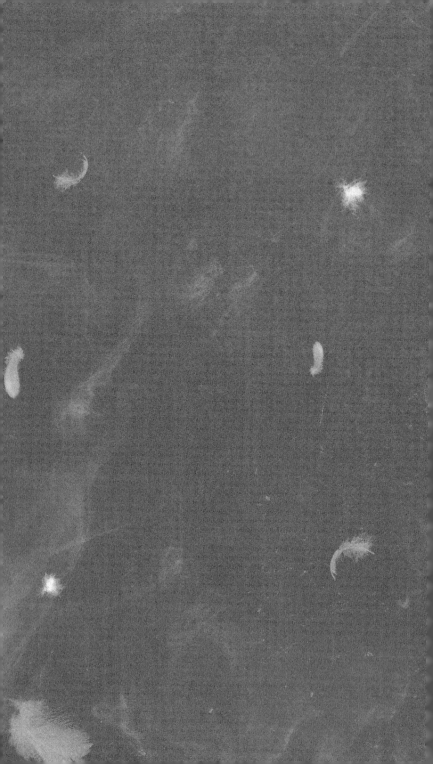

CHAPTER TWELVE

LUKE

THE THRONE I WAS LEFT IN CHARGE OF WAS SLIPPING through my fingers. I could feel it with each passing day, the distance and distrust that grew every time I showed up at the company.

It wasn't anything on the edge of treachery or even obvious, but the signs were all there. There was no joy as I watched pieces of the legacy that was entrusted to me be chipped away. Sure, it was everything I never wanted, but I would be dammed if I let it go.

My selfish nature had me holding on tighter just to spite everyone on the board. My reason for power was all thanks to a name that wasn't even mine, but even if I could have walked away, loyalty kept me rooted in place, fighting. And if I believed in destiny or fate, the reason for my refusal to quit was as clear as day, but instead, I chose to believe in my stubbornness.

Hector Bianchi was a cunning man who had been on the board since before I was born. He knew the ins and outs of Ferro Beauty Pharmaceuticals better than me, so he had the advantage.

The company's shares were used like a chess piece. Thanks to some disadvantage, we were currently tied. This was supposed to be my family, but the betrayal ran deep, and I couldn't believe he had been entrusted with a key piece. If I thought about it too closely, it enraged me, but then it didn't make sense, so I let myself indulge in the betrayal because it had never looked so tempting.

My whole life was filled with secrets. Too bad everyone that knew the answers to them was already dead —or dying.

Before Summer arrived, I was about to give up and sell it off. I already had enough money to live a privileged life, but I didn't want Hector to keep the company. I didn't have proof, but with Summer here, that would change. I knew he was connected to everything that had gone wrong, but I was too scared to pull the trigger on the information Summer carried.

I would be the one pulling the trigger, but she was the one who would deal with the fallout of the hit.

There was a knock on my door, and I sighed.

"Come in," I yelled, hoping it wasn't Hector. I was not in the mood to spar with him today. I knew my concentration should be here, but my thoughts were on Summer. A feeling I wasn't used to stirred in my stomach as I thought about the way she looked after her attack.

My fist clenched, but I was quickly distracted when my secretary walked in instead. Her eyes were bright as her gaze took me in. I didn't know how many times I had to remind her to stay professional. The way she smiled at me like she was privy to a secret I wasn't in on irritated the shit out of me. If that secret was the fact that she wanted to ride my cock, then it wasn't a secret at all.

"Yes?" I bit out.

No one here would dare say I was a pleasant person, and Elizabeth was no exception.

"Here are the documents you requested." She handed me a manila folder.

"Put it on the table," I instructed her. "I'm leaving. Filter my calls. Only reroute the ones that are pressing."

She nodded, then stood there biting her lip.

"Is there a reason why I have to suffer from your presence?"

"Will you be going to the company's New Year's ball?"

"No."

My irritation was palpable when Elizabeth didn't make a move.

"But it's a masquerade ball. We can..."

She kept on going, but I stopped listening to what she was saying, and instead, it gave me an idea.

"Sir, the heli is ready," Pedro informed me. Aside from Cecilia, he was the only other person I trusted. Both of them had been with me when it had all gone to hell. Cecilia even moved into the house permanently once my father died so I wouldn't be alone.

He was a couple of years older than me, tall with a wide frame. He looked more like a bodyguard than my chauffeur. In all honesty, he was more than a chauffeur, but that was neither here nor there.

"Perfect," I muttered, more than happy to get away from this place. "Any word on the academy?"

Pedro nodded. "You should have it on time. The day before, someone will debrief you and then come once the holiday passes and give further instructions, but you will be able to take it home."

Perfect.

Going from Upstate New York to the city was just one

short helicopter ride away. Years ago, this was where I stayed. My penthouse was still there, just waiting for the day I came back.

How eager I had been to make my own way and be on my own, yet here I was, barely living in the place I once wanted to escape to because I had been too broken to realize it wasn't fighting time anymore.

It was a short ride back to the house. Once we finally landed, the first thing Pedro did once he was unoccupied was hand me a USB drive.

"I didn't want anyone in the company to see me hand this to you."

My brow rose in attention.

"Everything your guy could find on Bianchi?"

Pedro gave me a slow nod. The smile that spread was filled with venom. I was close to discovering what I needed, and I knew it was time to start pushing for the answers. I had a feeling that at the end of this, I was going to hate myself even more, but if it brought justice, I'd say it was a sin I could live with.

The house was always quiet, so when I heard Cecilia yelling, blood drained from my face.

Not this shit again.

I could barely handle it the first time, and I wasn't sure I could do it a second time. I almost snorted as I rushed to follow Cecilia's voice. Who was I kidding? I would continue to do what it took to make everything right.

"Miss Summer!"

I didn't realize I took off running to where her voice was coming from.

"What's going on?" I barked.

Cecilia's eyes were wide, and fear was written all over them.

"I-I can't find Miss Summer."

There was no denying the affection Cecilia felt for her. It was hard to resist someone like Summer. She was like an eclipse. You could feel the warmth she emitted but kept hidden, and that just made you want to get closer to know more.

"Where have you looked?" There was an urgency in my tone that surprised even me.

"The greenhouse, kitchen, and I just came back from her room."

Shit, she wouldn't have gone to the left wing, would she?

"Have Pedro look outside, but if he finds her, tell him to call me. Don't engage—she doesn't know him. I don't want her to be startled."

Cecilia nodded as I took off, running toward the left wing.

There was no special lock in place since there had never been a need for it, but maybe I should invest in one. As soon as I opened the door, the air felt colder than it did the rest of the house.

I hated coming here, and poor Cecilia was the only one allowed to take it on. This area was forbidden to cleaners. I bypassed the old lab and sighed in relief when I didn't find Summer in there. I came to a halt before opening the two doors that led to one of the rooms in these headquarters.

The fireplace had been turned on, and I assumed Cecilia had already been here. She was much kinder than I was. I wouldn't even have brought an extra warm blanket. Everyone had to pay for their sins, but she liked to remind me that only God could do that.

I didn't say a word as I stepped foot in this repugnant

room, just looked around, and when I saw no sight of Summer, my shoulders sagged in relief just a bit.

Had she tried to run away?

That didn't matter. Even if she did, I would drag her back. It was her fault my head was fucked more than normal.

Last night, I couldn't sleep, so I went down to play, but that piano was now tainted. I couldn't stop thinking about the way she had looked on top of it. With every chord I struck, I would picture her body there, ready and waiting for me.

The way her hair fanned out like sunrays all over the top of the polished counter. The rise and fall of her chest as she anticipated what I would do to her. Or how her legs spread, begging me to take what she was so freely giving me. As fucked-up as it was, I wanted more.

I knew that even if she tried to run away, there was no fucking way I would let her. Two could play this fucked-up game she had started. If I had to drag her back here, I would.

With one last look at the bed, I curled my lip in disgust and walked away.

Cecilia was rounding the corner as I walked out of the hall.

"Pedro checked the front, and he drove around, and there's no sign of her," she rushed out.

She was always in her room or the greenhouse, not really knowing where anything was, and I felt like an ass for not bothering to show her more of the house.

Fuck.

I ran back to the greenhouse and prayed I was right.

The doors that led outside weren't locked.

I took off running and yelled her name as I went.

What if she got hurt?

A thousand things went through my mind, each new thought worse than the last.

I yelled her name, and each time she didn't answer, a part of me crumbled. This hopeless feeling was one I was too familiar with. The one that came with caring for someone other than yourself. It had been years since I felt like this, but it was as sickening now as it was the first time.

"Summer!" My throat burned from all my screams. The way my voice clawed its way out and my lungs adjusted to the cold air.

"Luke," she yelled, and I took off running, using her voice as a beacon. When I saw the entrance to the maze, I felt like I should have known better.

"What the fuck were you thinking!" I couldn't control myself. All I could still think about was the thought of her leaving—of her being hurt.

Eventually, she will.

Summer didn't answer. Instead, she took a step back. Automatically, I took one forward.

As shitty as it sounded after her attack, I was relieved because after what happened on the piano, I wasn't sure if I was okay with the boundaries being crossed. If she was someone else, I wouldn't have hesitated, but although she seemed like she was perfectly put together, she was a few secrets away from breaking.

One of my hands went around her waist to stop her from retreating any farther. My other hand cupped her cheek, and my teeth gritted when I noticed how cold her face was. She was facing me, but there was fear, and even though I had told her to run away from me, I didn't want her to fear me—not like this. This was not the reason I wanted her to run from me.

Despite everything going on in my mind, I did have her best interests at heart. And at this moment, I was glad she landed at my doorstep.

Summer's lips quivered as I rubbed my thumb over her face. Her nose was bright pink, going red. I watched her carefully to see if she wanted me to let her go, but her breathing was starting to even out—she was not going to have a panic attack because of me.

"What the hell were you thinking?" I repeated, this time gentler.

"I was just trying to explore."

Her answer left a sour taste in my mouth.

"Let's go," I said, trying to pull her with me, but she wouldn't budge.

"Do you want me to let go of you?" I asked, thinking that was why she had yet to move.

"What's over there?" she asked instead as she pointed to the place she had come from.

"Nothing."

"Luke, why won't you tell me anything?"

"Fuck this," I murmured before I reached down and carried her bridal-style. Her arms instantly wrapped around my neck, and fuck if that didn't make my chest swell. She trusted me just enough even though, at this point, we both knew she shouldn't. Even though I didn't deserve it, I had it. Her cane was digging into my back, but like hell if I would stop to fold it.

One thing I could count on was her self-preservation.

"Put me down," she hissed.

"No," I said as I began to take long strides back inside.

"Luke!" I heard her anger.

"You know how fucking scared we were. You can't just leave like that without letting us know."

"Is the house dangerous?"

"No."

"I'm blind, not an invalid," she spat.

I knew that, and I knew she was capable of a lot. She had survived way before I ever came into the picture. And even after I was out of it, she would continue to thrive.

I let out a loud sigh and kept walking. I didn't want to argue with her. Not after spending the last few hours sitting across from Hector and playing this stupid tug-of-war we had been partaking in, trying to see who had the bigger dick.

"Did you just spit on me?" Summer shrieked as we almost reached the door that led back inside.

"No," I scoffed.

That's when I noticed there were a few snowflakes on her hair, and one of them had landed by her upper lip.

"It's snowing," I told her matter-of-factly.

"Put me down!" she shouted, this time more enthusiastically.

"No," I repeated.

"Luke." She whispered my name like a plea, and although I didn't put her down, I did stop walking. She smiled at me. It started out slow but not sensual; it was the kind of smile that made a shit day be okay. The kind of smile you could get lost in. It transformed her stoic face and made it come alive.

"Luke, it's snowing," she gleefully said.

"It's a few snowflakes."

She didn't seem to care about the semantics. Her face was tipped up to the sky as snowflakes began to pepper her face. In the midst of winter, Summer looked at peace.

"Put me down."

"No," I simply stated.

She wiggled under my touch, trying to get me to let go.

Instead, I did something that surprised both of us. I twirled her around. Surprise was written all over her features before her face changed to one of delight.

God, did she look beautiful. Damaged people were breathtaking to watch. To see all those broken pieces being put back together and molded anew was a thing of beauty—perfection was so fucking overrated.

After a few minutes, she seemed to be content. She laid her head on my chest, and I hoped she didn't hear the way my heart was thumping like it was trying to come out of the cage it was contained in.

In the last few weeks, I had enjoyed things I never took the time to do. I forgot there was more to life than just existing. Just because you woke up each day breathing, it didn't mean you were living.

"Come on, little dove, let's warm you up."

Heat spread across her cheeks, and she bit her lower lip.

"Fuck," I muttered.

My cock grew at the sight. It didn't take a genius to figure out what was going through her mind.

She wanted me now, but that was because she didn't know all the pieces of me, and once she got the full picture, she was going to wish she never had.

The least I could do was hold back. I had already crossed so many lines.

"You could always warm me up," she said shyly.

"Summer," I warned, even though I was impressed at her for speaking her mind.

"It was a joke." She played it off, but we both knew it wasn't. Ignoring her so-called joke, I took her to the other side of the house where the library was located.

The whole time she was in my arms, she felt right. It

wasn't a burden to carry her; she fit perfectly like I knew she would. The things we wanted were the things that killed us, and there was no denying that Summer was killing me slowly.

To access the library, you could go about it two ways. The first was through the foyer. The empty space where the office used to be had a set of spiral stairs in the corner. Or you could take the main stairs to the second floor and access it from the side versus where the office takes you up to the heart of the library.

"I can walk, you know," she said as I started to head up the stairs to the second floor.

She could, but that would require me to let her go.

Once we had reached the second floor, I set her down. If she were to explore on her own, then it was better that she began to feel comfortable in the area.

"First door to the left, it's the library," I let her know.

I reached for her hand, and I heard her surprised gasp, but she immediately followed along.

"It smells like books," she stated as soon as we walked through the doors.

"It does," I agreed. "Remember, first door to the left."

"What else is on this floor?"

"Guest rooms, a gym, my office, and my room."

Her mouth parted in a silent O.

Summer tentatively began to explore. She stretched her arms out in front of her until she made contact with a shelf and stroked the spine of a few books.

"You know I have no use for this, right?"

"Knowledge is for everyone, isn't it?" I told her, and her brows scrunched in confusion. With the hand I still held on to, I led her to the area I had fixed for her. "This desk is for you. There's a computer to the side that has a system for the visually impaired. The touch pad in front of you is to take notes, read books, and write."

She pursed her lips, so I kept going before she thought I had forgotten what she had told me.

"After the holidays, you will have an instructor come three times a week to teach you how to read and write."

Her hands were now gripping the sides of the touch pad. I was worried I had overstepped, and I suddenly felt a bit at odds with myself.

"Don't worry, little dove," I muttered. "They will tailor a plan to fit your needs."

"Luke." She whispered my name as if it cost her to say it. She opened her mouth, but no words came out. I could see her thoughts play out on her face, and it was fascinating. She was like a kaleidoscope. So many different sides, and all of them beautiful. "Thank you."

My shoulders sagged in relief when she said those words.

I pushed the chair back so she could sit and then knelt in front of her. I took hold of her hands and looked up at her.

"You have nothing but time now."

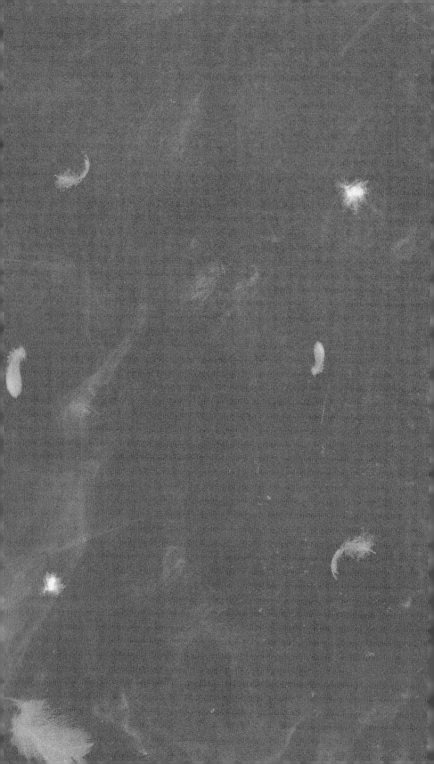

BEST SHOW

Tell me the truth, or feed me lies,
I still see all the things you want to hide.
You put on your best show so that I will not know,
all of the sins that have stained your soul.

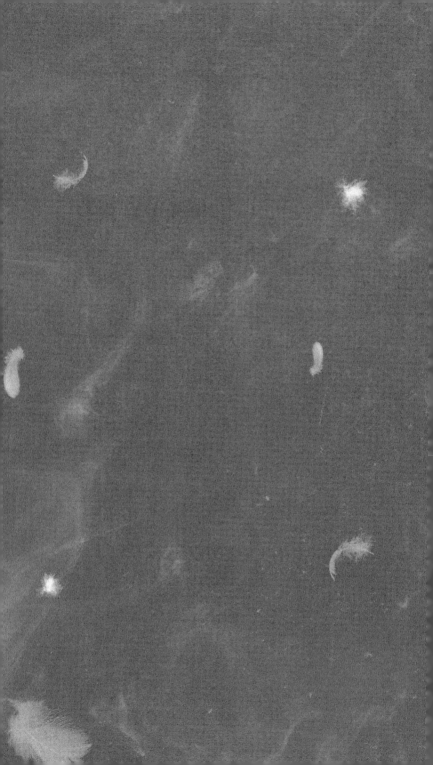

CHAPTER THIRTEEN

SUMMER

Have you ever felt like a fraud? That everything you have should not be yours? What had I done to deserve everything that was being given to me, and why? I was scared to let myself take the things that were being offered to me.

Sooner or later, everything we loved got ripped from us. It didn't matter if you tried to sink your claws in to try to keep them. All it did was create a bloody mess.

I lay awake last night, replaying memories that I no longer dared to visit. Had karma decided I wasn't a worthy punching bag anymore? Had I done my time, and did I dare to enjoy all the little things?

I had survived many things over the years, but each time, I lost a part of myself. And I had a feeling that if I gave myself completely to this, I might never recover.

Luke was right. I had nothing but time now. And that was a scary thing. To go from having to rush everywhere and live like every day could be your last to being at a standstill. The possibilities were endless—and intimidating.

When I was little, my father would play the piano for

me while I pranced around in a tutu and danced. What little girl didn't want to be a ballerina? When I finally got my wish, it came stained with blood and bad memories that I didn't allow myself to enjoy it.

Instead of going out and being grateful, I stayed locked in my room. Fear was rooted deep inside of me. I thought I was done running, but when it was all you knew, it made it hard to stop, didn't it?

You have nothing but time now.

The soft knock on the door startled me. I immediately took my slippers off, slid them under the bed, and then got up from the floor. My feet ached from practicing; I was just doing some stretches to end my session. I hadn't gone back to that empty room. Luke had already given me so much that I didn't feel right taking more. My room was big enough for some stuff. It wasn't much, but it was structure.

"Come in," I said, knowing it would probably be Cecilia.

"You didn't come out for breakfast, little dove."

A current of emotions washed over me at Luke's voice.

There was something physical that attracted me to him. Something that wanted me to give myself over to him, but I think a part of it had to do with the fact that he was the first man to pay any attention to me other than the sexual kind. He was giving me things without expecting anything in return. I figured my housing and a comfortable life came with whatever information he wanted, but everything else was extra.

With Nico, it was never like this. He was there for us but from a distance. Luke was everywhere in this house. I might not be able to see him, but I sure as hell could feel him.

He didn't call me out on the fact that I was hiding, and

for that, I was grateful.

"I was feeling under the weather."

As soon as the words were out of my mouth, his cold hand was on my forehead.

"You shouldn't have gone outside," he remarked.

If my mind wasn't a battlefield of emotions fighting for dominance, I would have smiled.

"You can't keep me locked in here," I said without thinking.

The hand that was on my forehead slid down until one of his knuckles tipped my chin up toward him.

"Don't try to test the limits of your cage," he warned.

My mouth went dry.

"One phone call to Nico, and I'll be—"

The words got cut off when his hand moved down to my throat. The pressure was just enough to make getting the words hard to choke out.

"You're never going back to him again," he stated, his hot breath fanning my cheeks. I could smell mint and a hint of menthol.

Something was being wrapped around one of my free hands. Felt like strings to a bag.

"Wear that tonight," Luke instructed as his hold on my throat loosened.

Instead of removing his hand completely, he slowly brought it up my face again and began to touch the scarring around my eyes. My heart rate sped up. I wasn't comfortable walking around the house without my glasses. It was hard to practice with them on, but I managed. I didn't want the other girls to see my scars when I never saw theirs.

In the comfort of my room, I felt safe to finally be able to practice freely.

"Don't wear the glasses tonight."

My mouth opened in protest, but he kept going.

"You're even more beautiful without them on."

Any words I wanted to say died on my lips at that moment. I felt the absence of his touch the moment he let me go. The door closed softly after him, and I was finally able to breathe.

By evening, I was still in my room, too scared to go out. Inside the bag, there were two boxes. One contained a dress. The material was warm and soft—velvet, I believed. The other one had a pair of shoes. Some sort of strappy sandals with kitten heels.

My eyes watered, and tears threatened to spill when I remembered the last Christmas I'd spent with my father.

"Mia principessa." My father's voice rang through the foyer as I made my way down the stairs.

Like always, I threw myself from the last step and jumped into his waiting arms.

"Papà, you're here!" I exclaimed excitedly. He had been working extra hard because they were set to launch a new product.

"Zio Luciano will be here soon. Remember, make his son feel welcome; he's been through a lot." My papà tapped my nose, and I smiled at him.

"Where's Mamma?" I asked as I peeked behind him.

"She's coming. She just had to set up a few things with the marketing department. Your zio—"

My father kept going, but I stopped listening when my zio Luciano walked in. I was about to take off and run toward him when I saw a shadow behind him.

As awkward as that dinner had been, it was still ten

times better than all the lonely ones I spent after they were gone. You really didn't know what you had until it was all gone.

Taking a tight hold on my cane, I made my way out the door. I refused any help today, reverting to the girl that thought she could handle everything on her own.

The dress fit me to perfection. It had a V-neckline with wide straps low on my shoulders. It was tight around my midsection but flared out below the waist with a slit on the right side. Every step I took made me feel exposed. The shoes weren't very high, but I was used to only wearing flats, so they made me nervous.

I didn't remember much of my mother, but when I did remember bits and pieces of her, it was always in nice clothing and beautiful high heels.

As soon as I made it to the foyer, the smell of cinnamon, oranges, and something else hit my nostrils. When I made it to the threshold, my head was down. I wore my hair loose, my bangs to the side to hide the worst of the scarring, but I knew it wasn't enough.

"Thank you for the clothes," I said as a greeting.

There was no answer. Maybe Luke wasn't here yet. I was about to pull back the chair when I heard someone else already dragging it out.

When I positioned myself in front of it, the back of the chair hit my legs, but before I could take a seat, Luke's fingers touched the side of my head that was covered. He swept my hair away and tucked a lock behind my ear.

"Better," he whispered, then allowed me to sit down.

I felt so exposed to him. It was like the more I tried to guard my secrets, the more he wanted to expose them. He found beauty in me when I couldn't see it myself, and the things that others didn't want to see, he wanted more of.

"I never celebrated Christmas," he said once he took his own seat.

"Not even as a child?"

A dark chuckle left his lips.

"My father cared more about his criminal empire than he did his family."

I bit my lip to stop myself from asking all the questions that were plaguing my mind.

"Do you miss your family?" I asked instead.

"My biological one, no, they were no family to me at all."

"I miss mine," I confessed. "I miss everyone."

Even the ones I shouldn't because they betrayed everything family stood for.

"I know." His tone was lower, gruffer, with an emotion I couldn't put a finger on.

We fell into a comfortable silence. I listened as he dragged plates across and brought them near me.

I leaned down and inhaled every single one before taking a bite out of them. I was chewing some steak when he finally decided to speak again.

"Tell me, little dove, how did you end up in *Casa del Silenzio.*"

The question took me off guard, even though that was the main reason why I was here. The only reason he had accepted to take me in. He had been wrong not to press me for information before because I was numb, but that numbness that had frosted over the years had begun to melt with each touch of kindness I received from him.

"Because my uncle killed my mother and then sold me off to the highest bidder."

I couldn't bring myself to tell him the other thing he had done.

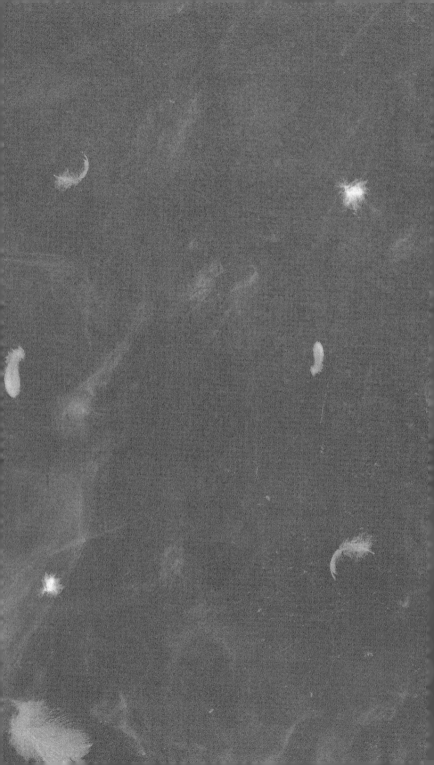

CHAPTER FOURTEEN

LUKE

We sat in silence while I figured out what the hell to say. Anger flared in every cell of my body, and I knew I had to cease it for now. Tonight wasn't entirely about that, about her secrets. It was about Summer as a person.

I set my eating utensils down. I knew I wasn't going to be able to eat any more.

"He did?" I managed to ask.

It took a second before she spoke again. Her lower lip wobbled before whispering, "I loved him. I still don't understand why he did that to me."

"Greed is a drug. You can't see anything but gold when you're on that path." The bitterness on my tongue was like poison. "My father fucked me over for some cash."

Summer was now scraping her food around on her plate. I sighed at how insensitive I had been bringing this up at what was supposed to be a nice dinner.

"We have a lot in common, don't we?" Her tone was almost teasing.

Taking a sip from my wine, I focused on her profile. It

had been a mistake to gift her a dress. It was distracting, the way the dress clung to her body. The dress was a royal blue, still dark but a stark contrast to the usual black she usually wore. The neckline was tasteful while being sensual.

"Misery loves company," I muttered, wanting to be done with the conversation I had started in the first place.

"If I may..." she began to say as she put down her utensils. "What is it that you need from *that* place?"

It was a fair question.

"I'm looking for some people who have wronged me."

She seemed to ponder on my answer.

"I was kept in a room," she began, and I gripped my drink. "Unless they would come to see me, I didn't have a way of knowing who that person was."

"You'd recognize them just by their voice?" It was an impressive feat, but with the trauma and the amount of time that had gone by, it seemed almost impossible.

A sad smile marred her features.

"By their voice, the way they smell, and how they interact with me..."

Fuck.

She already knew. And once again, she brought up the option before I did, so it would seem like she was the one in control.

My silence spoke volumes. She reached for her own wine and brought it to her lips.

"That's what you want me to do, isn't it? You want to parade me around as bait?"

My jaw was slack from how hard I was gritting my teeth. Her face was back to remaining blank, and the only thing that moved was a delicate eyebrow.

I set my drink down and shifted in my seat. "You aren't bait, my little dove..." My hand found its way to a tendril of her hair and twirled it. Her chest rose and fell, and my eyes went down to her cleavage and how it seemed to mock me. "You are a trap. I pity the man who underestimates you. You're not fragile, nor are you broken. Your jagged pieces are waiting for the perfect moment to strike."

She swallowed and then reached for another sip of wine. This time, the red stained her lips, making them appear lush and juicy.

"What made you arrive at this conclusion?"

"Because it's what Nico did. He paraded his broken ballerinas all over the world as bait to get the thing he wanted."

Regret washed over me. Would things have been different if I had gone to one of the shows?

I reached for her hand because I needed not only for her to hear my words but to feel them. She seemed surprised, but her small hand remained relaxed. I would say familiarity was to blame.

"Don't you want revenge? Don't you want every man and woman who hurt you to pay? I don't want to use you. I want to be your blade. Let me be your judge and executioner."

She was biting her lip and failing miserably to try and control her breathing. Was she scared? Had I gone too far? Then a lovely blush spread from her cheeks down to her chest, and when she shifted her legs, a thrill went through me.

My cock certainly appreciated the gesture. I wondered if she was already wet. My fingers itched to be back on her heat.

I cleared my throat.

"I'm not as strong as I appear to be—"

"I won't le—"

She put up a finger. "Let me finish... I'm not as strong as I appear to be, but for some insane reason, I trust you to keep your word—about this, at least."

Pride and regret swelled in my chest.

"I promise you, my little dove, you won't regret this."

She mumbled something that sounded like "I hope," but I pretended like I didn't hear.

"So, what's next?"

"There's a party for New Year's that my company is hosting..."

"You have a company?" she cut me off with intrigue.

"Unfortunately," I said. "You're to come with me."

That lovely blush was back, and if I could barely survive this, how would I do so the rest of the time?

"As your date?" She breathed the question.

"I believe men from my company might have...indulged themselves in *la Casa del Silenzio.*"

"Oh," she whispered. "Okay." She steeled her spine and tipped her jaw before turning her face toward me. "Luke." She spoke my name with conviction, and another jolt of lust went through me. "I want to make them all pay."

My smile was lethal.

"We will, my little dove. But enough of this, for now. It's Christmas, after all, so let us carry on with tonight's activities."

AFTER OUR MEAL, WE CLEARED THE DINING ROOM AND made our way to the foyer. It had been years since this house had been decorated, so when I told Cecilia to set up the decorations that adorned the foyer, she looked at me funny. This house used to shine bright in the holidays. It was a shame that Summer would never get to see it.

"Are you going to play me a song?" Summer teased as she let me lead her toward the foyer.

"Do you want me to play you a song?" It was something I did for myself, but the fact that she enjoyed listening to me play pleased me.

"Yes," she answered without hesitation.

"First, I want you to *see* the decorations," I told her in a way to refer to the way she saw things. I put her hand on top of the nearest tree branch.

The wonder in her eyes was refreshing. I'd seen it many times now, but each time, it slayed me just as it had the first.

"I hadn't realized the house was decorated."

There was a hint of something in her tone. Not sadness but an ache.

She got closer, and her foot kicked one of the presents out of the way. Upon hearing the noise, she bent to pick up what she had kicked. Her nose scrunched as she trailed the box, and then as her fingers pinched the bow, her face morphed.

"Open it. It's for you," I confirmed to let her know that the present was indeed hers.

"Luke." She breathed my name as if she had no idea what to make of me.

"It's nothing, Summer. Just open the damn present."

Her chest rose and fell, and I hated that I was standing because all I could see was her perfect breasts nestled in the cups of the dress, but damn if I wanted to move. I put my hands in my pockets while I waited and watched as she took her time. She was savoring the moment, the memory, and fuck if that didn't sting.

"What is it?" She gave a frustrated chuckle after a few seconds of playing with the contents inside.

"It's a collar," I told her.

Both of her eyebrows shot up, and I would have found that funny if it wasn't insulting.

"For me?"

"Fuck no."

This seemed to calm her.

"Some of the other ballerinas were treated as pets, so it kind of took me off guard."

The world was really fucked-up, wasn't it?

"Come with me," I said as I reached for her hand.

Once I had helped her get up, I walked with her to the old office. For some reason, her cheeks went pink again, and I really wanted to know what the hell she kept thinking about.

As soon as I opened the door, the dog started to pace, and his nails could be heard tapping the wooden floor. Summer hesitated for a second, but I kept pulling us through. I guided her to take a seat on the floor a few steps away from the dog.

"Don't be scared, okay?" I assured her.

I went toward the stairs, where I had leashed the dog just before dinner.

"Summer," I began to say as we got closer. "This is Bear, your new companion."

Her sharp intake of breath echoed in the empty room.

She reached out with both hands, and as soon as we were near, Bear began to sniff her and rub his head against her.

"The collar is for him," I told her.

A smile began to spread through her face as she petted the dog. When he licked her cheek, she laughed. Suddenly, it felt like I was trying to swallow sand. In the short time I had been with Summer, I hadn't heard her laugh once. The guilt hit me like a ton of bricks. She deserved to laugh, she deserved happiness, and even if it killed us both in the end, I was going to give her those things.

"Bear is one color versus the two-toned fur his breed is more famously known for."

"What color is he?"

"His fur is all black."

She kept playing with Bear, and he relished the attention, and since he wasn't in his harness, he knew it wasn't "work" time.

"Like a night with no stars?" Summer questioned.

"Yeah," I breathed.

"As you probably already guessed, I wasn't always blind." There was a sarcastic bite to her tone since we both knew the scars around her eyes weren't something she was born with. "Sometimes I still remember some things. Not vividly, but it comes like a gut feeling. Sometimes a color means nothing to me, and sometimes I know it all too well."

My nostrils flared, and I knew I would take my time to kill whoever did this to her. It would be slow and painful.

"And black means something to you?"

She hugged Bear close to her chest. "When I was a little girl, I used to think black was such an ugly color. Where I thought gray was sad, black was scary. Then my sight was gone, colors ceased to exist, and there was nothing. And all I could think of was that I was now in black."

I crouched on the floor in front of them.

"And how do you feel now?"

Summer licked her lips as her face turned toward me. How was it that even if she couldn't see me, she was still so attuned to where I was? And why didn't I mind that?

"I feel happy," she whispered, too scared to admit it louder, and I could guess why.

"How about if we call that feeling yellow."

The smile she gave me was blinding, and I relished the moment because there was a chance that next week things wouldn't be the same.

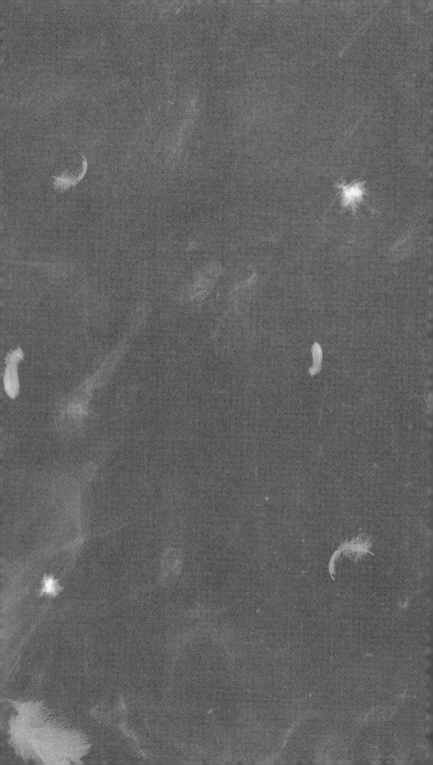

COLORS

She lived in black but loved in colors.
He lived at war but searched for summer.

They were chaos, and they were pain.
Willing to meet where sunshine met rain.

Because at the end of the day, everyone bled red.

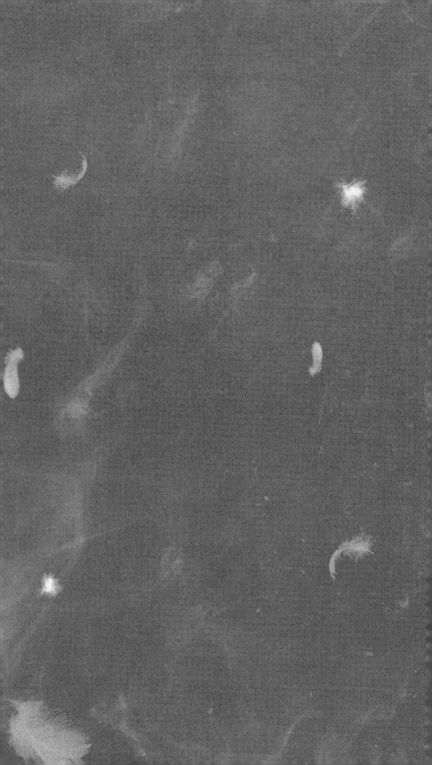

CHAPTER FIFTEEN

SUMMER

The days after Christmas Eve passed in a blur. Maybe it was the anticipation of going out. Not going to lie, it was slightly terrifying to do so. I'd been performing for years, but I had grown to love the peace that came with being secluded in this house.

The real reason the days seemed to go on faster was probably the furball sleeping next to me.

"Morning, Bear," I greeted the dog.

I could feel his tail wag, and I loved that about dogs. How you could tell they were happy from that one motion. They didn't need to talk and verbalize that to you, just like I didn't need to see it to feel it.

Luke had given me a brief explanation of how Bear worked. He had two leashes I could use on him. The first leash I used on him was when he walked with me to the greenhouse. That one was his off-duty leash. He still tried to guide me if I was walking into an object, but he was more relaxed. Then there was his harness. That one had a lever that I held on to and pulled so I could guide him where I wanted to go. In my ignorance, I thought the dogs guided you, but that was not how it worked. The human guided the dog, and they made sure they steered clear of objects that could harm them.

The first business day after Christmas, an instructor came to finish educating me on all things Bear. I got the feeling Luke bypassed protocols with money. This didn't really irritate me since it was something I had seen my whole life.

He knew some commands, and if I was in danger, he was trained to read my body language and go ask for help. After being alone for so long, it was nice to have a companion. Someone I could care for and take care of. Just like the plants in the greenhouse, it was something that was mine and made me feel a little more whole.

I knew it was stupid to place my self-worth on being able to function like others, but being able to have things to care for made me feel like I was normal.

If I felt like I couldn't use that empty room to dance before when Luke had gifted me a tutor and my own workspace, add a dog, and I had not been back there since.

Not that it mattered. Despite my panic attack and the occasional nightmare, this room was my sanctuary.

I started by stretching on the floor.

My muscles had been stiff from all the time I had ignored them when *Danza dei Morti* met its end by fire. Whatever part of me that integrated into the world ceased to exist when that company stopped playing.

After the last show ended, Nico was done with all of it. By then, there was an ease in him that had been missing before. He was finally at peace. So, all of his little swans followed him to sail the seven seas—and I hated every second of it.

It was months of constant sickness. While everyone else

felt free, no longer confined to the boundaries of land, I felt like I had no foothold in this world. Somedays, the waters were still, but their soft rocking could still be felt if you concentrated hard on it, and all I could do was focus on them.

There wasn't much I could do on a ship. I stayed mostly in my room, trying not to be sick. Then there were days when the waters were turbulent. I could feel every sway, the way the harsh winds scraped against my window, and prayed that it would end. I was jealous of the other girls who healed on that ship. Somewhere along the journey, they decided that they were ready to spread their wings and fly away. I said my goodbyes all while feeling like every time one of them left was like a nail rooting me in place.

When Nico finally announced that he would settle, I felt relieved. There would be no more sea, no more ship, no more rushed stops in a dock, and I wouldn't be so miserable.

Then he informed me of what would happen to me. And I couldn't blame him. He wanted his fresh start, and that fresh start couldn't happen if I continued to be a burden.

"Fuck," I groaned as I pushed myself to stretch past the point of pain.

Nico dropping me off at Luke's doorstep was the best thing that could have happened to me. He had done more for me than Nico did in the years he had me. Nico mended my wings, just enough to heal them, but not so I could escape.

"If you let me, I'll teach you to fly."

Bear jumped to attention. I knew someone was coming to my room before I heard the steps because Bear put himself in front of me in what I assumed was a protective manner.

I broke into a side straddle split and moaned as my body stretched.

"Morning, dove. I thought we could have breakfast in the—"

Luke's voice suddenly stopped.

"My apologies. I didn't realize you were busy."

Ignoring him, I stretched the opposite way.

"Breakfast where?" I asked in a breathy tone.

There was a pregnant pause before Luke answered.

"There's a small outdoor dining set in the greenhouse..." His voice sounded a bit stained. "I thought we could eat there today."

"Oh, that sounds lovely," I told him.

"I'll let you finish so you can get decent," he rushed out.

Decent? I was in long sleeves and a pair of leggings. I had not worn them before since they were worn-out from dancing. I didn't feel right wearing them past my morning practice, but they still covered me far more than the tutu and mesh dresses the dancing company had us prancing in.

"Wait," I called out after him. "Can you help me with two of my stretches? It's hard to do them on my own."

If it weren't for his footsteps getting closer, I would have thought he had left.

"What do you need me to do?" He sounded almost annoyed.

I bit back my smile.

"Can you sit in front of me?"

I heard him sigh, but I soon felt his presence in front of me. I wondered what he looked like, how he dressed. How he styled his hair. Did he make facial expressions when he was annoyed?

"Now what?"

"You help me stretch," I answered as if it was obvious.

I put my hands forward, wiggling my fingers so he would take them. "You're going to pull my body toward you."

He did as I asked, and I couldn't help but groan at the way my rigid body extended. It hurt, but it felt divine.

"Don't let go," I hissed once I felt his hands loosen. "It feels *so* good."

His fingers gripped into my palms, and I used that bite to focus on instead of the way my body burned. Just a few more seconds and I would move on to the next exercise.

"Okay, done," I breathed.

Luke let me go as if I had burned him.

"What's next?" he asked in a gruff tone.

I bit my lip as I lay flat on the floor and then lifted one of my legs and brought it as close as I could to my face while keeping the other straight.

"It's been a while since I stretched this much, so my flexibility is a little stiff."

Again, another pregnant pause.

"Luke?"

"Let's get this over with so we can get some fucking breakfast," he muttered.

The moment he fixed himself between my legs, the energy shifted. The air became heavier, and my body was hyperaware of his proximity. I'd done this before with another person, and it was all the same, so I didn't know whom I was trying to fool when I asked Luke for help.

My breathing was already labored, and I was trying to remain calm so he wouldn't stop. One of his knees was between my legs. I could feel the heat it emitted in my center. If he got closer, he could feel how wet I was starting to get.

His strong fingers wrapped above my ankle. Even

though I couldn't see him, I could feel his eyes on me. Without me having to tell him, he began to push my leg. My hands instantly went to his shoulders so I could ground myself, and I felt his body go still.

"More," I groaned as my muscles began to stretch.

He obliged, and then the back of his hand graced my cheek, and I held my breath at the contact. Every cell in my body rose to attention. My skin was buzzing with electricity. The hum of his skin was calling to me.

One of Luke's hands had moved and was now resting next to my head for better support. I was caged in between his body, and a thrill spread through me, ending at my core.

"Just like that," I moaned as the tip of my toe touched the floor.

Luke grunted in response, but his hold on my leg would leave bruises.

"Give me a minute, and we can do the other leg," I whispered, aware that his face was just above mine.

My hands were still on his shoulders. He removed his fingers from my legs but otherwise didn't move. I brought my leg up until the back of my knee touched his shoulder. The position was intimate, and I couldn't help but think back to the piano. A lot had happened that seemed like that time was an isolated incident.

I could feel his chest rising and falling rapidly. Good, I wasn't the only one affected by our proximity. Knowing that I had an emotional impact on him made me brave. My leg slid down the side of his arm until I lay on the floor. As I started to lift my other leg up, the hand he had by my head switched sides.

Now that neither one of us was speaking, I could hear his heavy breaths mixing with my shallow pants.

The longer we spent down here, the wetter I was becoming.

My leg had barely lifted when Luke snapped. And I knew he'd lost some control because he had been so careful before when he touched me. His fingers dug into my thigh, and he used the force to part my leg so he could have more room.

I bit my lip so I wouldn't moan. An ache was starting to take place, and if we didn't finish soon, he would notice the effect he was having on me.

Fuck.

My lip quivered between my teeth. I was biting so hard I was surprised I hadn't drawn blood. Luke's hand moved up my leg languidly. The moment he stroked the back of my knee, I shivered.

A whimper left my lips.

Luke hissed.

He began to stretch me, and I was careful not to make any further noises. With Luke, things could go one of two ways, and I didn't want to test him for fear that he would leave me alone.

"Like this, or can you take more, my dove?" he asked in a smoky tone that went straight to my core.

"More," I begged shamelessly.

I could feel the vibration of his groan through my body, enflaming the need I had for him. My toe was almost touching the floor, but the dull ache from flexing my muscles was forgotten the moment I felt Luke's breath caressing my cheek.

"Is this what you wanted, my little dove?" he taunted.

Before I could respond, his knee pushed against my core. It was barely there, but it ignited me. My body jolted at the touch, and goose bumps spread through my skin.

It took a moment to realize the needy sound came from me, but the heavy breathing was all him. We were at a standstill, seeing who would win, him or me. A broken dove or the dark prince.

"No," I lied.

He let go of my leg, and I missed the pressure of his fingers on my skin. Just like before, Luke did not back away. Once more, I lifted my leg until the back of my knee touched his shoulder. Except this time, I didn't slide it down his arm.

Sure, I'd started this to test him, but he was the one who broke first, and I wanted to see how much I could push him before I got burned by my actions.

I hooked my leg on his shoulder while the other went around his waist.

His hot breath moved up and down my cheek. I could feel the phantom touch of his lips, and it wasn't enough. Before today, I didn't think spearmint and aftershave was an intoxicating combination.

While I waited for the moment his lips touched my skin, I didn't notice when his hand moved until he was gripping my throat. His fingers added pressure to my pulse points, and my lack of oxygen seemed to heighten everything else.

"I can fucking smell you, Summer," he growled. And to prove his point, his knee pressed against my aching core deliberately.

I could feel the effects of my whimper on his body. His skin was vibrating with restraint. The hand that was on my throat tightened as if that were going to make my body stop responding to his.

Without thinking, I moved my hips against his knee.

My core was aching and tightly coiled. I couldn't remember the last time I had found relief.

"Fuck," he hissed but didn't stop me.

Instead, he pressed his knee deeper between my legs. I should have been embarrassed, but I was blaming my lack of shame on the fact that I was lacking proper air circulation to my brain.

"You're so fucking wet, Summer, you're making a mess of my pants."

If he was trying to make me self-conscious and get me to stop, it wasn't working.

"*Luke*," I whimpered as the ache grew.

"Fucking hell," he spat.

He let go of my throat and moved back, and I almost cried at the loss of contact as he removed my knee from his shoulder.

I opened my mouth to speak but bit my lip the moment he fixed my leg behind his waist where the other one was. As soon as my ankles locked, he gripped my hips and lifted my waist toward him.

"Is this what you wanted?" he barked as my aching pussy met his hardness. He ground against me, leaving no doubt that he desired this as much as I did.

"*God*." My back arched, trying to get him to press harder against me.

"I haven't even touched your needy pussy, yet you're ready to come apart for me," he taunted.

He let go of my waist, but my legs remained locked, keeping him in place. His hands moved up my body, causing me to squirm under his touch. His thumbs toyed with my pebbled nipples, but otherwise, he kept moving. I thought he would finally kiss me when the tip of his nose glided across my cleavage. He didn't. Instead, he slid across my beating artery, moving toward my chin. He shifted his hips against me. I imagined this was what he would have done if he were fucking me. His hands clasped my wrists, and he brought them over my head, pinning me down.

As if I were crazy enough to try and get away.

"Is this what you wanted, Summer?" He ground his hips against me. "To rut against me like a fucking animal—" Thrust. "—get your fucking wet pussy to come against my cock?"

Bear's bark wasn't enough to make either of us stop. My stomach was tightly coiled; I could feel how damp my core had become, but I didn't care. My clit was throbbing, and the way Luke was moving was driving me mad.

"*Please*," I begged him.

"Please, what? Stop?" he mocked me.

"No," I cried, trying to remove my hands from his hold, all while shifting my hips, but he had moved, and I couldn't find the friction I needed.

"What am I going to do with you, Summer?" he whispered against my lips.

I had plenty of ideas, but instead of voicing them, I tipped my head so I could finally kiss him, but he moved before my lips touched his.

He gave a soft chuckle. How could he be okay while I felt like I was dying if I didn't get him to touch me?

"You want my lips, dove?" he goaded against the shell of my ear. His lips moved softly, but they were there mocking me every moment they weren't where I wanted them. "You're killing me, love. I'm dying to taste you." As if to prove this, the tip of his tongue flicked my lobe. "My fingers itch to be buried in your fucking pussy again." He let go of one of my hands and trailed his fingertips down my arm and stopped above my ribs. "You were so fucking tight around them—" His hand moved lower to the apex of my thighs. My legs were shaking against him. This made Luke smile because I could feel it against my neck. And I knew he did it for my benefit because he moved his lips away right after, but he wanted me to feel his reaction. He let go of my other hand and began to glide his fingers until they met in the middle. "—I can only imagine how you'll feel when my cock pounds into you."

Luke gripped the cloth on either side of my legs and ripped it apart. I was so wet that I could feel a rush of coldness as my damp panties were exposed.

"*Luke, please,*" I whined when I felt him shift.

If he left me alone now, I would cry. I had never felt like this in my entire life. I was so turned on that it hurt.

"You look beautiful," he mused. "Hair fanned around you like a halo, your legs spread, and your pussy so wet, begging to be filled."

I didn't have to beg again or wonder if he would leave me. He hooked one finger into my damp panties and moved it aside.

Maybe later, I would be embarrassed by his sharp intake of breath against my core, but right now, it only turned me on even more. I lifted my hips toward him like I was some sort of offering. He wrapped his arm around my waist and pulled me higher until his lips teased my pussy. His touch was like a lightning bolt, making my core constrict.

"Look at the way your pussy is begging to be filled," he groaned before he finally licked me.

"*Luke.*" It was a desperate scream.

His tongue moved from my center all the way to my clit, where he used the tip to add pressure just where I needed it the most.

"You wanted a kiss, didn't you, Summer?" he asked, but before I could reply, I felt his lips kissing my clit.

I groaned, almost coming out of my skin. Luke slowed his ministrations, eating me out like I was a delicacy when I wanted to be devoured. His tongue teased my entrance while the tip of his nose pressed against my clit. My legs shook over his shoulders. I was so close now, and he was toying with me.

"If you—" Lick. "—want—" Another lick. "—to come—" He bit my clit. "—then fuck my face."

Oh God. My legs tightened around him, and I began to grind against his face, seeking the pleasure he was denying me. He hummed his approval into my core, and I felt it ignite me. I was almost there. I could feel it, and when he inserted two fingers in me and sucked my clit, the coil that was tightly wound snapped, and I screamed his name.

Time ceased to exist, and I felt like I was floating on air. Was this how it felt to fly? When I regained my hearing, all I could make out were my heavy pants. Luke was no longer between my legs, making me wonder if he was even here.

"Cecilia will help you change for the ball. I'll be back by then." Luke's voice came from across the room.

"So, no breakfast?" I tried to lighten the mood, waiting to see if he would say this was a mistake.

"I already ate." His voice drifted through the room, followed by the slamming of my door.

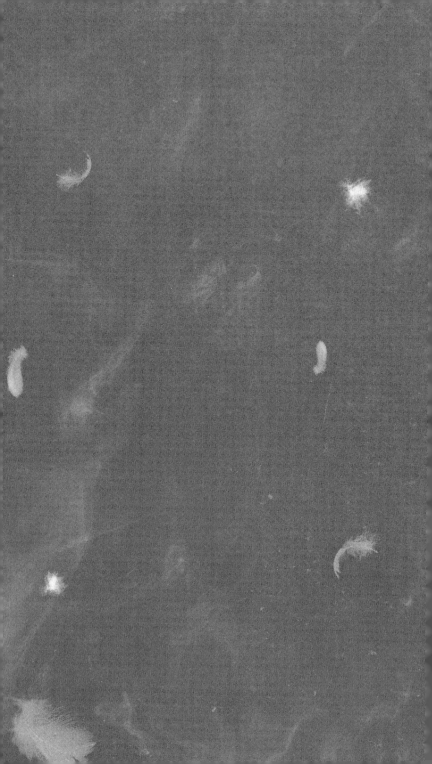

CHAPTER SIXTEEN

LUKE

I ARRIVED AT THE HOUSE JUST IN TIME TO GET READY for the party. My plan to run away had backfired when the smell of Summer's pussy was on my fucking skin. Retreating had seemed like a great plan, but my balls begged to differ.

She had been right there, and it would have been easy. I would have fucked her, but then what? Fucked myself over in the process?

Pulling a lighter and cigarette from the inside pocket of my suit, I sat on the edge of the bed and sparked. I was a real piece of shit, wasn't I? It didn't matter if her pussy was dripping for me. At the end of the day, I was the one holding all the cards, and that imbalance wasn't fair to her.

I caught sight of my profile in the mirror and laughed. I was a real fucking hypocrite. Acting like I had morals when this manor was dripping in blood. Ghosts haunted this place, and yet I refused to let go. The dead had more hold on us than the living because we refused to let go.

"Showtime," I mumbled as I grabbed my mask and the box that contained the one for Summer.

Since Summer wasn't in the foyer yet, I made my way to the left wing, but this time instead of going to that room, I ended up in the old lab.

As soon as I opened the door, the smell of ashes and bleach invaded me. It was everywhere, the odor too strong to be contained inside these walls.

On the far wall, a now broken sign still read *Ferro Beauty*. How was it that this company was full of dirty fucking secrets? I'd inherited a broken empire that was about to collapse with all the missing funds and a key to a box somewhere in the world that held the answers to all my problems.

When I walked back to the foyer, the first thing I heard was Bear's paws scratching against the floor. I put my hand inside my pockets as I waited for Summer to make her way toward me.

The dog trainers tried to persuade me to get a Lab and golden retriever mix since that breed had the most success. There were moments when I didn't trust my own shadow, so I felt it was best to get a dog with sharper guard instincts.

Cecilia must have stayed behind since Summer was alone. After what happened this morning, it wasn't wise— not that she'd care.

She looked divine. Her hair was done in some sort of half updo with waves. Her face had some makeup, but nothing over-the-top. Her lips weren't red, thank God for small miracles, but they were a soft pink.

Now her dress—that was another fucking story. It was black with intricate floral lace, and the underdress was the exact color of her skin. The top part of the dress consisted of a ribbed corset, while the bodice molded to her body and flared out at the bottom. The sleeves on the dress were made of lace, leaving you to wonder if she was actually naked.

Bear stopped walking until he was in front of me. When I gave him the command to sit, he did as he was told.

"You look beautiful," I told Summer as I stepped forward.

"The dress is long enough that I could wear flats. Thank you for that."

I tipped my head and then quickly realized she couldn't see. When I reached for her glasses, I could see the confusion on her features, but I cut her off.

"It's a masquerade ball. I got you something," I let her know as I put the mask over her face. Once that was done, I grabbed her hands and let her feel the mask.

The Venetian eye mask had trimmed lace all around and a small layer that covered the eyes. This was for Summer so she wouldn't be self-conscious about her scars, and the extra lace that covered her eyes was the perfect form of bait, ensuring we wouldn't raise suspicion.

"Are you ready?" I asked her once I had fastened the mask.

"Yes." Her voice lacked conviction, but it was too late to go back now.

BY THE TIME WE ARRIVED IN THE CITY, MY HAND WAS going numb. Summer didn't say much, but her grip told a different story. I didn't know if it was the altitude of the helicopter, the fact that she had to wear protective gear and it dulled her senses, or the fact that she would be going out to an event, but she was nervous.

She let me lead her to the elevator without a word. I

watched the numbers tick down toward the ballroom. Once there were three floors to go, I pulled her closer to my side, my arm wrapping around her waist, and I felt her lose some of the tension.

"I'm not very good with people," she rushed out as the elevator pinged, signaling that we had made it to our floor.

I leaned down and brushed my lips against the shell of her ear. "It's okay. I won't let anything happen to you."

As soon as we stepped foot in the ballroom, I could feel eyes on us. I rarely showed my face at these events, and I knew that was where Hector had the upper hand. The public loved him, while I was the recluse who had saved the company yet refused to give a single interview.

And here I was with a date. Not just any date—one that could bring this whole place to ashes with the truth she kept close to her chest.

"I thought you weren't coming." Elizabeth's accusatory tone was the first to greet us.

So much for being able to stay incognito. I already knew the mask wasn't going to do shit for me.

"Elizabeth." I tipped my head in acknowledgment but didn't bother with introductions, and Summer tensed when she realized I wasn't going to introduce her.

"And who's your date?"

"Come on, dove, let's go get a drink." I pulled Summer with me toward the bar.

"An ex-lover?" Summer asked with a bite to her tone.

Was it jealousy?

"She's my secretary," I explained.

"That you dated." Her question sounded more like an accusation.

"I don't do dates." I smirked, and even though I knew

she couldn't see my face, I knew she was irritated by my tone.

She left it alone for now, which I was grateful for. This would be amusing another time, just not now when I was using her as bait. Tonight, she was nothing but arm candy meant to get the people in my circles curious enough to come and brave a conversation with me. And if Summer would pick up on a clue or two, that would be a bonus.

It was our first go at things, so I knew not to get my hopes up, but also, a part of me didn't want her to find anything. What would be the aftermath if she did?

"Good evening, gentlemen," I greeted the men who were by the bar.

"Ah, Luke, we can't even pretend not to know who is underneath the mask," one of the more pleasant board members said.

I gave a humorless chuckle. "My cross to bear."

"I don't believe we had the pleasure of meeting your date," another man said, and I instantly recognized his voice. August—he was so far up Hector's ass that I was surprised he was standing here without him.

The smile I gave them was predatory. I dug my fingers into Summer's waist; in comfort or warning, I wasn't sure which, but she took it in stride.

"This is Summer," I told them as my hand moved up and down her side, handling her like she was an object.

Since I didn't use her last name, it could go one of two ways. The first, they would think she wasn't anyone of importance, just some random girl I dressed up, or she was someone I was trying to maintain anonymity with and was keeping her identity hidden. I mean, with a name like Summer, it would make sense.

Either way, it would pique their interest and keep them

talking while giving Summer more time to get familiarized with their voices. The conversation kept going for a few more minutes. I admired Summer; I imagined this could be very overwhelming, but she was taking it all in stride.

The mask she wore was perfect because none of them suspected that she was blind. She had perfected the art of turning to face whoever talked to her, and you could feel her attention on you. She didn't need to see you for her to analyze you.

"This will be Fe—"

"Excuse us, gentlemen." I cut them off before they could full-on get talking about the business.

Once we had stepped out of the way, Summer took a deep breath.

"Would you like a moment?"

Summer nodded vigorously.

I led her toward the hall so she could use the restroom. As soon as we stepped out of the ballroom, the noise lessened, and I could hear Summer's heavy sigh. Maneuvering her so she was against the wall, I put the hand that wasn't holding her above her head, caging her in.

"Hey, say the word and we can leave," I whispered in her ear.

"I'm okay," she assured me. "Which way do I go?"

Oh fuck—her cane.

"I'll take—"

"It's okay. I can manage on my own, Luke."

Of that, I had no doubt.

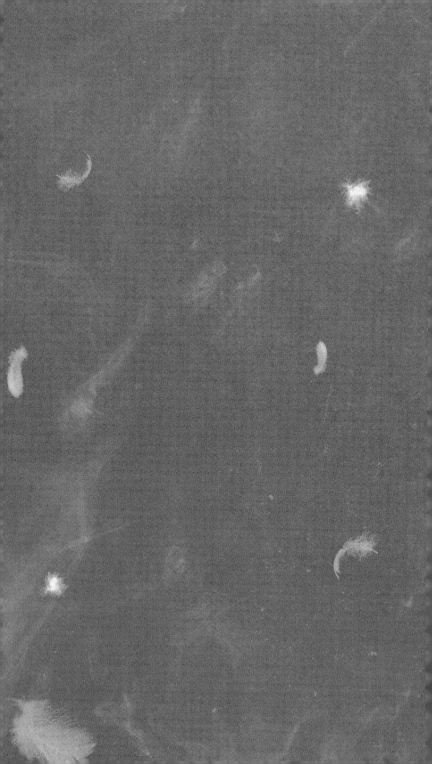

STRENGTH

I may be timid, but I'm not weak.
I may whisper, but I can still speak.
I might have been broken, but my pieces still fit.
I've reinforced them, so you better watch out for me.

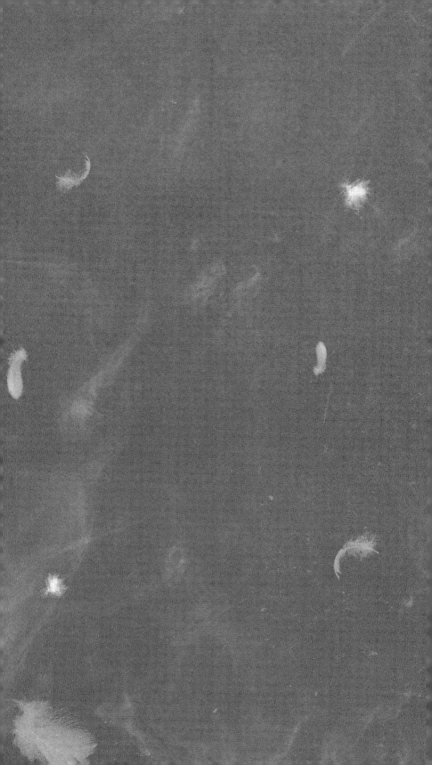

CHAPTER SEVENTEEN

SUMMER

It was overwhelming to be around so many people. Although I never saw the spotlight, there was something about being onstage that separated you from the rest of the world.

As I made my way to the bathroom, I realized I had been spoiled. I was not used to walking around without a cane. Roaming around like this reminded me of the first days in *la Casa del Silenzio*. Was it a compound or a mansion? I never bothered to find out, but I would trace the walls of my room over and over again as if, by some miracle, a door would appear and take me somewhere else.

The only other place it took me was the bathroom, where I learned to find solace in a scalding shower. I used to make myself believe that the burning water would wash away the sins on my skin.

I heard the door open as I was in the stall, and I quickly hurried up so whoever had entered wouldn't try and spark a conversation with me. I got out and walked straight to the sinks. I wished I had enough time to splash some water on my face. I was shaking my hands, trying to dry them since I was not going to waste time finding paper towels.

"Who are you?" a voice asked from my left, and that was when I realized I'd never heard a stall closing. The voice took me by surprise, and it made me jump.

"I'm no one," I whispered as I tried and failed to regain my breathing. I extended one of my arms and gripped the sink, needing to find a tether.

The tapping of a heel got closer, and I let go and took a step back. Luke was outside of those doors waiting for me. I knew that if I yelled, he would come in here, but there was no reason to overreact. This woman was simply asking a question. She wasn't threatening me, although her energy was strong and her tone possessive.

"No one?" She took another step forward. "I've never seen Luke treat anyone like he does you. One would think you were made of glass."

"Sounds like something you should take up with him, don't you think?" I tipped my chin up and squared my shoulders.

Without another word, I turned around and reached for the door, and then it took me a few seconds too long to locate the handle. It was enough time for the woman behind me to pull at the strings that held my mask together.

I felt it get loose as I walked through the door and hoped Luke was waiting right there for me to come out. The mask began to fall away from my face as I stepped into the hall. Luke did not call my name, but the woman turned me around by the shoulder and got a good look at me.

Her gasp felt like a physical blow.

If that wasn't enough, the man's voice that spoke didn't belong to Luke, but it was a voice I recognized.

"Are you ready to go, Elizabeth?" The French accent was just like how I remembered it.

My nails dug into my palms, and I had no hair I could use to cover my face with.

"What the hell is going on here?" Luke's tone came from down the hall, and he sounded furious.

Without turning back around, I ran to him blindly, trusting that he would catch me—pun intended.

Strong arms wrapped around me. I buried my face into his chest, and he didn't question it. One of his hands stroked the back of my head, keeping me in place.

"Why is her mask off?"

I could feel Luke vibrating with anger. When he spoke, each word was dripping with venom. He walked us toward the woman...toward *him*, while making sure I was still in his arms. The closer we got to the other couple, the more I wanted to imprint myself in Luke's skin.

"Elizabeth," Luke warned.

"*Mon amour*, what's the problem?" I froze, and Luke noticed.

"Fauché?" Luke seemed to question.

Before either of them could speak, Elizabeth did so.

"Who is she? And why are her eyes so fucked-up?"

Luke let go of me, and I felt cold. He stepped away but did it without turning me around, for which I was grateful. A few seconds later, he pressed my mask into the palm of my hand but didn't put it on me.

I was just about to tie it again when I heard gasping, and then *he* was yelling in French at Luke.

"You're going to kill her."

My shaky fingers weren't cooperating, and I couldn't get the mask to tie. I pressed it to my face and turned around to face the rest of the people. The beat of my heart was thumping wildly that it made it harder to focus on other things. If I needed further confirmation that the French man was the same one from my nightmares, his cologne was the final nail in the proverbial coffin.

"You stay out of this, Fauché, because you're next," Luke warned.

"L-L-Luke." My voice was shaky, and I didn't even want to bring attention to myself, but now more than ever, I needed to be far away from here.

"If I see you at the office on Monday, you're dead," Luke threatened. In seconds, I remembered the woman had talked to us earlier, but in my overstimulation, I had dismissed her voice, and what a mistake that had been.

A few seconds later, a loud thud hit the floor, and she was gasping for air.

"You've gone mad, Fe—"

Whatever he was going to say was cut off by Luke.

"If I were you, I'd tread very lightly, Fauché." Luke's voice was a harsh whisper, and I barely made out the words that he said. "*L'ora del silenzio è finite.*"

A chill went down my spine at the confirmation I didn't know I was looking for. I had hoped that my blind eyes were making me conjure demons that were not there, but my body remembered them all too well.

"Come on, dove, let's get you home." Luke's voice was much gentler now.

He tied my mask for the second time that night. Luke didn't take me by the hand. He held on to me tighter than ever before, that I was sure if we continued this way, my imprint would be left on his side.

"Pedro," he spoke, and I thought someone else must have been in the hall with us before I soon realized he was on the phone since the conversation was one-sided to my ears. "I'm taking Summer to my penthouse. I need you to keep an eye on Fauché."

The ballroom broke out in applause as we stepped foot into it. Some sort of video was playing in the background, announcing some new launch. As we walked away, we passed by a group of men who were speaking loudly. My knees buckled under the weight of the secrets that were threatening to be pulled out of me.

Luke was fast and didn't waste any time stopping. Instead, he dipped and cradled me into his arms. His hold was bruising, but I couldn't even respond to his touch because I was too busy being trapped in the past.

"If you tell anyone who you are...I will kill your mother just like I killed your father."

My mother wasn't dead, then? The hope that had bloomed in my chest quickly vanished. I was already condemned to my fate, but that didn't mean I had to give my mamma the same fate.

Any second now, the announcement that the house was open for the day would blare through the speaker system connected to this house.

It didn't matter that I had now heard it for a month straight; it still gave me chills as much as it did the first day.

"Benvenuto nella Casa del Silenzio."

Some house of silence this place was. My body shook, and tears began to fall down my face, proof that my eyes weren't totally useless and that they could still work. Maybe if I had a doctor, I would be able to see and not be shackled to this eternal nothingness.

I didn't ask for help because lives were at stake, and with one word, I could condemn them.

The door to my room opened, and I braced myself for the pain. This man always brought pain and even more shame with his use of words, but at least it was better than those who came before him. If I never saw him again, it would be too soon. As the days went by, I could almost convince myself that it was never him who brought me here. As the days went, I could lose myself in this pain and forget everything and everyone.

"Why are you crying?" *a different voice asked me.*

He was a different person. He wasn't calling me his dirty little girl. He didn't pull my legs until I was hanging on the edge. There was a kindness to him, and that made me cry harder.

"Mon amour," *his voice was closer than it had been a few seconds ago.* "You're breaking my heart."

I lifted my head, and I heard his gasp. My face had been deformed, and I looked monstrous now. That was what the other one said, and he preferred it that my face was to the bed when he brought me pain. It hurt more that way, but at least I was able to scream and beg for help without putting anyone at risk.

The bed dipped, and I hugged myself tighter, preparing for the worst.

"Don't be scared. I'm not going to hurt you."

A loud hiccup tore through me.

"You're going to help me?"

"Mon amour, I can't do that. You know what will happen if I do," *he said sympathetically, and I froze.* "If I help you, he's going to kill me too."

A strange form of kinship was forming because we were both being threatened by the same man.

"He was right. You are very lovely," *he murmured as he rubbed my cheek with the back of his fingers.* "Exquise."

He did that for a few seconds while my sobs subsided. I

kept waiting for the moment he pounced, for the pain to begin.

Something silky began to rub against my face after a few short minutes. My fingers came to investigate.

"What's this?"

"A tie," he told me.

I wondered what he was doing with it until he wrapped it around my eyes and tied it in the back.

"You are beautiful," he said in awe once my eyes were covered.

Then he was silent, and I was waiting for the moment he would pounce and bring me pain, but he surprised me when that didn't happen. Instead, he grabbed me by my waist and sat me down on his lap and cradled me.

Being in here, it had felt like I had aged overnight. When my father was alive, I was still being tucked in at night with a bedtime story, and once he passed, Mamma was too sad to keep the traditions going. I forgot how much I missed being hugged and having my hair stroked. This man was doing that, and I snuggled into his chest. His shirt was soft, and it smelled like fresh linen.

It didn't remind me of home, but it did remind me of more peaceful times.

"Oh, mon amour, you're covered in bruises," he lamented as he rubbed my arms. "I'm going to make sure you are as pristine as a porcelain doll."

I dozed off in that man's arm. When I woke up, he kissed my forehead and promised to come back the next day.

When the speaker system blared and the announcement was made, I was sitting on the edge of the bed with more energy than I had in days. It was the first night I slept without new pain.

"Mon amour," the man greeted when he returned, and I

perked up at the sound of his voice. "Were you waiting for me?"

I nodded eagerly.

This seemed to please him because he closed the door softly and then crouched by me and stroked my cheek. I was still wearing his tie around my eyes, having not taken it off.

"I got you something," he told me as he sat next to me.

He got me something. He laughed at my intake of breath and murmured something I couldn't hear, but I knew it was an endearment based on the softness in his tone.

"Come here," he told me, tugging me toward his lap.

Once I was seated, I waited to see what he had brought me. He didn't hand me anything. Instead, he pressed his fingers to my lips. The taste of chocolate exploded on my tongue.

It was a familiar taste, one that I loved but for a moment had forgotten it even existed.

"You like that, mon amour?" he whispered in my ear as he played with my hair.

What kid didn't like candy? He handed me a whole bag, and I beamed. He kept kissing my forehead, and I must have passed out on him from eating too many sweets.

He came back for me the next day.

"Mon amour," he would say, and I would go lax at his tone. "You're filthy," he told me, and I stiffened at the thought of displeasing him.

He noticed this because right away, he reassured me, "Don't be scared. It's nothing we can't fix."

He led me to the shower and fixed the temperature of the water for me. He helped me get out of my clothes and took his time washing the grime from my body. Once I was done, he helped dress me.

"The bruises are fading." He sounded excited as he said this.

He laid me on the bed and hugged me from behind. As I snuggled deeper into him, I felt something poking me from behind but soon fell asleep in the cocoon of safety he provided.

When he left that day, he didn't kiss my forehead but instead kissed right next to my lips.

"Goodbye, mon amour."

The next day, he came and brought me more of his ties with more chocolates but told me to save those and not gorge on them.

"That way, you can change them," he said as his thumb rubbed the edge of the tie wrapped around my eyes. Right below where the scars that made me ugly began.

"Okay," I said, knowing I would do it because I wanted to make him happy.

"Mon amour, I'm going to have to leave you for a little bit. Work is calling."

My face fell, and tears moistened the silk tie.

"Do you have to?"

"Oh, don't break my heart," he groaned.

His hands came to my hips and laid me on the bed. He rested his hands on either side of my face and peppered my face with kisses.

"I know what you can do so I can remember you every night," he said like he had a brilliant idea.

"I'll do it." I smiled as he kissed my neck, making me giggle.

Summer.

Summer.

Summer!

I snapped out of it. My body shook. The tremors

racking my form were trying to release the trauma I'd endured.

"Let me go," I said between gritted teeth. I didn't want to be touched. I wanted a shower; I felt so dirty.

"Just until we get to my penthouse," he managed to say.

We were moving. I hadn't noticed when we got in a car or how we exited the ballroom or the building we had been in. The ride was silent, and the weird in-between trance I had been in broke when the car stopped and Luke opened the door.

"Fuck," Luke hoarsely uttered when I reacted to his touch. "Let me guide you to the elevator at least...*please*."

I gave him my hand, and he squeezed it once, then carefully led me away from the car. He used his words, giving me directions as we went along.

The elevator pinged, and we went up floors. Luke didn't say a word, but I could choke on the energy he was emitting. My mind went back to that stupid memory.

I was so naïve. So small, I just needed someone to help me, not condemn me even more.

The elevator's door opened.

"Walk straight ahead. The place is open. There's furniture on your far right and a kitchen straight ahead with a dining room to the left. A set of stairs that lead to the second floor."

I followed the direction said in Luke's monotone voice until I made contact with a sofa.

As soon as I sat down, Luke began to speak.

"Fauché hurt you, didn't he?" Luke questioned, already knowing the answer.

A whimper was all that came out of my lips.

"Remember what I told you, Summer? I'm going to

make them pay." The lethal edge to his voice was not lost on me.

I began to speak, telling Luke pieces of what was done to me. My lips trembled as I got the last part out.

"He made me like it."

Luke's exhale of breath sounded painful.

"My little dove," he choked out.

He got closer to me. He wasn't touching me, but I still felt his presence all around me, and instead of making me feel suffocated, I felt protected in the cloak of his anger.

"I don't want to feel him, Luke," I whispered. With shaky hands, I reached out and touched his face, and my heart sped up because he had not allowed this before. His cheeks were a bit hollow, and his jaw was sharp. I tried to move my hands up, but he wrapped his palms around my wrists and brought my hands to his shoulders.

I could trust Luke. At least, this was what I kept telling myself, trying to keep a hold of the things I could control. The fragile remains of my sanity mocked me with my past transgressions.

It was like Luke knew I was having a silent war with myself because he pulled apart the ribbons, and once my mask fell, he kissed between my eyes.

A sob tore through me.

Luke's breath fanned my face.

"Anyone who ever touched you will die," he vowed against my skin.

I whimpered at his admission, my face getting closer to his warmth.

"Luke." I breathed his name with quivering lips because it was all I needed at this moment to pull me from the darkness that followed me around.

The trembling soon subsided, thanks to a surprisingly

soft mouth that held my bottom lip in place. My hands gripped his shoulders as I tentatively opened my mouth so I could kiss him. Luke didn't pull away and instead kissed me as I had never been kissed before.

There was something beautiful about kisses that you felt in your soul. Kisses that tasted like the sea that came from a moment when you felt wrecked, but instead of destroying you, they made you feel whole.

"Fucking hell, Summer," Luke cursed against my lips. "How am I supposed to stop now?"

I smiled against his lips. If I had the energy, I would have told him that I was fine with never stopping, but I was drained and feeling tired.

He was cautious as he wrapped his arms around my waist. When I leaned into the crook of his neck, he seemed to relax. He scooped me up in his arms and walked us up the flight of stairs he had mentioned earlier.

He laid me on the bed and wrapped me under the covers while he stayed above them.

"I'm sorry for putting you through that." He sounded sincere and full of regrets.

I gave him a weak smile. "I knew the score, Lu—"

Despite the covers, a chill spread through me. Luke went still next to me, being so attuned to my body language.

"Dove?" he questioned.

"Luke." I reached out for him. The moment I felt his hands, I grasped onto them like they were a lifeline. "I...I heard my uncle's voice tonight."

PART 2

Spring

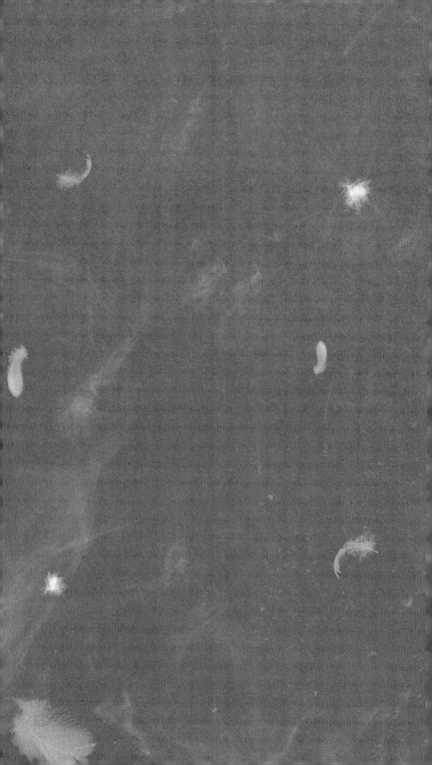

18

LUKE

I missed Summer.

What was supposed to be a short business trip turned into three months of torture. I supposed you could say the space was needed.

I certainly felt clearer about what I had been doing. My determination to see this through to the bitter end and get justice had been absolute. I was also able to think things through more rationally now that Summer was not lingering in every corner of the manor.

The weather here was much warmer than it was back home, but that wasn't enough to stop me from hating this place. The buildings, the roads, hell, even the way the sun set were all reminders of who I used to be.

Being back here, I couldn't help but think of my father. My hands were tightly fisted as if they could somehow contain the thoughts that were running rampant in my mind.

Taking a deep breath, I held it and then exhaled slowly, forcing my body to relax. It had been so long that I had convinced myself I had changed and that all those life lessons my father had given me had faded.

My hands were clean now. I had a business I ran. My money was legit, and there was no longer a need to be looking over my shoulder, wondering if today was the day the police would send my ass to prison.

"My son, you needed to remind them who we are. They think our name is weak, and we aren't going to take that," my father spat before he dismissed me.

I fought the urge to roll my eyes and tell him off. It was so easy to give directions without lifting a damn finger.

"I will make sure they know they can't mess with us," I assured him.

He took a drag of his cigar and waved me off.

What a joke this was. Even as I went about trying to collect debts that no longer had our names on them, I knew we were fighting a losing war. My father might have been someone back in the day, but now he was nothing. He was trying to hold on to a crumbling empire with both hands, and it wasn't enough to lift it to the glory it had once born.

Technology changed the game for every kind of business, and my father had been too stubborn to change with the tides. A new criminal regime was taking over, and sooner or later, we would all clash.

My mother was already dead, and I was grateful she was no longer suffering, even if she never did a damn thing for any of her kids. It was just my older brother and me, but he was so far up my father's ass that he would follow him to his death. I was glad we had no sisters. The more I saw of the world, I knew that as dangerous as it already was, it was ten times worse for women.

Those memories were as tainted as the crumbling building before me. I always knew following the man who had given me life would lead me to my death, but I didn't think either of us ever expected me to have a rebirth. And what a glorious new life it was, but life tends to cash in on all the things you owe it. The balance was uneven; I didn't deserve happiness when I was the cause of so much misery.

I had been paying for many mistakes, but I was determined to make it right. My first stop in evening the scales had arrived. My blood hummed with excitement.

Once upon a time, this estate had been beautiful, right under the Tuscany sun near vineyards. It was the perfect setup, if animosity and privacy were what you wanted. There were no neighbors for miles.

I felt sick as I took a step forward, but I reminded myself that I had wanted to do this alone. This was as much for me as it was for Summer.

The door to the house was unlocked. It probably had been that way since the day Nico stormed in and shut the whole place down.

The entrance was simple, yet I bet it had been elegant. Pieces of the furniture that decorated this place still remained. They were covered in dust but still painted a picture of how this place used to operate.

I walked around the kitchen and a billiard room that I assumed was more for the guests to talk about their "girls" and plan future meetings than anything else. I wondered just how many sick fucks stood around here when this place had been at its prime.

After everything that had happened, I didn't think I would have been the one to contact Nico and demand more information on Summer, but here I was. Learning all the sordid details of this fucking house, lamenting the fact that I wasn't the one who brought it down.

Every room was the same. A bed in the middle of the

room and a door that led to a bathroom. These girls never left their rooms, and the fact that they had to find solace in the same place they faced their nightmares made me sick to my stomach. To the right of the door stood a speaker, and I knew enough of this place to know that it was set up as a fear tactic. So the girls never forgot where they belonged.

Once I arrived at the room I knew had been hers, my fingers dug into the door hinges as if trying to stop me from stepping foot past the threshold. Unlike the other rooms, I did walk into this one. To understand her better, I felt like I needed insight into all the things she didn't say. An invasion of privacy, but it was too late to go back now.

I hadn't lied to her when I told her I had to leave for business. After our night in my penthouse, things changed, and although Summer seemed to be thriving with the shift in our relationship, I was still holding back. I told myself that I already knew what it felt like to have her cunt squeezing my fingers, the taste of her release coating my tongue. What was the harm in not putting a stop to it? We had already crossed the point of no return; we might as well bask in the pleasure of our sins.

It wasn't entirely a lie that I was on this side of the globe on business. If I was to take care of Fauché, then I needed to find a replacement for him. The look on his face when I walked in on a board meeting for our French division was priceless. He was on his toes, keeping his distance from me, and I let him think I had left, but one thing I was sure of was that he was not working alone.

I assumed the gray bed had once been white, but years of dirt and neglect had stained it. A tattered duvet covered half the bed, and I scrunched my nose as I shook it to see if any secrets still remained beneath it.

If there had been food in my stomach, I would have

thrown up. Stains still covered the bed, and although I already knew how this story came to be, seeing it was another thing.

I looked at my watch, and I knew the sun would go down soon. The door was wide open, and the only light was the one from the hallway since none of the rooms had windows. I swallowed back my anger for a moment and moved the bed around, then lifted the fucking mattress, and all I was able to find in the fucking room was the remains of a silk tie.

If it made me a bastard for mailing Fauché a picture of Summer I took when she wasn't aware, then so be it. She looked beautiful and radiant, and if he still remembered her, I was counting on the fact that he would show up here to tie up his loose ends because all it took was for Summer to accuse him, and his life would be over.

The envelope I had sent him had a picture of her, asking to meet in the place it had begun for them. Then I added that it was a reward for his loyalty.

I walked out of the room and back to the hallways so I could look out the window, and right on time, a lone black car was making its way down the driveway.

"House of silence, indeed," I muttered.

Murder wasn't something you forgot about. It was a clingy mistress that didn't want to leave you. The first taste of blood was traumatizing. It was enough to make you insane because putting your life above someone else's came with crippling guilt. Then anything after that numbed you because it was so easy to close your eyes and do what was expected of you. It was easy to play God when it wasn't your life that would succumb.

"What's your name, kid?" the man who found me asked.

Even though I was bleeding out in an alley, and he

looked way too extravagant to be here, he was the only one who stopped and helped me.

"I'm dead." I seethed, trying to contain the pain. "You should leave me before they come and finish me off."

The man cocked his head, and I flinched when his hand touched my cheek.

"You deserve so much more than this."

Maybe I did, and for a while, I enjoyed it as well. But now I had the means to make someone else's life a little better, and that was worth staining my hands for.

Since the door was open, I heard when the engine got cut off. I had left my car off to the side in hopes that Fauché thought whoever pulled his leash had left him a present and left.

I moved a little so I could get a better look and sighed when I saw him holding a gun with shaky hands. That certainly made things uneven since the only thing I had on me was a fucking spoon.

Lucas Greco died the day I left this continent and traveled to America. My life as Luke was different. Although it still had tragedies, it came with less blood.

The show had begun, so I fixed my sleeves and rolled them up.

On the plus side, Fauché had come alone. I moved silently to the room across from where Summer stayed and waited there with a barely closed door, just enough so I could peep from the small creek.

Although I was still, every part of me was racing. My heart was not used to this level of exhilaration, and my blood hummed, coming alive with adrenaline.

Perdonami, Padre, perché ho peccato.

I think, given the circumstances, he would understand and approve.

"*Mon amour?*" Fauché broke the silence that engulfed us. He was nervous, and that made me smile.

He walked deeper into the room, and I bet he had found the pictures I had left for him on the floor. It gave me enough time to open the door and get across the room. Pedro had been thorough in finding information.

Fauché was currently on the floor, ripping pictures of his extracurricular activities, so he didn't notice me coming in.

"You're not much of a fighter, are you, Fauché?" I mocked as I pressed my leg into the back of his neck and forced him to kiss the floor.

He whimpered.

Men like him, I knew all too well. The types that picked victims they could manipulate into thinking they were gods. He was a grown-ass fucking man with a good job—he could have an actual woman warming his bed, but that was not what got him off.

Summer had told me enough to know that his death wouldn't be slow.

"Mr. Ferro," he pleaded.

I watched as he grabbed the gun and turned it toward me. I added more pressure on his nape and braced myself when I saw him pull the trigger. I flinched when the shot rang out since it had been a while since I had been forced to be under a shower of bullets. The aim was nowhere near me, so I knew it wouldn't hit me.

"Did you come here to hurt Summer?"

"Summer?" he questioned. "That's her name?"

Mon amour.

My throat constricted in anger. He never even bothered to know her name. He aimed again and shot, and I knew I needed to get that gun away from him before he hurt me or killed himself.

"It must have been an *inconvenience* when this place closed down." My tone was laced with mock concern. "You had to do your perversions closer to home."

I added even more pressure, and it was immediately followed by the smell of piss.

"Who told you to come here? This place was invite-only, and we both know you lack the connections."

More crying and whimpers, and he was about to shoot again. This time, it was pointed toward me. I let go of his neck and kicked his side, but the asshole still shot. The bullet ended up ricocheting in the bathroom.

While he reeled from the pain to his rib, I broke his wrist and took the gun.

"Fuck!" he cried.

Fauché cradled his arm as he crawled to the wall. He flinched as I shot the remainder of the Glock's bullets into the hall.

"Now we don't have a use for this," I taunted him as I threw it back at him.

"You're not going to kill me?" he sobbed.

I smiled. "No."

He really was pathetic, and killing him would bring no one any joy. He might not have killed his victims, but he sure as fuck traumatized them, and killing him wouldn't even begin to get justice for what he had done.

"All you have to do is tell me who sent you here. That simple."

Fauché sobbed and seemed to consider my question.

"I don't know," he cried. "Someone found out about me, and they wanted one of my votes, and in return, they gave me an invitation here."

He whimpered as I took a step closer to him.

"Hmm," I hummed. "I guess I have no use for you."

More crying from Fauché. He brought his broken wrist to his chest and looked up at me.

"So, this is it?"

"I do have one more question." I raised one finger up. "You have been with the company for over fifteen years, right?"

At this, he tried to move and make a run for it. I stepped aside, letting him make it past the room and into the hall but pushed him when he got to the stairs. I watched him tumble down as I leisurely descended the stairs. As I did that, I undid the tie I had worn today and then pulled out the spoon that was in my back pocket.

"Oh, the sun went down," I told him. "It's too bad you won't get to see it again."

Fauché's eyes went wide.

"Y-y-you said you weren't going to k-k-kill me."

It was comical watching him try to get away. Before he could get up, I kicked the same side I had earlier, but this time harder, then kicked his upper chin. His moans and groans echoed in the empty house. There was nothing for miles, and what had once been his paradise was about to become his hell.

He was a whimpering mess when I gripped his jaw and pulled him closer to me.

"I'm a man of my word, Fauché. Death would be a mercy for you."

His brows were bunched in confusion. He couldn't comprehend that there were some things worse than death. The moment he saw me pull out the spoon, he tried to get out of my grasp. Too bad for him his body was weak, in pain, and overexhausted.

I taunted him with the tip of the spoon, adding enough pressure to where his crease met his eye.

"Please...please, I'll do anything," Fauché begged as he thrashed.

"Anything?" My soft-spoken voice had his beady eyes opening toward me.

Taking a deep breath, I ignored his pleas and pushed the spoon all the way, curving with the shape of his eye. His screams were deafening, but I pushed through. Liquid rolled down my knuckles, and it took a second to realize that Fauché had stopped screaming. The optic nerve was holding his eye out of his socket.

Using the fact that he had gone into shock, I did the same thing to the other eye now that he had stopped fighting me. If I had not seen some nasty shit in my life, this would have made me throw up.

I used Fauché's jacket to clean up the excess fluids from my hands and the spoon. While I did that, I felt his phone and keys through his jacket. I pulled them out since he would have no use for them anymore, and although the phone did ask for a passcode to unlock, it also gave me the option for a flashlight.

Better to get his phone dirty than mine.

Setting his phone in the middle of the stairs, I began to pull Fauché up the stairs. If I had known it was going to be this tiring to drag him back, I wouldn't have let him go downstairs at all. The life of luxury I now led had left me soft. The next time, I would think things through. I blamed my lack of planning on being out of practice.

I waited for what felt like hours for him to stir again.

"If their whores weren't deaf, then they were mute, isn't that right?" I asked, even though I didn't expect an answer back.

Removing his tongue would have been the wiser choice, but I didn't see how I could make that happen with my spoon. The next best thing was deafening him.

He didn't even fight me when I grabbed his chin. I took my spoon and turned it around to the other side and then plunged it into his ear canal. Blood was leaking out of his ears when I was done with him.

Fauché was still alive and would probably ease in and out of consciousness in the next few days. Grabbing his phone, I focused the light on him. He looked nothing like the man I had seen over the years.

I stood, and before I turned around to leave the room, I threw my loose tie at him.

"You'd look better with those eyes covered," I spat even though he would never hear the words, but I hoped that he felt the silk of the tie and would remember the words he had said to a scared blind girl.

I closed the door when I walked out and then made sure the house was locked. Nico had bought the property once he destroyed the place. He sold off all the other ones when he went into hiding, but this one he had kept, so until he was declared dead, no one would be coming to look.

Before I left, I moved the car to the back of the house so it would be out of the way. I could ask Pedro to help me get someone to take care of that.

Once I was back in my car, I grabbed my water bottle and cleaned my hands to the best of my ability and then used half a bottle of hand sanitizer to sterilize everything as much as I could.

Damn, the old me wouldn't have thought twice about disinfecting my hands.

I turned the car on, and as it purred to life, I pulled out my own phone and saw I had a missed call from Summer.

Smiling, I made my way out of *la Casa del Silenzio*.

"Hello? Luke," Summer answered the phone on the first ring. "I thought you must've fallen asleep early."

"I had to take care of some business," I told her as I sped my way out of the long driveway, the house becoming smaller and smaller in my rearview mirror.

"This late?"

"I'll be home tomorrow, my little dove," I told her, feeling better about having her with me since she arrived at my doorstep.

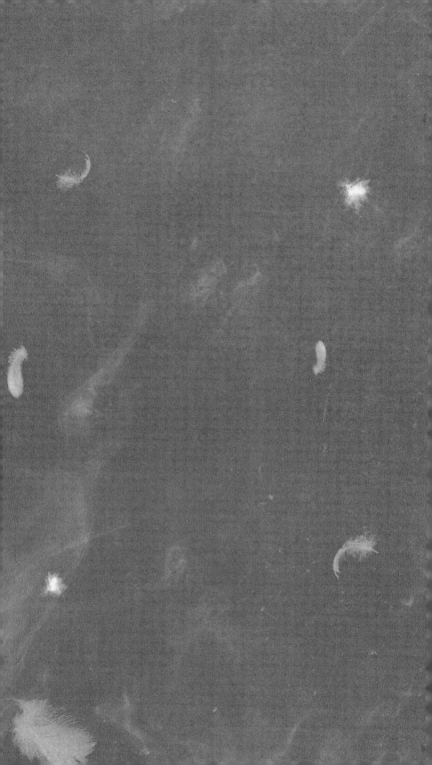

SUNSHINE & RAIN

Since I can remember,
there has always been something scary about you that I
couldn't explain.
Back then, I was sunshine, and you had always been rain.
We coexisted, but it wasn't the same.
Now I am changed and belong in your domain.
Too bad neither of us knows what to do with all this pain.

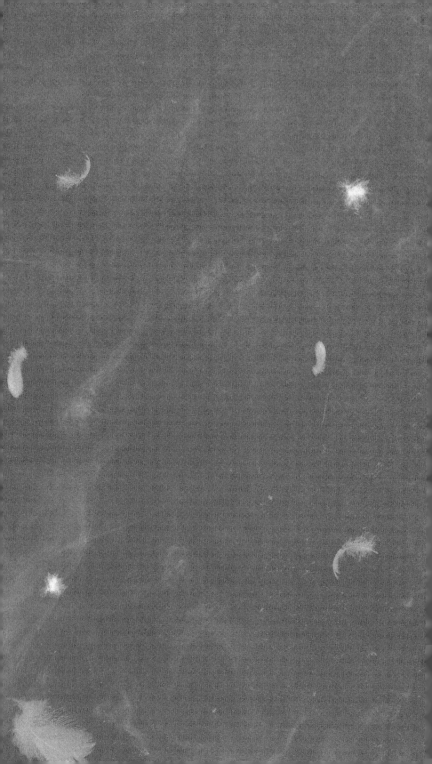

19

SUMMER

Bear's whining woke me, and I immediately sat up.

"I'm so sorry, boy," I apologized as I reached for my cane.

After spending more than an hour on the phone with Luke, I couldn't wind down to go back to sleep. It seemed like an eternity since I'd last seen him. Time seemed to move a bit slower. That was not to say I sat and waited for him.

My days were filled with learning and exploring. Now that Luke wasn't here, I had taken the time to get to know my surroundings a lot better.

Making my way out of the greenhouse, I opened the doors so Bear could go about his business.

The weather was getting warmer. I could feel the season changing from the way that the sun would warm my skin to how there was a new freshness in the air. Life was blooming again, coming alive with April's rain.

"Miss Summer," Cecilia called out for me.

Her distinct smell of lilies was dwarfed in the greenhouse, so I appreciated the fact that she let me know she was near.

"I'm here," I called out.

"Your tutor should be here in an hour. Would you like something to eat before or after?"

I had forgotten I had a session today. At least it would help in keeping my nerves at bay. Luke had left at the end of January, and I had not seen him in about three months. He said he needed to check the French division of his company.

I wasn't stupid. I knew this was related to *that* man, but I didn't want to know the details. I didn't want to hear his voice again. I had woken up cradled in Luke's arms the day after New Year's, and he had been holding me. I lay there awake until I felt the way his hand moved up and down my arm, drawing soothing patterns on my skin.

Then Luke proceeded to take off my dress. The fact that I fell asleep with it on was a testament to how bad my state of mind had been. After that, I ended up with Luke's fingers inside of me, bringing me to oblivion.

From there, things only got better. He wasn't as stand-offish as before. What had happened in that ballroom definitely brought us closer. I sought his warmth, and he let me, and maybe a part of me took advantage of the fact that he wouldn't turn me away, knowing that I wanted to be closer to him despite the fact that I hated when others touched me.

A couple of other times, he helped me stretch before my morning practice, and once I was done, I ended up with either his fingers or tongue inside of me.

I shifted my legs at the memory. Just when it seemed like I was getting somewhere with Luke, he had to leave. At least he had been here when my tutor first started coming and helped ease me into this new transition.

The first week after he'd left was the hardest because I went from talking to him daily to having no communication with him for a whole week. It had been incredibly lonely being in this house with just Cecilia.

Even though it had hurt, I knew it was his way of keeping distant from what was happening between us.

After one week, my tutor showed up with a cell phone. She had added a text-to-speech option so it would be easy for me to navigate it.

That same night when it said Luke was calling, a smile broke out on my face.

"Hello?" I said to the phone. I had practiced with my tutor how one worked since I had never used one before.

"Summer." Luke's voice made my belly flutter. "How are you?"

"So, you do remember I'm alive," I said before hanging up.

He called again and again until Cecilia barged into my room sometime in the early morning, handing me her phone and pleading for me to take the call so she could get some sleep.

It was something I would have never done before, especially in the earlier months, but there was a familiarity with Luke now. I felt stronger, but not physically, although my dancing was better than it had been. Mentally, I felt like I could weather storms without succumbing to their harsh winds. Luke made me feel safe to have my own voice.

When Bear scratched the door, I let him back in. He happily trailed behind me as I made my way to the breakfast table that was in the greenhouse. Now that the weather was changing, I liked to start my days here.

You could feel the sun from the windows, and each day, the rays got warmer. This greenhouse, my classes, Bear, and even my dancing brought me joy. A happy life wasn't just monumental moments that made an impact but a cumulation of the little things that made you get up each morning and greet the day, being thankful that you got to live it.

This was the peace I had prayed for.

I was such an anxious mess that I didn't eat much. When I made my way to the library, Cecilia informed me that the cleaning ladies would be here today so I wouldn't be startled.

After that first scare, they had been good with keeping their distance from me. I had also been good at keeping my panic attacks at bay. The last one had been on New Year's, but the worst one had been the first one in this place.

"Good morning, Summer," my tutor yelled as soon as she opened the library door.

I waited until she was near me to return the sentiment.

"Hi, Eve. How are you today?"

My tutor was in her late fifties. She was incredibly patient and kind. She and her husband were high school sweethearts, a term she'd had to explain to me, and he knew he would lose his sight young, so this had motivated Eve to learn as much as she could in order to help her visually impaired spouse. There was something beautiful about that kind of level of dedication for someone else.

It was easy to give a person vows and promises of a happy life when you had good health. The test of that love was what happened when that health got threatened? Some people didn't know how to love, and when they faced imperfections, all they saw glaring back at them were their shortcomings, so they left instead of rising up to the occasion.

"I'm great and a bit excited too."

"Why is that?" I asked.

She cleared her throat.

"You've been doing amazing, pushing yourself for the last few months, and the test I had you take last week marked you high enough that I can move you out of elementary classes."

"Really?" I whispered.

It had been embarrassing but not surprising when my testing had put me at elementary level. I knew nothing of the world. The only kind of lessons I had taken were the ones life had given me.

Eve called it street smarts, but it was just another thing she did to make me feel at ease. Educating me was not something anyone had thought to do.

"It's going to get harder and more frustrating from now on, but I know you can do it," she told me.

I nodded vigorously because of that, I had no doubt. Eve had taught me how to download audiobooks. It was something I'd had no idea existed. As my world kept growing, I often found myself trapped in the glimmers of the past. I let myself remember and feel like I had been stuck in time, and while everything had advanced, and I was running, trying to catch up. The books I listened to got confusing, even though they were targeted at people my age, but words sometimes threw me off or the things they talked about because I had no idea what they looked like. Still, I pushed myself to finish them because even if they humbled me with how little I knew, I still ended up learning a thing or two from them.

"You seem nervous today," Eve noted after a few hours.

I bit my lip and felt heat creep up my cheeks.

"Luke comes back today," I admitted.

She was quiet for a few seconds. The chair creaked when she shifted her weight. She was contemplating something.

"Eve?" I probed.

"It's nothing. I shouldn't ask." She added the last bit hastily.

"Ask what?"

My brow was furrowed. The air was almost uncomfortable, and since Eve had been here, she'd done everything in her power to put me at ease.

"My contract states I am not allowed to discuss your past, but I just want to know if you're okay here. Does Luke treat you well? He's not the most courteous man, but he seems to make sure you have everything you need to thrive."

What she said made me smile. I always thought Eve was aware of what had happened to me, but knowing Luke had not shared about my life or made it something that shouldn't be touched because it would make me uncomfortable warmed me.

"Luke has allowed me to live and not just exist."

This seemed to placate her, and the rest of our time together passed smoothly.

IT WAS ALMOST DINNERTIME, AND I WAS AS RESTLESS AS Bear was waiting for our daily walk. Luke said he would be back today, but he didn't mention a time. I had to take into account the time difference, so if he slept and then took the plane ride he should be here, right? I shook my head and instead grabbed onto Bear's leash and guided him toward the side door from the greenhouse.

Luke had promised me that as soon as the weather was a

bit warmer, he would get me plants for the outside garden. It was bear with signs of neglect. He said no one had bothered to revive it once the plants had died.

"Miss Summer." Pedro's voice caught me by surprise, and he noticed by the way I jumped.

It made him laugh.

"And here I thought we were friends now." His tone was light and teasing.

Were we friends? Or was he just keeping me company on Luke's behalf? Either way, I was thankful.

"I'm just surprised you're here," I told him.

"Why wouldn't I be? I remember we had a pending conversation."

I cleared my throat. Right, how could I forget? Unlike Luke, Pedro had done research on Nico's company. He wanted to know why I was still dancing if it reminded me of the past I no longer wanted a part of.

"When I was dancing in the company, it was to survive, but now I do it for myself."

Pedro hummed. "You are one strong girl, Summer," he said and, as always, broke my name into two distinct syllables.

I bent to stroke Bear's head. I didn't know if it was supposed to be a compliment or not. Pedro was easier to read in some ways, but in others, he left me confused. His company, as weird as it had been at first, had been welcomed.

"I would have thought you'd be in the city by now," I stated after a few minutes.

"So, you don't want my company anymore?"

I shook my head before replying, "I assumed you would be picking Luke up already."

Pedro laughed, and I was always fascinated by the way

it was louder and more vivacious since his voice was low and breathy. "Impatient, aren't we?"

I couldn't help the blush that spread through me. I had been impatient all day, trying to make time go by faster.

"Don't worry, Summer, your Luke will be here before you know it," he told me as he walked me outside the maze.

From there, Bear and I made our way to the house. Dinner and the rest of the night passed by slowly.

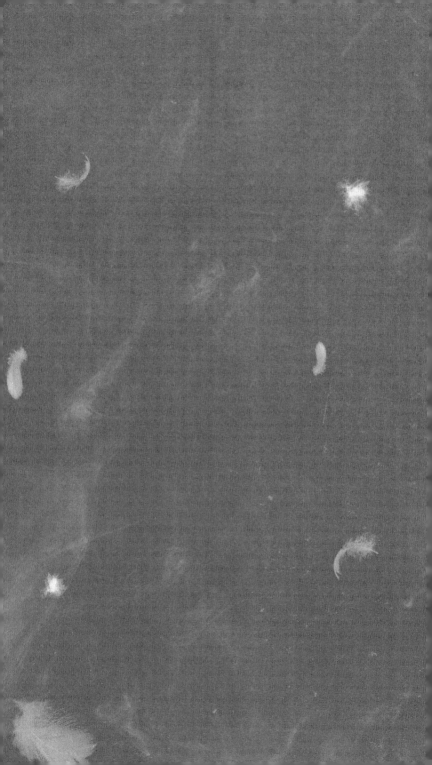

20

SUMMER

The cold air on my skin was what woke me up. I had not intended to fall asleep because I was determined to wait for Luke. I fell asleep on top of my covers, and my nightgown was not warm enough to stop me from breaking out in shivers.

I reached for my phone, and there were no notifications. I didn't know if I should be worried or angry. Without bothering to check the phone for the time, I commanded it to call Luke.

The phone fell from my hands when I heard a faint ringing coming from outside of my room. Although I depended more on Bear nowadays, I still made a habit of leaving my cane next to my bed.

"It's okay, boy, go back to bed," I instructed Bear.

My door was open from when I had refused to close it earlier, wanting to hear when Luke returned. The last time I checked the clock, it was nearing midnight.

Was that why he didn't wake me? Because it was late?

The midnight strolls to the foyer started to feel like déjà vu. My steps were soft, and the cane barely made any noise.

It wasn't until my cane made contact with the bench that I wondered if Luke was still there. Nothing was said, but I could feel a presence, but if he was here, why wasn't he saying any words? I lifted my chin and inhaled, trying to see if I could smell a cigarette being smoked, but nothing.

Next to the leg of the bench was another object. I tapped it with my cane, trying to see if it sounded hollow.

"Why are you hitting me, Summer?" Luke's voice sounded amused.

My loud intake of breath made him chuckle. I had longed for him since the moment he had left, and now that he was back, I didn't know how to act.

"You're back," I said aloud, stating the obvious.

"I told you I would be."

I brought my cane back to my side and used it to support myself and stood straighter.

"Actually, that was a lie. It's technically another day today."

Luke's laugh took me by surprise. My saliva felt thick when I tried to swallow. I guess I had expected him to be dismissive of me like before. I had come here expecting him to tell me to go back to bed.

"There were some things I wanted to get from the office before I came home."

I supposed that made sense, and since I didn't speak, Luke kept going.

"That way, I don't have to go back there until Monday."

A smile tore through me. There was something lighter about Luke. I couldn't place my finger on it, but I wasn't so ignorant as to not have an idea of what could have caused the shift.

"I missed you," I admitted shyly.

"Have you now?" he murmured.

Feeling brave, I took a step forward, and another one, until I could feel his heat on either side of me. I didn't need to see to know I was standing between his spread legs.

My heavy breathing was the only thing I could hear.

Shivers went down my body when I felt fingers on the back of my knee trailing up my thigh.

"You didn't come to say hi." I tried to control my voice so it wasn't obvious that I was panting because of his proximity.

"Hi," he teased in a husky tone as his hands trailed higher, playing with the hem of my nightgown.

His actions made me feel even braver, so I reached for him. He didn't tense when my hands landed on his shoulders.

"How was your trip?" I hissed as one of his hands rested between my legs, squeezing my inner thigh.

The hand that was working between my legs stilled, and the other wrapped around my waist. He turned me around so I could face the piano and the other side of the bench. I was about to protest when he guided me to sit on his lap. He removed the hand that was between my legs and brought it up so he could move my hair back.

"Have you been practicing?" he murmured against the shell of my ear.

The action had me grinding myself into him as I threw my head back against his shoulder.

"A little." My breathy tone had him tightening his arm around my waist.

"Show me," he commanded as he took hold of my hands and brought them to touch the keys of the piano.

I knew he was changing the subject, but for now, I would let him because I didn't want him to stop whatever it was he was doing. We had practiced before, but not like this. While he let Eve teach me all other sorts of things, he was the one who was teaching me to play.

He put my thumb right over the C note. With my right hand, I started off with the first four chords, and they sounded perfect, but when I was going to switch it off to A, I pressed another by accident.

Luke's hand was in between my legs again, this time cupping my pussy.

"From the beginning. You almost had it before I left," he chided.

My body was hot, and when I took a deep breath, I shifted, and all it did was press myself more into his hand. I bit my lip so I wouldn't make a sound.

I went back to pressing CC and GG, and this time I got AA and G when Luke moved my panties aside and stroked me with one finger. I couldn't help the whimper that escaped my lips.

"Keep going, Summer," he groaned against the curve of my neck.

When I went to play the next line in the song, my notes were being pressed too slowly. My DD notes weren't consecutive since I couldn't focus.

"You were doing so good, my dove," he taunted as he stopped his ministrations.

An annoyed huff left my lips, but I started over from the beginning. Luke pressed a kiss to my neck and began to stroke my clit with more pressure.

My hands trembled with each note I forced myself to play in rhythm. Playing "Twinkle, Twinkle, Little Star" should not have been this hard.

When I pressed C, I immediately let go of the note, feeling frustrated despite the fact that I had played the whole song by myself.

Luke teased my entrance with the tip of his finger. He stroked me, then murmured, "So wet for me."

All I could do was whimper as he sunk two fingers into me. He pulled them out, only to slam them back in.

"Did this tight little pussy miss me?" he growled before nipping the bottom of my earlobe.

My response was to grind my hips against him.

"Did you touch yourself thinking of me?"

I shook my head, and he stilled.

For all the experiences I'd had, I sometimes still felt like a virgin. The last time I'd had sex had been in *that* house. I was more than ready to do what I had to do to survive in Nico's ballet company, but I didn't have to do so being on my back, so my sexuality was buried in piles of trauma and guilt. There was no one who enticed me enough to want to try.

And although I got frustrated with Luke, I was grateful for how things had unfolded, even if it felt selfish that all the pleasure was on my end.

"Please don't stop," I hissed.

Luke began to work me slower, taking his time with my body. He held me tight against him as if he was trying to keep me from disappearing.

My soft whines turned into loud moans as he began to pick up the pace. Luke curled his fingers, and he hit a sensitive spot that had me arching my back against him.

"Luke." I cried his name with desperation.

"So fucking beautiful," he spoke against my cheek, his lips moving delicately against my skin.

I was so close my hips shifted faster, fucking myself against his hand. He began to trace circles against my clit with his thumb, and I was ready to snap.

"That's it, Summer, come for me."

He tilted my head, kissing me softly as I screamed my release against his waiting lips.

My chest heaved as I came down from my high. Luke had shifted me so I could sit up straighter, but at this angle, I could feel his hardness press against my ass.

"My trip was productive," he murmured as he tipped my chin up so he could kiss my forehead.

I didn't know what to say, or if he wanted me to acknowledge what had transpired over there, but before I could formulate a train of thought, he spoke again, surprising me.

With his thumb, he stroked the edges of one of my eyes. The scarred area around them had been desensitized to touch, but I could feel his caress on the outer corners.

"You have beautiful eyes." It was a statement.

"I don't remember what they look like," I admitted.

"They are a bright blue-to-green color."

My smile was sad. Not exactly how my mother had them, something that used to make me jealous as a little kid.

"Like the Caribbean Sea," I said without thinking.

"What?" Luke went still.

I cleared my throat. I couldn't remember the sea or the sand, but I did get a feeling of beauty but sadness attached to it. "My mom used to take me to the Cayman Islands a lot."

The pregnant pause continued, and Luke's body was still stiff.

"Too bad my eyes are wasted on me." The admission left my lips before I could filter it. Luke finally spoke in response to my words.

"Listen to me, my little dove," he started to say in a grave tone. He cupped my face with one hand and traced his thumb over the scars, down my nose, and to my lips. "You are beautiful. The color of your eyes, your nose, and your pouty lips are factors." He took a deep breath. "There's a reason why the beauty industry is worth over five hundred billion dollars globally. People are always looking to fix something, to cover up marks, to change things they don't like about themselves." He brought his hand right above my chest and pressed down so he could feel the beating of my heart. "True beauty starts here." He tapped my heart. "Beauty fades, but the heart remains, and that kind of beauty doesn't ever go away."

"Thank you."

Luke kissed the top of my head once more before speaking. "Whoever said your scars were not a thing of beauty doesn't deserve to live."

My breath hitched.

"And are they...living?" Despite not wanting to know earlier, I needed the answer for my peace of mind.

"You don't need to lose sleep over people who are beneath you."

I swallowed my curiosity and left it at that, but a part of me felt relieved to know I would never hear those two words again.

"Can I *see* you?" My question was hesitant.

He brought my hands to his cheeks, and I felt the changes that had happened since the last time he let me touch him.

"Not yet," he said, and it almost sounded sad.

I stroked his cheeks and smiled at the feel of his stubble. Instead of going up, my hands went lower toward his neck, touching his Adam's apple lightly, then down his shoulders.

My ass wiggled just to test to see if he was still hard, and I bit my lip when I noticed he was. I kept my hands on him as I stood up, gliding them down his arms as I knelt on the floor between his feet.

"Summer," he warned.

I ignored him, my hands now going down to his middle. His dress shirt clung to his body. Even with the cloth as a barrier, if I pressed hard enough, I could feel the ridges of his skin.

The man had carried me enough times for me to know that he was in good physical shape, but feeling it was another thing.

"I've never done this," I told him, knowing he would understand the meaning behind my words. I had never done it as a woman to a man. And although I wanted this with him, a part of me was also looking to reclaim what had been stolen.

"You don't have to." He grit out as I unbuckled his belt.

"But this is the first time I want to." I faced him so he could see the sincerity on my face, even if I couldn't see the uncertainty on his.

Luke stroked the underside of my jaw.

"Say the word, and we can stop."

I didn't bother responding as I began to pull his pants down. He helped me by lifting his hips. My hands felt clammy as I pushed his boxers down with them. I swallowed my insecurities and fears and reached for him. Luke was long and thick, and the head of his dick was swollen and leaking. I wrapped my hand at the base and then stroked up, then down again.

Luke's hiss was indication enough for me to keep going. I did that a few more times, noticing how his body stilled, how the air shifted, and those soft growls that left his lips. All signs that he was enjoying this.

"Fuck," Luke groaned the moment I took him into my mouth.

The moment I began to swallow him, one of his hands wrapped around my hair, but he instantly let go when he noticed what he had done. I bobbed my head once more as I used one of my hands to signal that I was okay for him to have his hand there.

Luke wasn't taking anything from me. All he ever did was give, and I wanted to give this part of me to him.

"Summer," he said in warning.

I could tell he was close by the way his hips shifted, how he growled when I deep-throated him. He tried to get me to pull away, but I didn't let him.

"Fucking hell," he grunted as he spilled into my throat.

I let him go with a soft popping sound. He immediately hooked his arms under my own and lifted me up.

"Welcome home," I told him, and he laughed.

And although it was my second time hearing that sound, there was something about it that made it feel familiar.

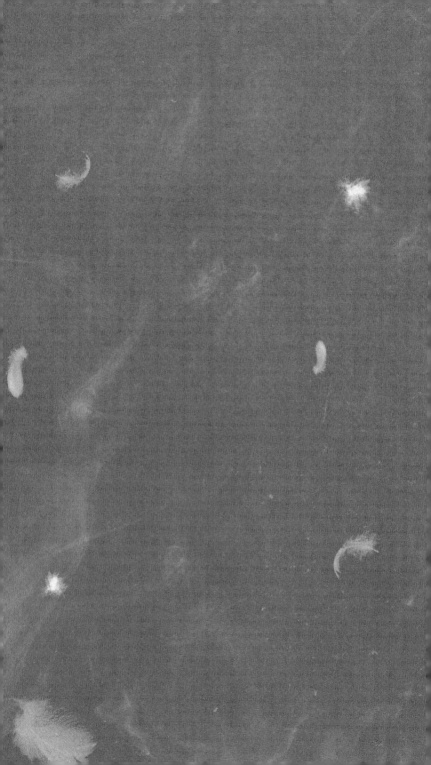

MISTAKES

I am not labeled by the choices that I have made.
I am more than a few of my mistakes.
Because every single wrong path I've taken
Has been a lesson that I've gained.

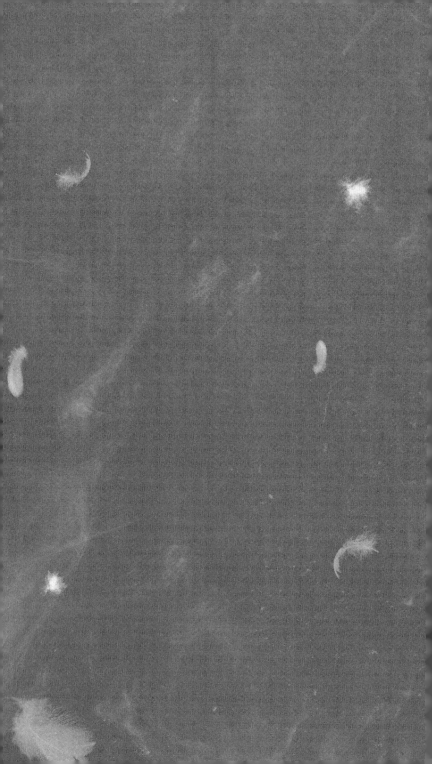

"Principessa," my uncle's cheery voice greeted me the moment I walked into the dining room.

"Zio!" I yelled as I began to run and throw myself at him until I noticed he wasn't alone—lately, he never was.

I scrunched my nose, and he laughed.

He said I was jealous, but I didn't think I was jealous of someone a lot older than me. I was used to being the center of my dad's attention. Something my mamma used to playfully complain about. After my papà died, my uncle took over all the things my papà would do with me. Though he overcompensated in the affections department.

"You look tan," he commented as I finished making my way toward him.

My zio Luciano pulled at my hair and winked at me, then nodded so I could turn to say hi to the guy next to him.

Feeling compelled to greet our guest, I turned and forced a smile. His usually blank face seemed amused. His skin was golden no matter the season, and his brown eyes had an intensity to them that I didn't like.

He greeted me by my first name, and I just stared at him. Family or not, I didn't trust him.

"Where did your mamma take you?" My uncle pulled me to his lap as he pulled a plate of fruit toward us. I ignored the fruits and reached for the waffles.

My zio didn't complain about the things I ate, unlike my mamma.

"We went to the beach." I was excited as I told him about the surprise business trip where my mamma let me tag along. "The water was like my mamma's eyes."

"Some cold-ass fucking waters, then."

"Shh." My zio shut the stupid jerk up.

I was adding more syrup to my waffles when my mother walked in.

"Annalisa, get over here." She snapped her fingers while she glared at my uncle.

My face fell, and I tried to get up, but my uncle didn't let me go.

My head was pounding today. It was becoming more exhausting to run away from all of my mistakes. I couldn't help but think back on my memories and notice things with a fresh perspective.

Had my mamma known what my zio was capable of, and was that why there was so much hostility between them toward the end? And if she knew, why didn't she try harder to snap out of the dark hole she fell into after my papà died?

My body was shaking, but I was otherwise proud of myself for not losing it completely after that memory came to the forefront of my mind. My feelings were still slit in two when it came to that man. My fragile mind had a hard time separating the man I remembered before the accident from the man he became afterward.

Or were the memories I had of him nothing but a perfectly crafted illusion he had me believe?

Either outcome brought bile up my throat. I'd trusted him after my papà left me. He was the person who hung the moon and stars for me, and for him to be the first person to visit me in my new world killed me.

I hadn't lied to Luke when I said my uncle was the one who sold me to that place, but I also hadn't told him the truth. Zio Luciano was the first who took from me.

Tears spilled onto my arms, and I didn't realize that I was crying. I felt like I was floating. Instead of a panic attack approaching, there was an odd sense of calmness in me. A stillness that was deadly.

"Are you sure you heard your uncle's voice?" Luke couldn't hide the concern in his tone.

"Over the years, I've forgotten a lot of things, but his voice is something I can't escape."

That was the last time I talked about the ordeal. Luke seemed displeased about the fact that I didn't want to talk about my uncle but seemed to leave it alone.

"If you tell anyone who you are...I will kill your mother just like I killed your father."

Even years later, I couldn't believe he killed my papà. Had the signs been there, too, and I missed them? Now that I was older, I could find the silver lining in my tragedy. The reason why I was able to bury the biggest betrayal in my life was because I didn't see it happening.

Maybe that was what made him brave. Maybe that was why he took advantage of me because he knew my eyes could not see. Did he stare at my empty eyes while he defiled me? Did he look upon my face and not feel an ounce of remorse while I cried?

My body shook and shivered. I wanted to come out of

my skin. I didn't want to be alone anymore. I didn't know what time it was; I didn't even bother to check.

"Come on, boy," I whispered, hating how broken my voice sounded.

Bear let himself be put on the leash. Once he was secure, I led us out of the room. Things had been okay with Luke since he returned. Just like he said, he stayed home, although he did say he had work to do. I didn't mind because Eve kept me on my toes.

The house seemed emptier than usual. I was a little disappointed that I could not hear the faint sound of the piano being played. Midnight talks were when I felt closer to Luke.

There was a darkness to him that didn't make me feel scared. It was in that darkness that I could see his true self, and although some might find it terrifying, I found it comforting.

I was about to turn toward the stairs when I heard a soft humming. Chills went down my spine. I held on to Bear's leash tighter, and in doing so, I felt a little more at ease. If something was amiss, Bear would have barked, right?

Instead of going up to the second floor, I went back toward the greenhouse, where I was sure the noise was coming from.

As I made my way back, I could almost convince myself I had imagined the humming. Just as I was about to open the door, I heard it again. My heart began to beat erratically, and it made Bear uneasy. I pushed open the doors and felt a current of wind that should not have been there.

I made my way toward the doors to try and investigate if they were open. No one had called out to me, and Bear still seemed to be okay, so I kept going. The moment I got closer to the doors, I knew they were open because I felt a cool breeze caressing my cheeks. When I smelled a hint of lilies in the air, I relaxed.

"Cecilia?"

"*Dio mio!*" she yelled, and I jumped back.

"I'm sorry for stalking you," I quickly added.

"It's fine," she said, out of breath.

"What are you doing?" I asked. "And what were you singing? It sounded familiar."

Cecilia was quiet, not answering me. I heard some shuffling, and then Bear growled lowly.

"I'm so sorry, Miss Summer," she rushed out. "You gave me quite the fright. I dropped the yarn I was working on."

I took a step forward again. "Do you need any help?"

I might not be able to see, but I could find objects on the floor with ease.

"No, that's okay. You better go back before you catch a cold. Mr. Luke won't be pleased if that happened." The last part was added with a bite I had not heard before from Cecilia.

"Okay." I absently nodded. "Are you sure you are okay, Cecilia?"

"Yes, I couldn't sleep, so I figured some fresh air would do me some good."

That made sense. "Would you like me to keep you company?"

"I think you should go to bed, Miss Summer. It's quite late." There was an urgency to her voice that put me on alert.

My throat constricted, and it was difficult to swallow. Why was she being so cold to me?

"Good night, Cecilia." I managed to choke the words out.

Just as I was about to leave, she spoke again.

"It's not appropriate for you to be spending so much time with Mr. Luke."

My chest felt heavy as I walked back out of the greenhouse. Here I thought she liked me. Were her feelings personal, or was it because I was a guest in this house and Luke had given me more than was appropriate? Did she think I was taking advantage of him? Of his generosity?

My body felt cold, and although I didn't want to go back to my room, I knew that if I got rejected by Luke in this state, I would not be able to handle it. So, I started to make my way back to my room when I heard footsteps coming my way.

Was there more Cecilia wanted to tell me?

Bear was calm. However, I was not. The lack of lilies in the air made me cautious.

"Luke?" I called his name, but the chuckle that followed wasn't his.

"I'm sorry to disappoint you, Miss Summer."

Upon hearing Pedro's voice, my shoulders lost the tension they had been holding.

"I'm sorry, I didn't expect you to be up at this time," I told him.

"I was just checking on Cecilia. Making sure she locks up for the night."

"Right," I said. I pulled on Bear's leash so he could begin the trek back to my room. "Well, good night."

"Couldn't sleep?" Pedro asked as he began to walk with me.

Maybe it was just my nerves or my dream, but something about this encounter made my skin crawl. I just wanted to be alone—I wanted to feel safe. I regretted going into the greenhouse because that was my happy place, and tonight, it got tainted.

"I'm okay." I tried to sound relaxed.

"Well, if you need me to watch over you, all you have to do is ask."

Bear's leash was burning in my palm from where I was gripping it tightly.

"I'm kidding, Summer," Pedro teased. "Sweet dreams," he added in his low, breathy voice.

I mumbled, "You too," and then closed the door in his face. I didn't know how long I stayed there, sitting on the edge of the bed, just keeping watch over my door. It seemed like all my demons had come out to play today.

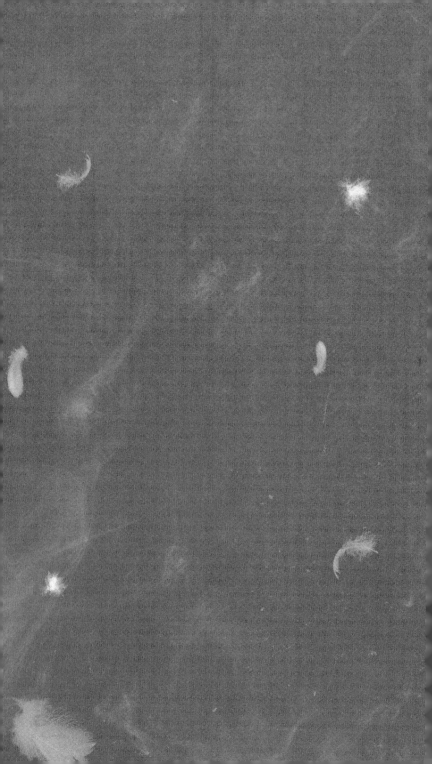

BLISS

If ignorance is bliss, then let me bask in it a little longer.

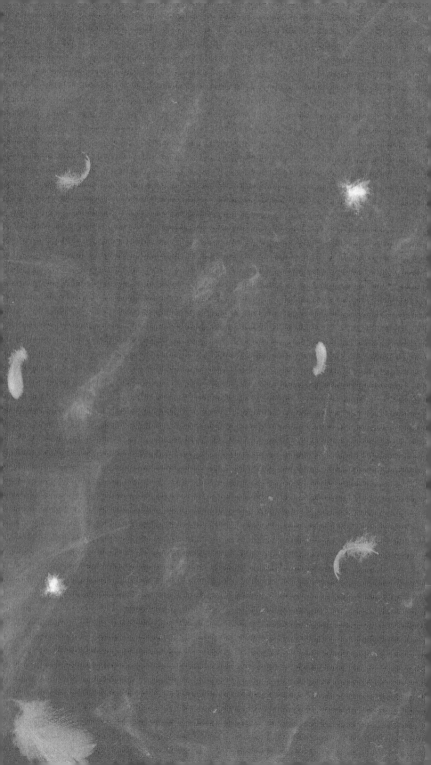

22

SUMMER

Summer.
My body swayed from side to side.
Summer.
Another gentle shake.
"Summer!"

I was startled awake by someone's hands on my arm. The hand felt nice and warm, and that was when I realized I was still on the edge of the bed, huddled into a ball.

"You're freezing." Luke's tone was displeased. His hand rubbed up and down my arm. "Is there a reason why you slept this way?"

I felt uneasy letting him know what was going on in my head the night before. Now that he was here, last night's worries didn't seem as severe. A part of me kept saying that it was all in my head.

"I couldn't really sleep." I shrugged, trying to play it off.

"Why didn't you call me?" Now he sounded annoyed.

I bit my lip before I could tell him the truth. He was silent, clearly waiting for my answer. "It didn't seem that important."

Luke made a humphing sound.

"I was going to have breakfast in bed this morning, but I've changed my mind. I'll meet you in the greenhouse. There are a few things I need to talk to you about."

He sounded like he was mad at me, and I couldn't figure out what I had done to make him upset.

"We can't have breakfast in the dining room?" The question slipped out of my mouth before I could filter it.

"No." His answer was immediate.

Luke left my room without another word. Sighing, I got ready, lamenting the fact that I wouldn't have time for my morning practice, but if Luke had come for me, it must be later than I had thought.

He didn't have to say he cared—it was always in the little things he did, and usually, I found comfort in that, but something in me was screaming, telling me to listen. Didn't I pride myself in the fact that I could see without my eyes? That I could find deceptions in plain sight? Was I going crazy? Had the years of running finally caught up to me, and because I avoided every memory from my past, was there even anything left of me?

I took my time getting to the greenhouse. There was no breeze this time around; the air was even lighter than it had been at night. I was about to take my seat when Luke's hand took hold of my own. My brow furrowed in confusion as to why he stopped me from sitting. Was he going to make a big deal about the fact that I wore my glasses today?

He didn't give instructions, not verbally, at least, but his intentions were clear. He pulled me toward the place where he usually sat. One of his hands wrapped around my back, and then he guided me down so I could sit on his lap.

That ache between my legs that only he could summon instantly appeared. Despite the conversation I'd had with

Cecilia last night, my cheeks still warmed. I couldn't help but recall the last memory I had of my uncle and the paradox of this moment.

There was some scraping going on as Luke fixed me a plate. Once he was satisfied, I heard the plate being placed right in front of me before he put a spoon in my hand.

"Eat." It was a command.

Up until I lost my sight, I didn't realize that, for most of us, eating was a visual experience. It was the first thing we noticed, followed by the smell. Even when trying new foods, we are guided by our sight before opening ourselves to new things.

I'd learned to adjust by using my sense of smell, but sometimes I missed something as simple as a fruit spread, pancakes, or a birthday cake. That last one made my throat clog up. I couldn't recall any of my past birthdays, not the theme, not my parents, not one thing.

As soon as I scooped some food into my mouth, Luke seemed to relax.

"Why didn't you call me, Summer?" Luke asked.

My oatmeal suddenly felt thicker in my mouth.

"Is this because of what has been happening between us?" His voice was hoarse.

"No." I quickly faced him. "I...I was actually going to look for you, but then..." I sighed. Luke was patient, waiting for my answer. "I didn't want to intrude in your life more than I already am."

That was answer enough. I wouldn't be throwing Cecilia under the bus either. She was just looking out for her boss's well-being.

Luke's silence spoke volumes.

"Luke?" I squeaked. If I wasn't sitting on him, I would have been sure he had left me.

"Oh, I'm sorry, Summer. I'm trying to figure out how my tongue in your cunt gave the impression that you were intruding in my life?"

That was a good point. Still, I didn't back down, though maybe I should have.

"You always leave me alone and tell me to go to bed."

Except on New Year's, but I was hysterical then, so that didn't count.

"That has nothing to do with you," he told me, and I snorted.

Luke did not like this because his hand was gripping my chin and forcing me to face him fully. He then removed my glasses from my face and threw them across the room. I could hear the thudding noise they made.

I took a deep breath.

"Oh, my little dove," he chided. "I send you away not because I can't wait to get rid of you. I do it because I want to fuck you."

My mouth parted in a silent O.

"I knew I shouldn't want you. I knew that in this life-time or any other, you weren't meant for me, but I've always been selfish and self-serving, and you, my sweet dove, are one of the most beautiful things I've ever laid eyes on."

I sucked in a breath.

"For someone who can't see, you haven't lost sight of the important things. Witnessing life through your eyes has made it impossible for me to stay away from you. For over a decade, all I could think of was revenge. There was no future, just the past."

I licked my lips.

My stomach was fluttering with wings I didn't know existed inside of me. I was floating, but I wasn't scared because I had a tether, and it was Luke. He said he would teach me to fly if I let him. I finally felt like my cage was open, waiting for me to leave and never return back to it.

"And now...do you see a future?" *With me?* I didn't add the last part, but my hand moved to his chest and over his heart. I wanted to feel his reaction. Was his heart beating as wildly as mine? Were his hands clammy from the excitement racing through his body?

Luke let go of my chin and cradled my body, so I was forced to rest my head on his chest. I held my breath waiting for his answer.

"The past is going to bury me alive." His voice was somber, and my excitement quickly faded. His hands, however, wrapped around me tighter so I wouldn't let go.

I slowly slid my hands up his neck, and he stiffened but otherwise didn't throw me off his lap. I stopped until I made it to his jaw. As much as I wanted to feel him, to know his face, I would not take what was not freely given to me.

"Let me help you," I whispered.

Luke kissed my forehead before chuckling without emotion.

"Isn't that why we are here in the first place? So you can help me?"

I didn't back down.

"And you're the only one who cares about getting justice for me." I took a deep breath before continuing. "I am nothing special. I'm a simple statistic. I can't even say that I got lucky because what happened to me before was not luck. It doesn't matter what you need from me because what you have given me has been so much more." I took another deep breath, and this next part almost felt silly to admit, but I wanted him to know. "*He* used to kiss my forehead all the time. It was how he gained my trust. He brought me comfort when I was at my most vulnerable.

And he twisted that for his own pleasure... You, Luke, have shown me with your actions that you put my well-being above your own."

Luke's hand was at my nape, and he lightly pulled so he could control the movement of my neck, causing my face to tilt up. I heard his heavy breathing before I felt his lips.

If his kisses before were to make me whole, this one was to break away the pieces of myself that no longer fit. This kiss was the sweetest form of salvation. He tasted like regret when his lips met mine, but to me, they felt a lot like freedom.

"I was so wrong about you." His words sounded pained.

No one could accuse Luke of being a stupid man. He seemed to sense my hesitation about being in the greenhouse, so he made it a point for us to stay there. He didn't say a word as I watered the plants. He didn't complain when I touched the roses.

"Someone promised me an outdoor garden," I said after a while.

I had just put the hose away and was now making my way to the swing.

"Just tell me what to get, and I'll get Pedro to get it."

"What doesn't Pedro do?" I questioned. Did the man ever have free time? I might have pressed more on the nature of their friendship, but I just wanted to push last night to the back of my mind.

Luke chuckled, and I stopped to concentrate on the sound he made. Something about it made me nostalgic, like an old tune you forgot the words to.

"It's just him and Cecilia for all these grounds?"

"Yes." His voice was a little clipped. "Other than the cleaning crew that comes once a week, there's a lawn crew that starts in a few weeks and then stops once summer leaves."

I nodded because I got the impression that he didn't wish to talk about it further.

"There's an event tonight that we have to go to." His words had rushed out without emotion.

I wasn't looking forward to it, but I was ready. If there was one thing I was sure of, it was the fact that Luke would protect me.

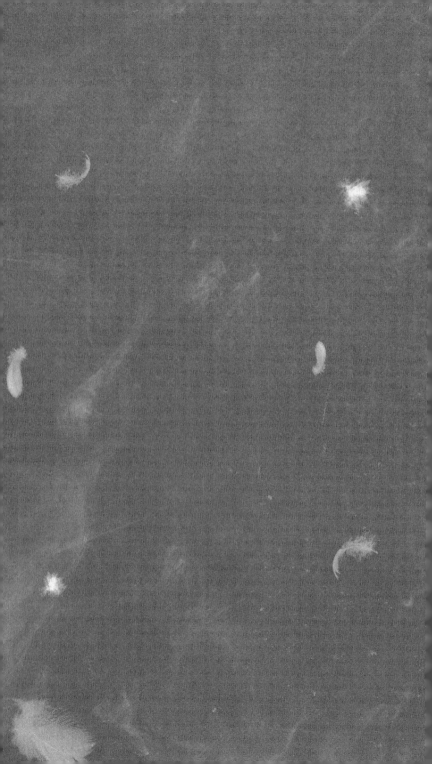

23

LUKE

I gave up on the notion that Hector Bianchi would slip. All these years, I'd been blindly chasing bank accounts based on information that was not valid on information I didn't have the whole picture of.

I knew Hector was a piece of shit, but even I thought there were some lines one did not cross. He was the businessman, and I was the street thug playing dress-up.

For years now, he held the shares that belonged to me over my head, and I grew bitter, resenting everything about that and how it came to be, but now I knew those shares he held over my head couldn't be possible.

The accounts were real—of that, I was sure—but everything else I thought I knew was incorrect. I had all the pieces to the puzzle, but the parts were all wrong.

Tonight, I would end it.

My hands shook as I fixed my bow tie. Hector was hosting a party today with the board members, foreign investors, and other influential people. It was the perfect place for me to show the ace up my sleeve, but I knew it would cost me greatly.

Summer had suffered the last time I'd brought her out. This time, it would nearly kill her. Regret marred my features as I finished fixing my suit.

Although I knew she was hiding something from me and I couldn't stand it, for now, I left it alone. The barrier I had set for us was crucial, even if it was only for my sake. After tonight, if she still wanted me, then I would give myself to her completely.

It was the most fucked-up thing in the world that I was brought down to my knees for a broken dove.

Summer blindsided me. The intrigue I felt for her fucked me over in the end because who wouldn't fall for someone who looked like an angel and tasted like sunshine?

When my phone rang, my chest grew tight. The weight of my sins was starting to weigh me down.

"Are you on your way?" I asked Pedro.

"Yes, sir. I think we should take precautions for the blowback."

"I don't want to disturb Summer's way of life," I let him know.

"Better her way of life than her actual life." He was brutally honest. Then again, he was a man of few words. He always got to the point and didn't bother himself with useless chatter.

"Let me know when you're back."

He hung up, and I made my way downstairs. This house was about to feel smaller in the following hours, I could already feel it. I pulled a pack of smokes as I made my way to the left wing. Perhaps it was bad taste to gloat to the less fortunate, but it felt like karma was finally being served.

When I opened the double doors that led to the hall-ways, Cecilia was making her way out of the room.

"Is everything okay?" My tone was harsher than how I usually spoke to her.

"Yes, *sir*." Her tone had some bite to it.

Cecilia had been very fond of my father. She took care of the house to the point that sometimes I felt like she thought this place was more hers than it was mine. After all, I had been the intruder in all of this.

"Is now a good time to go in?" I took a drag of my cigarette, and although Cecilia looked annoyed, she nodded.

Cecilia began to walk away when I spoke again.

"Anything I should know about?"

Her eyes widened, but otherwise, her face remained impassive.

"No," she said confidently, but it almost felt like a lie. I felt like I was starting to become paranoid.

I dismissed her with a nod and continued to make my way forward.

There was a sick joy I felt when I pushed open the doors to let myself in. Usually, I was in a gloomy mood, but today, I felt content despite the impending doom on the horizon.

"I would ask how you're doing, but we both know hell is not a fun place to be."

There was no reaction, just wide eyes staring at me, full of shock and mania. Stuck in an endless loop of misery.

I got closer and ashed my cigarette on the bed. It would piss off Cecilia, but it was the little things that made me feel at peace for not being able to execute my revenge sooner.

A small wheezing noise came from her chest, and it made me smile. Some would say this was cruel—inhumane. I called it justice.

"I hope that not even in your dreams you find peace, Mrs. Ferro."

The small piece of joy I had found minutes ago was gone the moment I was back in the foyer, waiting for Summer.

Playing the piano always helped me clear my head. It was the first thing I'd learned to do for myself when I got my second chance at life. I knew that with enough time and dedication, anything could be possible. It was why I had faith in Summer that she could conquer the world given the right tools.

People like Summer and me, who had lived in hell, would do anything to claw their way into paradise.

As I sat on the bench, not even playing could relax me because all I could think about was Summer moaning my name while my fingers played with her wet pussy like she was the world's greatest symphony.

After a few seconds, I gave up, but it was just in time when I heard the footsteps from Summer and the light thumping from Bear.

She was a sight. Her hair was down and flowy. The dress was made for her, and the sunglasses were designer. Today, we both had a role to play, so it was better that she showed them the version of herself she was most comfortable with, even if it was not the version of her that I liked the most.

"Beautiful as always," I let her know, and then I kissed her because I might not get the chance to do it anymore after today, and I wanted the taste of her lips to linger along with the pain.

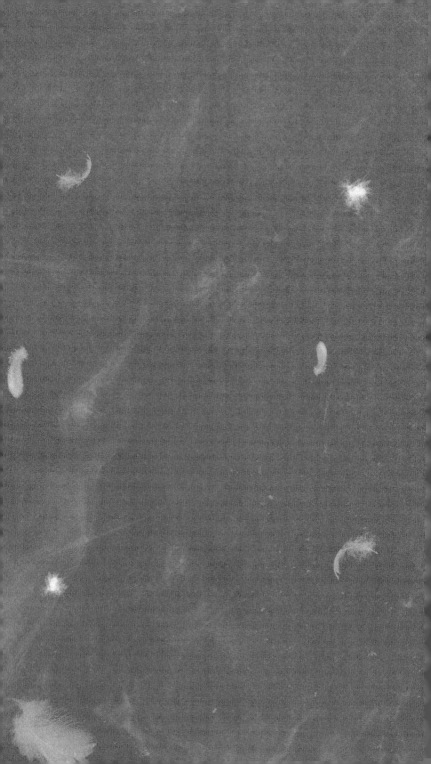

HURT ME

If you knew you could hurt me,
Why did you take the time to make me melt?

If you knew you could hurt me,
Why did you make me care?

If you knew you could hurt me,
Why didn't you warn me?

That by the end of this, you would destroy me.

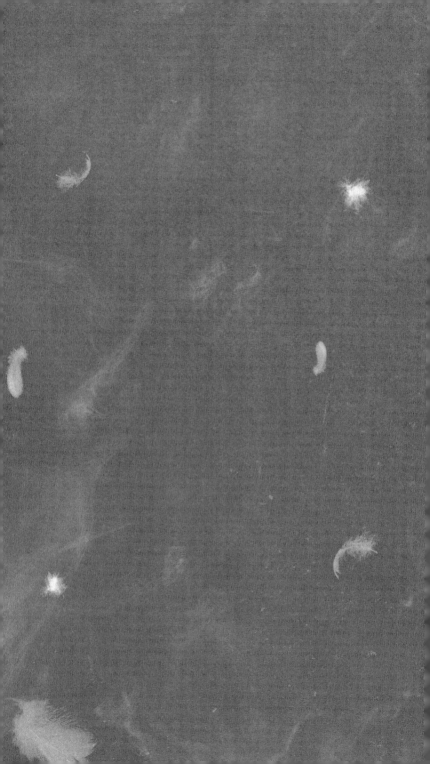

24

SUMMER

Everything about today had been intense. And it wasn't just my lingering thoughts from the previous night that followed.

After the conversation Luke and I had this morning, you would have thought we would have grown closer. But those remaining walls that should have crumbled seemed to be reinforced. Perhaps he was as nervous as I was? While I was new to his master plan of revenge, this had been his lifeline.

I couldn't imagine putting all of my energy into revenge. It was something that ate at you every single day. What would be left in the end?

Luke led me to his helicopter. There wasn't much time to talk while we made our way to the city. I knew he had money, but I hadn't pressed about what it was he did. I told myself it was because I didn't want to bite the hand that was feeding me, but deep down, I knew that maybe I wouldn't like the answer.

I had lived in delusion most of my life. What was the harm in doing it a little longer?

When we arrived in the city, Luke was even more withdrawn. He led me to the car and guided me into the back seat when someone else opened the door for me.

"Thank you, Pedro." My voice was perhaps too cheery. I blamed the silence. It was starting to make me feel uneasy.

"You don't have to thank Pedro for things he gets paid to do." Luke's words had a bite to them.

I waited for Pedro to say something or acknowledge me, but he didn't do it and instead took off driving. Was he this withdrawn because of Luke? Had I messed up by talking to him during work hours? Soon enough, I heard the sound of something moving, like a window being rolled up, but it was internal.

To pass the time, I traced the patterns of my dress. The dress I wore was off the shoulder, formfitting lace that flared out mid-thigh.

It was long enough to hide the fact that I was not wearing heels. There was only so much trust I could give out, and all of it was now on the man next to me. For the next few hours, he would be my crutch, and I didn't think he realized just how much I was giving in by allowing him that position.

He squeezed my hand as if to assure me that he would be my strength.

"What's wrong, my dove?" He shifted, getting closer to me.

"Nothing," I lied. "So, where are we going?"

Luke used the opportunity to lift me and sit me on his lap.

My stupid heart started to beat faster. The intimacy we shared had not been like this. It was felt but not seen. It touched your heart without needing anything physical or more concrete.

This time, it was me sucking in a breath as he wrapped an arm around my waist. I tipped my chin toward him, wondering how he looked at me. I rested my head on his shoulder and bit my lip when I felt the evidence I had been hoping for.

He was hard for me.

He wanted me.

And that proposal I had made in the beginning was now haunting me. I ached to lean up and touch him.

I wanted to push past his boundaries and obliterate every wall he had set up in my wake. My fingers came to his throat and lightly grazed the way his artery throbbed. Moving them, I traced his Adam's apple and felt his long swallow.

Daring to be bold, I moved my fingers higher, and he went still beneath me. That arm that was wrapped around me was like a steel band, cautioning me without words. His fingers dug into my hips as a final warning.

I ignored this.

I knew pain and what he would dish out would not hurt me. A thin line existed between pain and pleasure, love and hate, because they were the same side of a coin. All I knew was the negatives, and I didn't care what I had to do to get the positives.

My heart was now beating fast. It was like a tune of drums spurring me on as my fingers glided to his jaw.

It was sharp—strong. The skin was smooth in some areas, with a hint of prickliness in others. Before over-thinking it, I leaned in and kissed the underside of his jaw.

Dull pain bloomed in my hip from where he now dug his fingers in deeper, as if trying to steady himself, prepare to pull me away, or brand his hand there so I wouldn't go anywhere.

"What are you doing?" he hissed.

When I pulled back, he relaxed a bit. I ached to see all of him, but I didn't want to push him. Things lost beauty when they were not freely given. And I knew better than anyone what kind of scars the things you were forced to do left on you. They were not only physical, but they went skin-deep. I could feel them with every breath I took. With every trip down memory lane, they were there, always with their arms wide open, ready to grab me in their clutches and sink me back in.

I didn't reply, for he knew and remembered from our past conversation what my intentions were. All I wanted was a small part of him. Even if he didn't realize it, he had stolen a part of me already, so it was only fair I got something in return as well.

With my thumb, I traced his lips. They were smooth, the bottom one a tad bit bigger than the top one, with a wide and defined Cupid's bow. I liked the feel of them on my lips, and I couldn't help but remember the way they felt moving between my legs.

I shifted in his lap, trying to find some relief from the feelings he had awoken in me.

He parted his lips, and I was prepared for him to tell me it was enough, but instead, he took my thumb into the cavern of his mouth. He waited until it was all the way in, then wrapped his teeth around it and began pulling back.

"Luke," I moaned as the feeling between my legs intensified.

He swirled his tongue against the tip of my thumb before wrapping his mouth around the digit and letting it out with an audible pop.

"We are here," he groaned with regret.

The door opened, and he sat me astride him while he

wrapped the coat over my shoulders. Although spring was here, the air was still chilly.

Luke got out of the car first, then took my hand and guided me out. As soon as my foot touched the ground, he had a possessive hold on me.

"I won't let you fall," he promised.

I nodded as he began to lead the way.

"Will you tell me where we are now?"

"Soon," he told me as he led us over a threshold.

The first thing that hit me was the smell. It was a mix of perfume, alcohol, and cigarettes.

My mouth went dry.

It couldn't be, right?

This should have smelled like a bar, but it was far too classy for that. The cigars were only the best, alcohol top-shelf, and the perfume and cologne designer.

Although I said I felt nothing and nothing mattered, that was because I thought I had escaped my first cage and the flames that had branded me would never touch me again.

The murmur of people stopped the moment Luke and I stepped fully into the room, their soft gasps enough to let me know we had been unexpected visitors.

"Lucas," a familiar voice drawled, and it came from directly next to me.

I jolted with fear, trying to wrap my brain around it so I could pinpoint the place and time I had once heard the voice, although I already knew the answer all too well. I almost made myself believe that the last time I'd heard it had been a fluke.

"Run!"

My mother's chilling voice rang, sinking into every pore

of me, and instead of spurring me into action, it made me immobile with fear.

"Mamma," I screamed as I ran toward her. The man who had her stopped and looked at me, and I sucked in a breath when I recognized his face.

Tears welled in my eyes as I really took in and saw the way he was holding on to my mom. He wasn't helping her. He was the reason why she was in pain. His hands were on her neck, and my mom pleaded for me, but I didn't know what to do.

They were my world, but I was beginning to realize that perhaps it wasn't big enough for both of them.

Without thinking, I grabbed the first thing I could find. It was a container from the lab, a tray with tubes on it, and maybe I should have wondered why it was home and heeded my papà's caution never to touch it, but I just wanted to help in any way I could.

I threw it up, the contents spilling as it went. Screams echoed all around, and it wasn't until I gasped for air that I realized that the haunting sounds were coming from me.

My hands came to my face, and I couldn't even open my eyes from the pain. Someone rushed to me, and they tried to pick me up. They said words I did not care to hear. I needed to open my eyes. More than anything, I needed to get away. Since my eyes were closed, I couldn't see what I touched, but I pushed away from the arms trying to hold on to me.

"Fuck," the person roared.

"Mamma!" I yelled, but her answer never came.

With my eyes closed, I made my way through the house, knowing where everything was from memory. The lab led out to the dinner area, and if I made it to the kitchen, I could rinse my eyes in the sink.

I got knocked back when my body collided with someone.

"Where's your mom, little one?" I instantly recognized my padrino's voice.

As I gasped for air, I tried to beg him to help, but instead, he carried me away.

"We have to get out of here now," he rushed out. "He will kill you next."

As my heart broke, I could feel the pain of every jagged end that was currently shattering before me.

The chaos and the pain had lulled me to sleep. When I woke, everything was now black. A thundering voice echoed through every corner of where I was currently lying. If the devil had a voice, his would be it.

"Benvenuto nella Casa del Silenzio."

I was surprised my body wasn't convulsing as violently as I felt on the inside. Five words were on my mind on repeat like a broken record, but the tone of it was all wrong.

The fragments of my memory were chipped and altered. If it weren't for Luke's fingers digging into my side like he was trying to claw his way into my skin, my feet would have failed me.

All I could do was stay still, reminding myself that Luke was next to me, and as long as he was here, I would be safe. He had already slayed one of my demons; he was about to do the same to the devil I couldn't escape.

"I hope we aren't interrupting anything," Luke drawled lazily, but I knew underneath his tone that his body was tense because I could feel the rigidity of it next to mine.

"Of course not," he spoke, and I almost threw up at the memory of his voice.

Luke's fingernails bit into my skin. I didn't know whom he was trying to keep together, him or me, but right now, that little bit of pain he was giving me was all I had to hold on to. Maybe he knew it, and that was his way of telling me he was here and he had not forgotten about me.

"Excellent, because now that I see almost everyone is here, I do have one question." Luke's words were met with anticipation. I could almost taste the nervous energy. Slow murmurs were going on everywhere, and I knew that the overstimulation of it all was about to get to me.

"And what is that?"

My hands fisted at my sides. His voice was like being abused all over again.

"How is it that Annalisa Ferro signed over her shares of the company when she's been under my care this whole time?"

When Luke said he would teach me how to fly, I never thought it would result in this. With my mangled body on the floor and my wings ripped and thrown into the sky. If I could have left my skin and never return back to it, I would have done so in an instant.

I almost believed I was free, but a gilded cage was still a cage.

Annalisa Ferro was one name I never thought I would hear again.

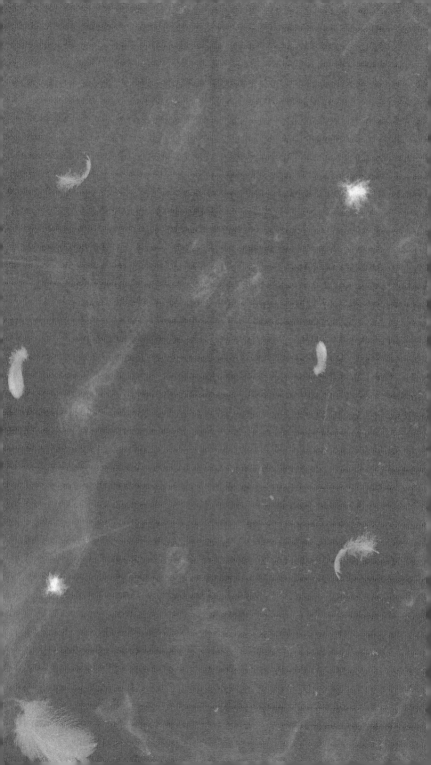

25

LUKE

REVENGE WASN'T ALL THAT IT WAS MADE OUT TO BE. I didn't feel victorious calling checkmate in this long game. Despite knowing what it would cause, it had to be done. Summer had been still a few seconds ago, and now she had gone limp. My arm around her was the only thing keeping her together.

It took me by surprise when she first walked through my door. I recognized "Summer" the second I looked at her face. There was something familiar about her features. They were etched on a face I'd grown to hate. They were not exactly the same, but similar enough. I had been looking for answers from someone who might have a clue in which direction I could look, and the key to it all was right there.

My dear cousin was in one of her family's estates, and she didn't seem to have a clue. I kept my poker face on because I didn't want Nico to know he had delivered my revenge on a silver platter.

Still, I wasn't sure. How could she have signed over the shares when she was one of Nico's broken swans? My mind immediately raced with what I knew of the act, and dread filled me.

Was she really blind, or was it all an act? I didn't trust Bianchi, but I knew I could trust Nico. We lived by the same moral code.

I needed to be sure that Summer was Annalisa, but without alerting her. It was something Cecilia didn't agree with. She'd worked with Luciano for years, had known Summer since the moment she was born.

Summer was family.

Annalisa had signed over her shares to Hector the moment she turned eighteen. All his paperwork seemed to be legal. I didn't know what to think of it all because everything about *that* day had been a blur.

Hector glared at me while everyone murmured and gossiped. Their eyes were on Summer, filled with shock but mostly pity.

Her father had made groundbreaking formula discoveries in the beauty industry, and his legacy was not what they considered beautiful.

Fuck them—fuck them all.

"As lovely as this has been, I think we will go now. We didn't mean to impose," I mocked as I began to drag Summer away.

My point here was made. Everyone knew that his power at the company was gone. I didn't need to call for an emergency board meeting—the fucking board was here. Everyone was smart and self-serviced that Bianchi would want to save his face, expecting him to resign quietly.

As soon as the chilly air hit my face, it was enough to blow away the façade I had been clinging to. Summer was cold, tense—comatose.

Guilt spread through my body; it was a feeling I wasn't

used to, but one I had been living with since the moment Summer came to the manor.

"Sum—"

"Don't. Talk. To. Me." Her words were like ice shards cutting me up to the core.

I kept my mouth shut as I led her to the car. Pedro had already known this wasn't going to end well, so I didn't have to tell him to take us to my penthouse as he was one step ahead and already on his way there.

Ironic that my personal space was now marred with bad memories. The walls in the house haunted us, and now my place would be a reminder of the things I had put her through.

I knew I would have many sins hanging over my head; I just didn't realize how heavy they would get. In my master plan, I'd never let myself think about what I would do after I hurt her because I never entertained the idea that I would fall for her.

My plan had been so simple: find someone who knew those who frequented the House of Silence and get all the information I could from them. I should have known that you couldn't just throw money at a wound and expect it not to hurt.

Summer's knuckles were white from squeezing her hands into tight fists. Her jaw was taut and her shoulders rigid. Good—anger was better than being numb. I now knew her enough to know that she hated the fact that she was holding on to me like I was a crutch. That was what made me feel like shit—her trust was gone.

As soon as the elevator door pinged open, Summer pulled away from me, getting as much space between us as possible. I took off my jacket as I watched her go toward the living room.

She had no safe space here. There was nowhere for her to run off to.

"Summer." I said her name tentatively, and her face instantly turned to face me.

Fury was etched in her features. You didn't need to look into a person's eyes to see the loathing they had for you when their body language said it all.

"Summer, is it?" Her voice was low and restrained. She didn't want me to hear her pain. "You're a piece of shit."

"Would you prefer I call you Annalisa?"

Her face contorted in pain at the mention of her birth name.

"H-h-how long?" She gasped for air as the words left her lips.

"How long have I known?"

She clenched her teeth. I could see how tense her jaw was. Her nod was slow, and her fist had begun to shake—she looked beautiful.

I was proud of her for standing up to me, knowing that I held all the cards to her way of life. There was no point in hiding anymore, so I took a step toward her. She tried to step back, but the backs of her legs hit the couch, and she was forced to stop.

"I'll show you," I let her know.

She didn't unclench her fists as I took one in my hands. I rubbed my thumb soothingly over the top as a small form of comfort.

As soon as she noticed that I was bringing her fist to my face, she tried to pull away.

"I don't want to see you anymore." She seethed.

I wasn't going to lie, that stung. Did she think it was easy for me to see her face fall each time I denied her touching my face and getting to know me? So she could see me in the only way she knew how?

And now that I was offering myself up to her, she wanted nothing to do with me.

"I was almost positive the moment my eyes landed on your face," I admitted, and fuck if the hurt whimper that escaped her lips didn't slay me. "I was one hundred percent sure the moment I laid eyes on your scars..." She tried to pull her fist back, but I didn't let her. I grabbed her other hand and attempted to force both palms open, placing her hands on either side of my face, where scars similar to her own ran down my jawline. "...because they are just like mine."

Her intake of breath was so sharp that I was surprised she didn't double over in pain. Tentatively, she began to open her fists. Her fingertips were tense as she began to do the one thing I had denied her because I knew that if she'd felt my scars so similar to hers, she would know.

"You marked me that day, little dove." My admission was met with deaf ears.

She touched my eyes next, but unlike hers, mine weren't scared. The only reason my scars weren't as harsh and deep was because I was able to rinse them, which told me no one had bothered to clean her face.

It made me sick to my stomach thinking of the pain she must have been in while the chemicals worked their way down to her skin. Beauty comes at a cost, and many of the chemicals used in beauty serums must be diluted. Unfortunately for Summer, the ones she picked up that day were part of testing for new formulas and, therefore, were not yet stable.

"You didn't bother to tell me?" she spat as she let her

hands fall to her sides. Her shoulders slumped, and her head fell.

I hated how defeated she looked, but not as much as I hated that her whole life, she had been used as collateral.

She took deep breaths as she finished processing everything. Her downcast face snapped up, and then she lunged for me. Summer began to hit me as she cried.

"How could you, *Lucas*?" My name was like venom on her lips.

"It's Luke," I corrected, even if it didn't make a difference.

"What's your name, kid?" the man who found me asked.

Even though I was bleeding out in an alley and he looked way too extravagant to be here, he was the only one who stopped and helped me.

"I'm dead." I seethed, trying to contain the pain. "You should leave me before they come and finish me off."

The man cocked his head, and I flinched when his hand touched my cheek.

"You deserve so much more than this," he pressed on.

I couldn't figure out why a man like him was even having a conversation with someone like me. Or why he was even on this side of town. He didn't reek like filth but high class.

If I could, I would have laughed at his words. Those with privilege were so easy to cast stones at everyone else. Thinking that changing your life was a matter of want, disregarding all the other bullshit that followed. No one deserved their tragedies, but we all played the hands life gave us the best way we knew how.

"Let me help you," he pressed as he took off his jacket and draped it over my chest.

He pulled out his phone and made a phone call.

"L-L-Lucas," I coughed out my name.

His smile was warm, and I didn't think my own father had ever looked at me with any sort of affection before. "Luciano."

Apparently, having names that began with the same letter was like a sign from the universe that he was supposed to help me.

26

LUKE

I stood there, hating myself with each tear that fell, knowing that I had made this bed and we were going to lie in it. Her hits lessened in force but not her cries.

"You're sick, you know that?" she spat at me. "We are family. Is that what Luciano taught you? That it was okay to—"

"Don't," I warned as I gripped her chin and forced her to face me.

I knew she was hurting and that she thought she knew things in this whole clusterfuck, but Luciano didn't deserve her hatred. He was one of the best—if not *the* best—men I'd ever met.

"I didn't do anything you didn't want me to. Hell, you were fucking begging for it," I hissed, ignoring the pain it brought to look at her tears. "Do you know how hard it was not to give in to you? I knew you'd never forgive me if you didn't know the whole truth."

She scoffed. "How noble of you. I mean, if my uncle raped me, what difference does it make if my cousin does too."

My hold on her chin got tighter; I knew it was causing her pain. I knew she said she thought Luciano sold her, but to have raped her? Fucking shit. She had already lost so much, but to have her memory of him ripped like that —fuck.

"If I remember correctly, *principessa*, you refused to acknowledge me as family. I am not your cousin. Luciano was my father in name only, but not blood." My face was closer to hers, just a few breaths away from kissing. I wanted to soothe her, but I knew she wouldn't let me.

She was fucking strong. No wonder there was real terror whenever she thought she heard his voice.

At some point, she stopped crying, and instead of hitting me, she had my shirt in tight fists.

"Fuck you." Her rage was mixing with my own.

"Oh, I want to."

"Just like Luciano? Following Daddy's footsteps? Is he going to walk in here and take me after you?"

My other hand wrapped around her waist while the hold on her chin softened. This was what made me sick, what filled me with rage, and there would be hell to pay. The fact that her memories were so distorted, she really believed a man who adored her would seek to destroy the most innocent part of her.

"Luciano didn't rape you, Summer. He loved you as if you were his own."

Summer was shivering as she shook her head vehemently. "You don't know the things he did to me!"

"He got arrested that same day!" I yelled back over her hysterics.

She stopped moving, her lower lip trembling like crazy.

"He died a few months later, and his biggest regret was not being able to say goodbye to you."

Her forehead fell to my chest as she tried to control her sobs.

"S-s-so it wasn't him?" she whimpered. "H-h-e w-wasn't the o-one who to-o-k me first?"

Both my arms wrapped around her protectively.

"He would have rather died than hurt you."

"Then why was he choking my mom?"

Fuck, this next part was going to kill her. Summer lifted her head, and I took the opportunity to remove her glasses. There was no point in keeping barriers between us anymore. All of our secrets were about to be bared.

"Because your mom's lover killed your father."

A lone tear fell from her right eye as her beautiful, life-less eyes were aimed at me. She was not surprised by this news.

"Deep down, you knew, didn't you, Summer? You knew nothing was as it seemed. The way you got comfortable so quickly. Why you always wanted to be in the greenhouse, loved going into the maze..." Her breathing got heavier. "Why you didn't go looking for me the other night... Is it that you would have known exactly where to go? And lastly, the fact that you didn't even bother to investigate what was on the left wing."

Summer was shaking.

"I didn't want to hurt you, Summer."

"I hate you." Her voice was filled with loathing, but fuck if I was backing down now.

"Yeah?" I said against her lips, giving her enough time to back away, but instead, she took a deep breath that made her breasts press against my chest. "I think you're full of shit, my little dove."

I kissed her softly, with no restraints, tasting the lingering effects of my betrayal, and fuck me, it was intoxicating. Since she didn't pull away, I nipped her bottom lip gently.

I was fucking hard, and if she didn't push me away, I would give in to what we both wanted. My hands played with her waist, sliding down to cup her ass. Her shiver was sign enough to keep going.

"What did I tell you the first time we were in the greenhouse?" It was a rhetorical question I didn't expect an answer to. "Doves are smart. It doesn't matter the distance. They always find their way back home. So yes, Summer, I omitted the truth, but only because you seemed desperate to run away from your past. But I still gave you enough clues to question everything, and you chose to ignore them—you chose to give in to me."

I kissed her again harder, this time letting myself possess her in a way I hadn't allowed myself to do so before—not when she wasn't giving in to things with a clear head.

Summer moaned into my mouth, and there wasn't anything delicate about it. She was angry and hurt, but at this moment, she was feeling just as impulsive and careless as I was.

Keeping a hold on her ass, I maneuvered us so that this time it was me against the sofa. She didn't fight me when I began to slide down the zipper on her dress. I leaned back, my legs spread, and watched as the dress pooled at her feet. She wasn't wearing a bra, and my mouth watered at the sight of her tits.

Maybe I was taking advantage of the situation, but I didn't know if come tomorrow she would still want me. If she wanted me right now, I was going to take that and let myself have her, even if it was only for one night.

"You're so fucking beautiful," I told her as I kissed her breast.

My tongue flicked her nipple, then sucked it. Summer's hands flew to my shoulders as she threw her head back in pleasure. While I removed her panties, I did the same with her other breast.

Her panting, her heavy breaths, were the sweetest fucking melody I had ever heard, but even I knew nothing would compare to her cries as she came for me.

Summer whimpered as my hand trailed down her stomach toward her folds. She was soaked already, and we hadn't even started.

"So fucking ready for me," I groaned.

I kissed the arch of her neck, making my way up toward her panting lips.

When I brought her down to straddle me, she didn't protest. My lips kissed every inch of skin they came in contact with while I worked on unbuckling myself.

My dick was hard and leaking precum, more than ready to finally be sheathed in her pussy.

"You're..." I kissed her neck by her ear. "...going to fuck me." The last part was a growl as I aligned my dick with her wet heat.

I pushed down on her hips so she could take me, and her mouth parted with pleasure.

"Your pussy is so fucking wet...tight...squeezing me so fucking hard." My groan was pained. It was the sweetest kind of torture.

Summer's head rolled back as she finally took all of me.

"Is this what you wanted?" Thrust. "To be so fucking full of me?"

"Shut up," she breathed as her pussy clenched all around me.

With her hands using my shoulders for support, she began to ride me. God, she was magnificent. She was focused on her pleasure, and I was lucky enough to be along for the ride.

"Why?" I grunted as her hips rolled. "You don't want to hear how perfect I think your pussy is? How it gets wetter by the words coming out of my lips?"

She moaned at this.

"You can't see the ecstasy on my face, but you sure as fuck can feel it." I met her thrust with my own. "And I'll be damned if I don't tell you just how much I love—"

Summer cupped my face and shut me up with a kiss. I could still taste her anger, but her lust was overpowering everything else.

If she wanted to use my body, then I was too happy to be at her mercy.

"Fuck, Summer," I whispered against her lips.

"Luke." My name finally fell from her lips the moment her pussy began to spasm against my dick.

"Oh, fuck," I hissed at the sensation. I needed to pull out before I came in her.

She came softly as she bit her lip, denying me the pleasure of having her fall apart for me. As soon as I felt her orgasm stop, I tried to pull her up, but she rolled her hips, and I couldn't help moaning.

"No one was ever allowed..." Her words were soft, but the meaning behind them was what had me finishing inside her.

We were both breathing heavily, our beating hearts in synch for the first time since she arrived in my life. After a few seconds, she finally spoke, and I wished I wasn't as surprised by her words.

"I want you to take me back to the house," she let me know as she pulled away.

She faced away from me as she got dressed and made it clear she'd stopped thinking of the estate as home.

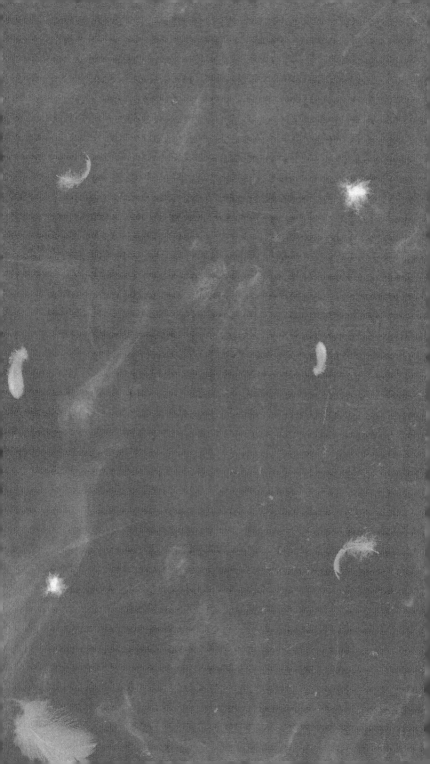

FOOL

Maybe I'm the fool for refusing to see what was right in
front of me.
My bad for thinking you actually gave a fuck about me.
Congratulations on making a laughingstock out of me.
Do you feel better now that you killed off a part of me?

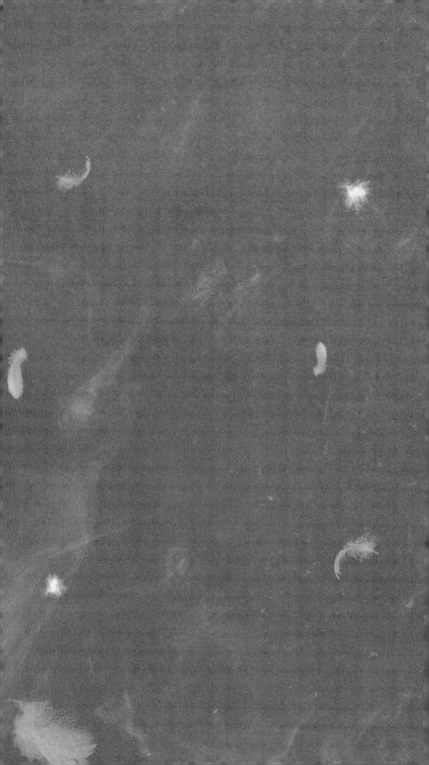

27

SUMMER

THE HOUSE FELT DIFFERENT NOW THAT I KNEW THE secrets that it carried. When Pedro dropped me off, he didn't even attempt to talk to me. I stood in front of the door and just touched the wooden panel, not bothering to turn the knob. I knew Cecilia had to be expecting me. I was spent; I didn't have the energy to spar with her. It sucked that it took one conversation to sully the relationship we were starting to build.

I was fucked-up. I told myself pretty lies so I would feel like I had survived, but I was a coward. Too scared to look into my past because I couldn't face the fact that my perfect family, my perfect life, had been a lie.

Luke was right. Deep down, I'd felt a kinship with this place that I had never felt before. It had felt like coming home because it once had been. That was why I didn't want to know where in the world I was because if he had said it, the illusion that I was nowhere near home would have been shattered, and I would have been forced to face my demons.

The house felt different as I stepped in. The magic it held was gone, and all that remained were the demons I tried running away from. I didn't call for Bear, nor did I go to my room to get my cane. Instead, I made my way to the grand piano.

My hands traced the edges as I walked around, letting myself sink into the feelings it gave me. Letting myself remember things I had wanted to suppress. Even if most of the things weren't bad, they were still painful.

My stomach was coiled with unresolved feelings as I sat on the bench.

I bit my lip so I would stop myself from crying. I felt relieved that my zio had not violated me, but there was no denying the fact that he had tried to kill my mother. Don't even get me started on her having a hand in my papà's death.

I lifted the cover and stroked the keys. My zio had loved this piano. He said it brought him peace and helped him work through his ideas.

I guess it made sense why Luke had taken it upon himself to learn. My zio must have made one hell of an impact on Luke for him to hold Luciano in such high regard.

Zio Luciano had been right—I was a jealous little kid when Luke came along. My uncle's affection wasn't solely mine anymore. He had a kid, one I refused to acknowledge out of pettiness. I loved the manor, but my mamma preferred to stay in the city, so that was where we spent most of our time. My zio and father loved the manor, so in our absence, the house was more theirs than it had been ours. My dad was a chemist, and he had a lab in the house since he preferred to work on new formulas away from the company.

Once he passed away, our visits were less frequent. I would be dumped here when my mom had things to do, and

Cecilia would watch over me as I played around in the greenhouse. The house wasn't the same once my papà passed away, but it was still the place where I found his presence lingering—a sort of safe haven. I'd have never imagined this place would bring so many bad memories.

How wrong had I been?

I sighed, already knowing where I would be off to next.

The fact that you didn't even bother to investigate what was on the left wing.

Luke was right again. I stayed safe and confined to my gilded cage that was rid of any attachment that would trigger me. Maybe it had been sub- conscious, but I stayed content with my limitations.

The lab was on the left wing—the beginning of my end. I got up and made my way toward my room and called for Bear. Even if he was just near me, it would make me feel safer, like I had some sort of support with me.

I didn't feel secure walking these halls on my own anymore. This place made me feel like there was a shadow clinging to me, waiting, watching for the perfect moment to strike.

Bear's paws tapped against the floor. I was still lucky enough that I had not encountered Cecilia. Let's hope it stayed that way. I wanted to finish looking at the ghost of my past in my own way. My interaction with Cecilia the other day made a little more sense as to why she was acting a little cold with me. To her, Luke and I were family.

I paused at the closed doors that led into the left wing. My heart beat faster, waiting for me to push its limitations by diving headfirst into this past that I was unsure I was ready to face but knowing I was tired of running. I lost my sight, and I took off running into the unknown before I took a look back to see what I was leaving behind.

Cold. This side of the house was colder than the rest, as if it had known that nothing but misery resided here and it needed to neutralize the hell that was trying to escape with ice.

The smell of flowers and chemicals was amiss, and the only thing that remained was something bitter in the air. It was like death was lingering. The metal doors that led to the lab were cool, and a chill spread through my body. Every part of me told me to go back, but I had ignored my instincts thus far, and I wasn't about to do it again. There were none so blind than the one who would not see, and I had no excuse for that. The answers I had been looking for this whole time had been right in front of me, and I refused to acknowledge them.

I made it to a table. It was bare, no longer filled with machinery, test tubes, or paper. My fingers traced the surface, and a tear fell as I allowed myself to think back to that day.

I missed my papà. Trips to the beach with him were always fun. Mamma and I had been traveling a lot to the islands, but she never took me to play in the sand. It was always meetings and the signing of papers. She was always in a rush, looking over our shoulders.

It was probably because Papà made her feel the safest.

My knees were drawn to my chest as I sat on the floor of the greenhouse. My back was pressed to the window as I watched how the noon light illuminated the whole room. This place seemed to be more vibrant when Papà was alive. He loved his flowers. Although he said Zio was the better chemist while he was in charge of making the money—or so that was what Papà had said.

"You didn't have a fun time at the beach?" The lazy drawl made me scrunch my nose in annoyance.

I turned to look at my zio's new son. Maybe what annoyed me the most was the fact that he looked more like a Ferro than I did. He had the dark skin and hair, with deep brown eyes. He could pass for Zio's son. Maybe I was feeling left out now that my mamma was wary of my uncle. If she wasn't fighting with him, she was arguing with my padrino.

"It was okay," I lied. I got up and began to walk away.

I was going to go find my mamma.

"It gets better," he said after me.

I ignored him and made my way through the rooms, looking for my mamma.

"You're a fucking cunt, Melissa." Someone's angry voice filtered into the foyer.

"He found out, didn't he? He wouldn't have given a shit about the affair, but the money—"

My mamma spat something too low for me to hear, almost like she was struggling.

"Run!" My mother's chilling voice rang, sinking into every pore of me, and instead of spurring me into action, it made me immobile with fear.

"Mamma," I screamed as I ran toward her. The man who had her stopped and looked at me, and I sucked in a breath when I recognized his face.

Bear's bark snapped me out of my memory. He was pacing the room, and fear began to take hold of me. I tried to breathe, but just like last time, I couldn't. Someone screamed, and I heard a crash, followed by Bear's whine. It took me a second to realize that his body was no longer next to mine.

My back hit the ground first, followed by my head.

"No," Cecilia screamed.

"What's going on?" a voice I couldn't place asked.

My neck hurt from where I tried to gasp for air, and I

couldn't. The pressure in my chest was too much that I couldn't get up. I began to go in and out of consciousness until it felt like I had broken the surface and was able to breathe. It burned, the way life filled me, as it scratched my insides, not letting me have a moment of peace.

I lay on the floor for minutes, or it might have been seconds. Bear's whining started to drift and sound farther and farther away.

"What are you doing?" Cecilia shrieked.

Was she expecting me to have an answer for her?

"This is the second time. He won't allow for it to happen again. Make sure she's okay. I'll be right back."

Who was this man? I couldn't recognize his voice.

"Are you okay, Miss Summer?"

Lilies. I could smell lilies.

Was I dying? Had my past finally caught up to me enough to kill me?

Cecilia sat me up, and I could hear her soft cries as she massaged my neck, trying to ease my pain.

Her phone rang, and Cecilia's voice was shaky.

"N-n-o, now's not a good time," she rushed out. "She's not lucid now."

Cecilia left the room to finish the conversation. I used the opportunity to finish getting up. I couldn't breathe here, even with the pressure around my neck easing. With shaky legs and holding on to the walls, I made my way out.

I felt like a toddler who was learning how to walk as I made my way across the wing. I needed fresh air. It took me a few tries, but I got the front door open. Who was in that house?

Who was that man, and did he want to hurt me?

The most foolish thing I could ever do was to keep walking away, but my legs wouldn't stop. It wasn't until a few minutes later I heard a car. I braced myself, ready for the pain.

"Summer?" It was the first thing they said as they opened a door.

I tried to back away the best I could.

"Are you okay, Summer? Where's Luke?" This time, I recognized Pedro's nasally tone.

"Luke?" I questioned. Hadn't he left him in the city? "There's a man in the house," I managed to choke out. Some of the adrenaline that had been spurring me on was beginning to leave my body.

"Is there really?"

I froze.

Pedro's voice no longer sounded low and breathy, but it was one I knew all too well. The voice that haunted my dreams. The voice I heard as I was being torn and shredded.

The voice I put my trust in to keep me safe.

"Where's your mom, little one?" I instantly recognized my padrino's voice.

As I gasped for air, I tried to beg him to help, but instead, he carried me away.

"We have to get out of here now," he rushed out. "He will kill you next."

In reality, it was Hector Bianchi who was out to kill me.

"My dear Annalisa, it would have been better for you to stay dead," he mocked before he pressed something to my face, and everything else went numb.

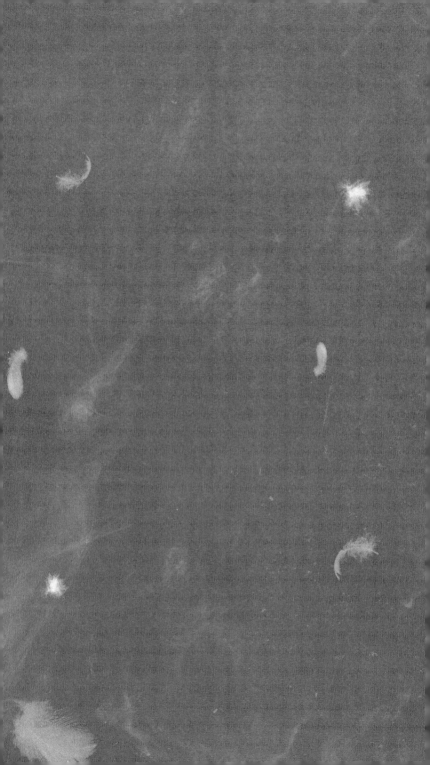

BEAUTY

He looked at my demons, and he told them to run.
For he was not scared of the damage that they had done.
He looked into my eyes and fell in love with my scars.
Because beauty was more than just a pretty front.

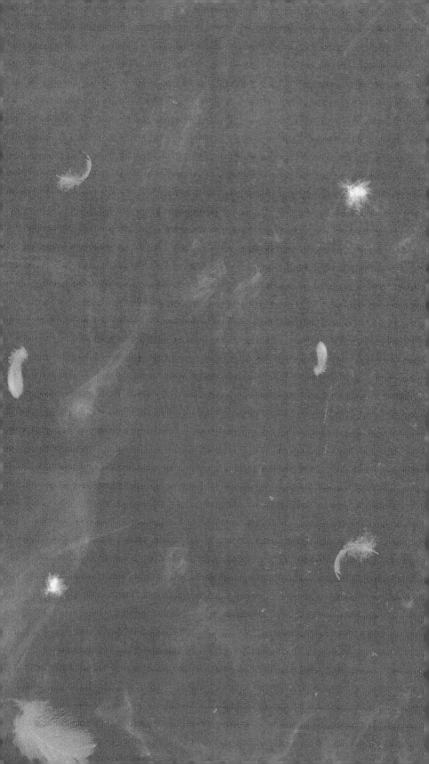

28

SUMMER

My eyes burned. I wanted to scream, but I didn't know how. My hands clung to my padrino as he took me away from the house. I wanted to tell him that my mamma was in trouble, but all I could hear was "He's going to kill you too."

Why would my zio want me dead? It made no sense.

A silent scream tore through me as my padrino threw me inside the car. That seemed to snap me out of the numbness I had felt.

I screamed so loud I felt it shake the car.

"Shut up!"

I couldn't help it. My eyes were burning worse than before. I opened them, and it was blurry. Was I crying? Could I not see through my tears? The sun was still shining on the horizon, and the only reason I knew this was that I could faintly see the orange glow, but it was growing darker by the second. Was time moving that fast?

"Padrino," I whimpered. "Take me back."

My godfather didn't listen to reason and ignored me.

"I can't see!" I began to scream as I realized there was

nothing. I forced my eyes to remain open, as if that would make my sight come back. I refused to blink, and they burned even more. The pain around my eyes was worse.

My hands had a tingle to them too, but less. Everything was dark, and all I was left with was pain.

I went in and out of consciousness for what felt like days. As soon as I started to feel somewhat coherent, someone would get near me, and then I would feel drowsy again.

"Unfortunately, I will need the little bitch. No one knows I was there that day, only Melissa. And since Luciano's little charity case won't let her go, all I have is this little golden ticket."

My body felt numb again, and I drifted off.

When I was finally lucid, I found myself in a strange bed. A deep-rooted ache was the first thing I felt as soon as I became conscious. I wasn't in pain per se, but the feeling that engulfed me wasn't a pleasant one. My eyes were closed, and they wouldn't budge. It was like having a nightmare you couldn't wake up from. Was I dreaming? I didn't think so. I could feel the coldness of the room grazing my exposed skin. I could feel the sheets beneath me. They were coarse. At least, they felt that way since I was used to my soft ones. My fingers began to move when I willed them to, even though my eyes refused to do so. I also felt the stillness of my feet, and when I wiggled my toes, they moved instantly. All of this pointed to me being awake. I brought my hand to my face, and it was covered in some type of bandage. I traced the material, and it went all around my head. Fear spread through me in an instant.

"Mamma," I yelled.

Panic set in when I couldn't remember how I had fallen asleep. I sat up, trying to remove the wraps that hindered me from seeing.

Suddenly, my hand stopped at the last wrap when my memory came back to me. My mamma had been gasping for air as her eyes begged me for help.

A thundering voice echoed through every corner of where I was currently lying. If the devil had a voice, his would be it.

"Benvenuto nella Casa del Silenzio."

I whimpered as fear like I had never known spread through me like fire, trying to burn me enough to make me forget.

"Zio?" I questioned.

Was I still at the house? Had he killed my mamma?

"My little principessa." He spoke in a tone unlike his own, or maybe this was because I had finally seen the kind of monster he truly was.

I couldn't see a thing, but I could feel tears falling down my cheeks.

My zio was next to me, and the bed dipped with his weight. He was speaking nonsense, and nothing he was saying made sense.

"Melissa should have trusted me more." He said my mamma's name with anger. "You were going to be beautiful just like her, and now you're deformed."

He touched my eyes, his nails scraping against the scabs around my eyes, and I whimpered in pain. Then he touched my leg, and that was when I realized that it was bare. His hand trailed higher to a place no one should touch.

I cried, my hands trying to push him away, but he was so strong, and my body hurt. It hurt so much that I blocked it all out. Just the ache remained.

"If you tell anyone who you are...I will kill your mother just like I killed your father."

For the second time in my life, I woke up in a strange bed. You'd think that by now, I would be used to it. The sense of losing yourself and wondering if this was finally the time that you would snap. Was there even a point to keeping going? There wasn't any fear on my part—not this time.

At this point, there wasn't anything new shy of death that could be done to me. There was some sort of fucked-up peace that came with that realization. If I had survived my demons once, could I do it again? Or was the first time merely practice, and this time, it was sure to kill me?

Thinking back on it with my newfound memories, I could see how things didn't make sense. There was no way Zio Luciano could have been the one to rape me when Hector had been the one who had taken me. He had been my mother's lover and responsible for my father's death. But why was my zio trying to kill my mamma?

My head was throbbing, and my mouth tasted like chemicals. I might have woken up alone and disorientated once again, but I was not *that* scared little girl who was frightened because she couldn't see. My life ended there because I thought the life I had was nothing to live for if I couldn't witness it with my eyes. Now I knew that life was felt through all your senses, not just one. One of them failed me, but I had four more to fall back on.

If this was my end, I would not go down without a fight. I was sharper and wiser, and death was always lingering, so maybe it was time to meet that old friend. I was hurt, but I was also angry, and I let that anger fuel me.

I could hear a doorknob twisting, and I remained still on the bed. Making sure my eyes were closed, I tried to be as calm as possible.

I made sure not to move, not letting my body betray me. I'd lived with fear, regrets, and pain—I could do this.

I was holding out for something—no, I realized I was holding out for *someone*.

Luke.

Then his face was there, the one I barely remembered—the one I envied because I felt like he was stealing someone from me when I had already lost so much.

And then there was his face now with scars that mirrored my own. I was holding out hope that Luke would find me.

A part of me called me foolish for putting my trust in someone who had betrayed me, while the other argued that he had kept true to his words.

Footsteps came inside.

Hector's voice was harsh and angry.

"Not my problem, Elizabeth," he spat. "It's not like he will kill your mother. That little bastard doesn't have it in him."

There was more being said on the other side of the line, and my heart grew restless. My palms were sweaty, and I could feel perspiration trickling down my forehead.

"No," he snarled. "The deal was for your mother to find that damn key so I could access the accounts she left, but she couldn't even do that."

My mother?

"If she had done her job, then I wouldn't have to resort to such drastic measures. You're on your own."

He hung up the phone, and I felt his steps get closer. Bile began to rise as the bed dipped. I was waiting for my panic attack to set in like it always had lately.

Hector's hip pressed against my own. His hand came over my waist, and he leaned into me.

"You would have been more beautiful than my Melissa." His cold fingers touched my smooth cheek.

I flinched at the touch.

Hector gripped my chin, and his fingers dug into the hollow of my cheekbones. When Luke did it, it was to get my attention, but this was to bring me pain.

"Should we take a trip down memory lane, Annalisa?"

Tears pooled in my useless eyes, but I refused to say a word to him.

"I need you in one piece for the bank, but maybe after." His words were laced with retribution.

"Get up. We have to go to the bank. Fauché was a useless piece of shit, but the moment Luke went after him, I knew he was hot on my trail, although he would never make the connection between us."

Once he moved, I sighed in relief. I was safe—for now.

I had many questions, but for now, I'd keep them to myself. Hector was the last person I wanted them answered by.

Elizabeth...he had said her name, and something about it nagged at my brain. Of course—she was Luke's secretary. But what did she have to do with all of this?

Everything that had gone wrong in my life could be traced back to Hector. He said my mom's name as if he loved her, but you didn't defile the daughter of the woman you supposedly loved. He didn't love my mom; he was or had been infatuated with her, but what he wanted was power.

Was throwing me in *la Casa del Silenzio* a power play to know I was alive while everyone thought me dead?

If my uncle had killed my mom, where was he? Or was she dead? And I didn't think Luke had just stopped looking for me, had he?

My head throbbed even more.

How much time had passed? I hated this disoriented

feeling. It was uneasy, and hopelessness filtered through all the cracks.

A bit later, Hector came back.

"Put those on. No one wants to see that face," he spat as he threw what I assumed were glasses at my chest.

No sooner were they on when he grabbed my arm and began to pull me along. I heard people—kids. The air was different here, more humid. As soon as we were outside, I heard seagulls in the sky. He had brought me somewhere tropical, and I felt dread at the thought of not being anywhere near Luke.

He spoke to someone and then made us get into a car. As scared as I was, I knew that going wherever it was that he was taking me was my best bet. I didn't want to be with him at the hotel, nor near a bed.

The idea that Luke would rescue me didn't seem very plausible.

The car stopped, and he paid. My stomach was in knots as he began to pull me along with him. Why wasn't I asking for help? Should I attempt to run away or scream? Would it make a difference? I had nothing to my name; I didn't know any numbers by memory.

I knew I had to scream or do something. It was the only shot I had, but for now, I bided my time.

We were back inside a building, where the air-conditioning here was cool, and the floor was smooth and recently waxed.

"Hello, good afternoon," Hector greeted with a charm I didn't know he possessed. "We would like to access an account."

"May I see an ID?"

There was some shuffling going on with Hector, but then I heard something slide across a counter.

"My goddaughter lost her parents and her sight in a terrible accident." He added pressure to my arm so I would stay silent.

So, the account was mine? He had the documentation needed. Money—was he after the money my uncle and mom had been fighting about?

"She's old enough to handle the assets her family left her."

"If you'd come to the back with us, there's just a few more things we have to go over first," the lady at the counter told us.

Hector pressed his mouth to my ear. "One wrong word and you'll regret it."

My lips moved of their own accord. The fight in me had not died—at least not yet.

"There are worse things than death, Annalisa." His voice was stern. "I could take you away and have you every night and make sure your precious Luke sees the videos in the mornings."

It would kill him.

It would kill me.

I felt like throwing up.

He was going to get the money and then probably kill me, right? Death sounded like a mercy compared to the other option. Neither Luke nor I would survive it.

We sat there while they went over the paperwork. He claimed to have lost the keys to a safe, but since they had my documents and my fingerprint matched, they could go ahead and access the account.

Life had been cruel to me, giving me a taste of freedom only to have it ripped away. Life made me fly and had me crashing back down the second I was ready to spread my wings like I never had before.

"I'm sorry, Miss Ferro, but the contents in your account can't be accessed," the bank teller told us.

"What do you mean?" Hector's voice had gone icy, and I could feel his anger.

"The contents have been cleared out."

You could have heard a pin drop by the silence in the room.

I was fucked, wasn't I?

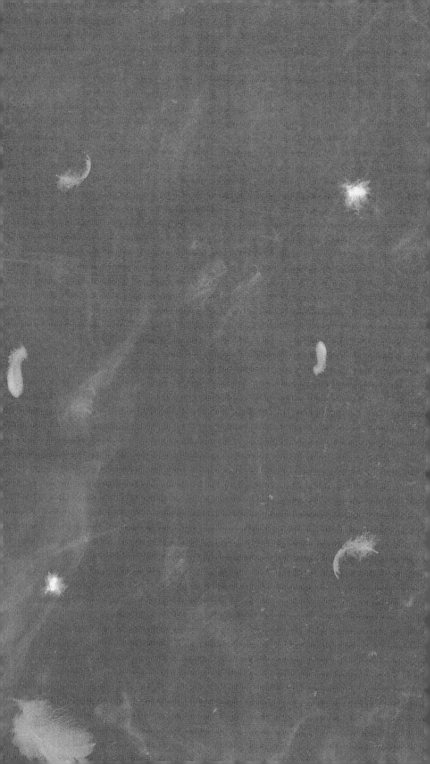

29

LUKE

THIS DREAD AND THE DESPERATE FEELING WAS ONE I had forgotten existed. It sunk into every pore of your body. If you let it, the fear would paralyze you.

When I got the call that the Summer was missing, I was about to go out of my damn skin. I came back to the house to find Pedro had Cecilia on a chair, and she was in hysterics.

"Are you going to tell him, or should I?" Pedro asked.

"What. Happened?" I seethed, barely being able to hold it together.

Fuck, this was my fault. I didn't expect the retaliation to be this way. Maybe if I had listened to Pedro earlier and contacted the security firm before now, this could have been avoided.

"Cecilia has been letting Hector come into the house and visit Melissa," Pedro spat with disgust.

My knees shook with that betrayal. Any affection I might have felt for the woman died in that instant. I should have pieced it together. That familiarity Summer seemed to have with Pedro—fuck. It made me sick.

"Please..." she begged. "I didn't mean any harm. I just wanted to bring some joy into her life," she pleaded.

"I might have forgiven that incident, but this, I cannot. I don't give a fuck if Luciano loved you like family because if you were family, you would have never done that."

"Oh, that's not all," Pedro scoffed as he handed me Cecilia's phone.

There were calls upon calls to Hector, but there was one name there that I didn't even know existed in her contacts.

I pressed Call, and right away, an all-too-familiar voice answered.

"Mom, he's mad—he doesn't want to give us our share. He said you had years to get the information, and now he doesn't need us anymore."

"Well, this certainly makes sense," I drawled, and Elizabeth stayed quiet. I hung up the phone and looked from Pedro to Cecilia, who was crying and begging.

I felt like an idiot. Why Bianchi wanted her close to me, the way she smirked at me like she knew something I didn't. Hell, the reason Cecilia moved in with me was with an ulterior motive. She didn't do it so I wouldn't be lonely but to spy on me.

"Why?" I managed to look Cecilia in the face long enough to ask.

Her chest was rising and falling rapidly. "I had been employed for years, taking care of Luciano's house before you came in the picture, and what did I get in return? Nothing."

This was all about the damn offshore account. I snorted because everyone was going to be in for a rude awakening.

"Had you asked me for money, I would have given it to you," I told her, and it was the truth. She was family. Had

Luciano known about her daughter? Did it even matter now?

"Anything else I'm missing?"

Pedro began to speak on Cecilia's behalf, telling me what he had walked into earlier, and all I could do was swallow my pride at the fact that I had put my trust in the wrong person.

"Bianchi has her," I confirmed what Pedro already suspected. "He's taking her to the island."

I felt somewhat relieved at that last part, and I thanked my fucking stars that Summer had begun to open up to me and had let that slip. Knowing where to look made things a hell of a lot easier.

"That's good. It gives us time to get over there." Pedro looked at the time. "Even with the hour lead he has, the banks will be closed when he arrives. It gives us a good window, so stay calm. He won't hurt Summer before then. He needs her to cooperate."

My jaw was set in a tight line.

I was going to come out of my skin if he abused her as he had done all those years ago. Making her believe it was Luciano who did it was his little revenge for not having access to the accounts.

Melissa had known not to put her full faith in him and created a fail-safe. The account was in both their names, and until Summer turned of legal age, she would always need Melissa to access it. After that, they needed a key or to have Summer's paperwork, but the key bypassed all.

Since the beginning, only I had the key.

While Pedro arranged for our flight and everything else, I went to go check on Bear. He was lying down on his bed, his eyes looking up at me with sadness.

"He's going to die." I rubbed his head. "For putting his hand on both of you."

Bear gave a soft whine as I patted his head.

W HEN I BECAME LUCID, THE FIRST THING I NOTICED WAS *the antiseptic smell that surrounded me. The second thing was the beeping noise of a monitor. Third, I could feel IVs connected to me.*

So I hadn't died?

I tried to sit up, but a groan left my lips.

"Don't move," the man said.

So I hadn't imagined him? I was racking my brain, trying to remember his name. "Luciano?"

He smiled at me.

"You're okay. You'll be discharged in a few days. Luckily, you didn't pierce any vital organs."

I snorted.

How lucky was I?

I was alive, but what did I have to live for?

"You ever been to America?" he asked.

All I could do was look at him with a raised brow. I could barely survive here. What made him think I could travel anywhere at all, least of all out of the country? That was the thing about rich people, wasn't it? They were out of touch with their reality.

Luciano smiled. "Would you like to join me?"

"I'm not gay," I blurted out now that I thought about it.

"Neither am I?" His answer sounded like a question on its own. He cleared his throat and spoke again. "I haven't settled down enough to get married. I don't have kids, but I do have a niece. She's special to me. Family is very impor-

tant. I have a little brother with a wife I can't stand, so we've grown apart."

"She's a bad wife?"

"She's a cunt."

If my biological father had taught me anything, it was that we needed to adapt in order to survive. There was nothing left for me in Italy. My brother was too far gone in my father's shadow. There was no point in me staying. All I could do was close that chapter in my life. Here was a stranger doing more for me than my own blood ever did. Luciano got me everything I would need to start my life fresh in the United States. He was clean and did everything by the book. Being with him, there was no looking over my shoulder, and it felt nice. He was too wise, like an older brother but too caring to be considered so. He was like the father I never had.

His brother was nice, but that wife of his was a cunt, and his niece didn't like me, but she was just a spoiled child. When his brother died, Luciano confided in me that he was sure he was murdered.

I made it my mission to help him get his justice.

Luciano was too clean and played by the rules. And the one time Melissa goaded him and he snapped, all hell broke loose.

"We have eyes on all the major resorts," Pedro assured me.

All I could do was nod.

We left Bear back at the penthouse, along with other essentials we brought from the house. Cecilia was being watched, and now the only thing we had to take care of was Hector. After exposing his charade with the shares, he took a sabbatical from work. Everyone knew he wasn't coming back. After this, it would be over—well, almost over, but that was the least of my worries.

It was ten minutes after the bank had opened when Hector got out of a car, and he was dragging Summer along with him. I took a step forward, but I was immediately pulled back. The team I had hired for this didn't fuck around.

Pedro was with me and reminded me that we were playing it safe. Especially if I wanted my revenge, I needed to do things their way. I could storm in and get Summer, but with so many people, Hector would use it to his advantage to get away.

"Okay, we are in position now," one of the men told me.

Fifteen minutes later, Hector walked out, and I could see the fury in his eyes. All of his plans had failed. He wanted money the easy way. Wanted things that he didn't work hard for. It was why he hated when Luciano brought me under his wing. In his eyes, I was undeserving—he had been there longer. Some people wanted the world to hand them blessings without having to earn them.

"We got him." Pedro patted my back, and I clenched my fist as I watched him throw Summer into the back of the "cab."

I wanted to kill him once and for all.

"Let's go. She must be terrified" was all I managed to say to them.

I really wanted a fucking smoke, but now was not the time for one. I sat on the passenger side as we made our way toward the airstrip.

"The situation was neutralized the moment he tried to get off at the hotel. The woman was notified of the situation. They should be arriving within five minutes."

As soon as we got to the airstrip, I saw the rest of the team waiting. It was important to me to clear the damage Bianchi had done to the Ferro name. It took years and patience, but I finally had everything to fuck him over. Everyone always left a trail.

Once we made it back to US soil, the cops would be waiting.

I saw the car come into view, and I finally felt like I could begin to breathe. Last night was one of the longest nights of my fucking life.

No sooner was the car parked than the door opened, and Summer rushed out. Her head moved everywhere, trying to decipher where she was and her surroundings.

"Luke." She whimpered my name, and I took off running toward her.

I wrapped her in my arms the moment she was near enough for me to hold her. Her fist bunched my shirt as she buried her face in my chest and cried.

"Shhhhh." I brushed my hand down her hair. "It's okay now, my little dove. You're safe."

She cried harder.

"Did he hurt you?" I said just loud enough for her to hear.

She froze, and I closed my eyes so tight I saw stars but tried to remain calm.

"Not like that..."

I exhaled in relief.

"He didn't get a chance."

My throat constricted, and I turned to look at the car and watched as they escorted Hector out.

I cupped Summer's cheeks in my hands and tipped her face to meet mine. I pressed my forehead against hers, and amidst all the people, I began to make promises I knew I would keep.

"It's going to be okay. I know you don't have reason to trust me, Summer, but I swear I'm not going to hurt you.

Not anymore. Not ever again." My breath fanned her skin, and she sagged against me.

"I knew you'd come for me," she whispered, and for now, that was more than enough for me.

"I love you, Summer." I confessed the words she had stopped me from saying the other night.

Before she could say anything else, the feds began to speak. Summer froze, and I just held her tighter, letting her know I was there.

"Hector Bianchi, you're under arrest for embezzlement, along with the kidnapping of Annalisa Ferro."

I silently added the murders of Amado and Luciano Ferro, but I didn't want the fucker to go to a maximum-security prison. I wanted him locked up somewhere that would give me access to him. Kidnapping and embezzlement weren't as severe as murder charges.

Bianchi almost looked relieved to know that he would be going to jail. That I would not be killing him today. That I didn't have enough on him to put him away for murder.

"Pedro," I called. "Stay with Summer for a second." She shook her head, and her fist tightened against my shirt once more.

I kissed the top of her head. The last thing I wanted was to hurt her, but it had to be done.

"He will stand close enough that you can feel him, but he won't touch you," I let her know, and this seemed to placate her.

Once I untangled myself from her grip, I walked toward the jet, where they had Hector seated and ready to take him back to the US.

"I'll make this quick," I let the men know.

Hector Bianchi was cuffed, and he had nowhere to run anymore.

"Don't look so smug, Bianchi. I'm going to make sure that wherever you end up, they know what you did to a child." His face blanched. "How many years was Summer in that place?" I pretended to count with my fingers. "Almost a decade?" I looked into his eyes. The gloating was now gone. "Then, after I keep you alive for that long, I'm going to make sure you receive the same treatment you gave Luciano."

Yeah, I knew the fucker had him killed off in jail.

You see, now *I* could see the full picture. Since he was Summer's godfather, he was close enough to the Ferros, and it must have killed him how they had more than he did. Maybe he did love Melissa, or maybe she was just a trophy, something he took away from Amado.

He found out about the money, so they killed him. It would have been a good amount for him and Melissa to disappear, but I bet he wanted more. Greedy people always did.

Hector and Melissa were probably ready to dip when Luciano found out about it. Melissa was never the same after that, and since she was under our care, he took Summer away, waiting until she turned eighteen. In the meantime, he went back to the company and framed Luciano for attempted murder against Melissa and Summer's disappearance. At the time, it just looked like Melissa's lover was looking out for her.

With both Ferros out of the way, he thought it would be easy to overtake the company, but he never counted on me and the trust Luciano set up under my name.

It wasn't until Luciano was murdered in prison that I began to suspect more was at play. Nico destroying the House of Silence put a wrench in his plan, but he figured that Summer was most likely dead, so he faked the fact that she handed over her shares to him.

Neither of us expected Summer to walk back into that place that took everything from her would be both of our downfalls.

Except I had never felt better.

"See you in hell, Bianchi." I flipped him off as I walked back toward Summer.

She was standing stiffly next to Pedro, and the moment I spoke to her, she rushed to my arms, and I knew then we would be okay.

"Let's go home, my little dove."

IT WAS LATE BY THE TIME WE ARRIVED AT THE penthouse. Bear rushed to greet Summer, and she fell down to her knees and hugged him. Tears streamed down her eyes, and her body shook. I had filled her in on what had happened, laying all our secrets bare.

"Luke?" she said after a while.

I walked toward where she was with Bear and crouched next to her.

"If Luciano went to jail for my disappearance and my mom's attempted murder, where is she?"

Although I should have been expecting that question, I still felt like shit when I lied to her about it. But I didn't want her to think Luciano had murdered her. She had lost enough, and if I could preserve the memory she had of him, it would be worth it.

"I don't know."

There was no use in opening another wound. It was time for her to leave the past and begin to move forward.

ENDLESS SUMMER

It was in my darkest moments that I searched for an endless
summer.
Something to take away the pain, to overshadow all the rain.
It was in my darkest moments that I needed one single
reason to live.
Something to make me feel pure and whole.
So I wouldn't give up on the world.

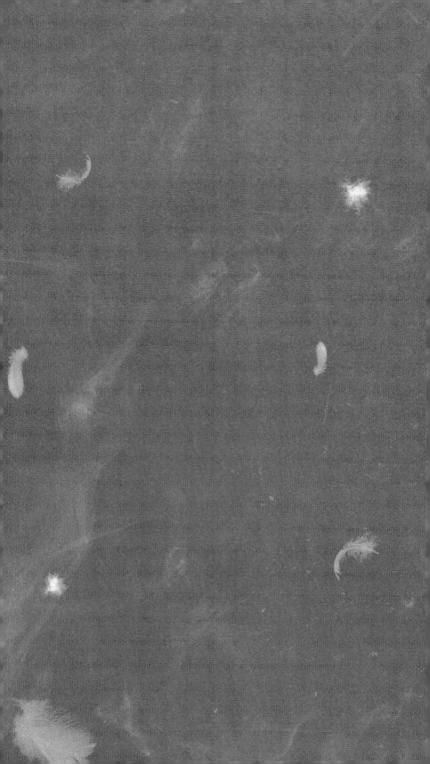

30

SUMMER

Spring was supposed to represent a fresh new start, but I always thought there was something magical about summer. The sun would burn a little brighter; the heat waves would incinerate any lingering feelings you wished to forget. Summer was fun and full of mischief, full of life and vibrancy.

Summer was full of late nights under the sky, mistakes that we looked back on somewhat fondly. I wanted to forget everything, including my own name, and let myself find solace in one endless summer.

Perhaps I had been a bit delusional about putting all my energy into maintaining my façade, but at the time, it was all I had left to give. Annalisa Ferro had died the moment she lost her eyesight. Summer was born on a dark stage, wearing a white tutu. It was like the time I had spent in the House of Silence never existed. There was no point in having any lingering feelings for the girl I could have been—the heiress to Ferro Beauty.

Luke's breathing was calm and spaced out, an indication that he was sleeping. We got home late last night. He didn't ask me if I wanted to go back to the house; he brought me to his penthouse and carried me to his room. Maybe he did it for himself, or maybe he did it for me, but that house was already tainted with too many bad memories. Luke bathed me and then changed me into one of my night-gowns. He kissed and held me tight until we fell back asleep.

It might have been hours or days, but it was the best rest I'd had as of late.

Luke had an arm wrapped around my middle. It was possessive, even if he wasn't lucid. One of my hands came up, and with the pad of my finger, I traced the outer edge of his face. Our scars connected us more than our familiar ties did.

Where would we have been if I had accepted help from him? I was blind before I even lost my eyesight; I think most humans are. We let ourselves get blinded by hate, grief, and anger, not keeping sight of the things that were important. Life passed in the blink of an eye, even if you weren't ready for it to go by.

Now that I was allowed to touch him, I couldn't stop—not until I knew his face like I did all the bumps and ridges on my own hand.

"Good morning, my little dove," he murmured.

In the end, forgiving Luke had been easy. His words were intended to maim me, and perhaps they would have if he had not done everything in his power to enable me to stand stronger than before.

After all, he did warn me and riddle me with clues, I had been the one who refused to trust their instincts. I didn't need to see to recognize when every part of me flour-ished in the Ferro estate because it was home.

Luke nurtured me and forced me to grow, letting me get

my strength and confidence back before he tore it all down with hopes that it wouldn't kill me.

"Hi," I whispered, still not entirely convinced that everything had been one hell of a dream.

"How are you feeling?" Luke asked as he began to play with my hair.

For someone who had been closed off, he was incredibly touchy and affectionate, even if he didn't say so with pretty words. At the end of the day, pretty words were just words with no meaning unless actions were behind them.

It was easy to forgive Luke because I felt and witnessed the actions of his love, and that was something I would not have been able to do if I had my sight. Because the facial expressions of his betrayal would have been etched in my brain, making it near impossible to move on.

All I had were the words he had said, but his words did not align with the actions he had shown me.

"I think I've had enough excitement for a lifetime," I let him know.

Luke pressed his mouth to my cheek and gave me a half smile. "No more, my dove. I can promise you that."

And I believed him.

What a pair we were.

My hand went from our matching scars to being entwined in his hair. There was something so freeing about being able to kiss someone just because you felt like it. His lips against mine felt divine. They made me feel whole— Luke made me feel beautiful.

He took control of the kiss, and as my arms wrapped around him, he laid me on my back with him on top of me.

My legs spread to accommodate him. Now that there were no boundaries to stick to, my hands touched every part of his skin they came in contact with. I was learning every scar, every ridge mapping his body, with my hands and lips.

His chest was firm, with a light sprinkle of hair around his pecs, and his abs were taut and defined. There were scars on his body from when he used to be Lucas Greco. Pain was the easiest thing to *see*, even for a blind person. It left all kinds of marks. The physical ones were easy—you could touch them—but the internal ones were still there, defining a person from the way they talked to you, how they breathed, and all the things they left unsaid.

My hand stopped at the hard ridge that was on his side. This was the scar that brought him into my life.

Luke kissed between my brows as I caressed his scar. His breath hitched when my hand explored lower into the light trail of hair that disappeared into the waistband of his pajama pants.

"Summer," he warned.

I bit my lip and wrapped my legs around him, tilting my hips until I met with his hardness.

Our first time had been frenzied and full of anger, but I didn't regret it. At the time, it was what I needed. Even if it wasn't ideal, it was something that helped me feel like I was taking back my power.

"Luke." My hands cupped his cheeks.

I liked the stubble and the way it felt against my palms. I could feel his lips pull into a grin as I kept rubbing my hands against him.

"You like that?" His voice had dropped in tone, and my core clenched in anticipation.

Luke's hands went under my nightgown. His warm palms slid up my thighs, and he hooked his index fingers on either side of my panties and began to draw them down. He kissed under my chin, then my neck. He pulled back so he could finish ridding me of my underwear.

"You'll like this even more," he rasped as he began to kiss his way up my legs.

He bunched my nightgown to my hips. My legs quivered with anticipation for his next move. My back arched when I felt his hot breath at my core. Luke pressed soft kisses into the apex of my legs, then my thighs. I could feel how wet I was getting, how I was spread eagle for him, and I felt my cheeks heat.

"Luke," I whimpered.

His tongue slid between my folds, seeking my clit.

"Shh, I'm about to have my breakfast," he groaned into my pussy before he began to suck on my clit.

My body jolted at the contact, and he used this to his advantage and gripped my hips, then moved them closer to his face.

He alternated between kissing me and licking me, his stubble rubbing against me each time he moved. When he inserted two fingers inside of me, I cried out. Luke hooked his fingers at the same time he began to suck on my clit.

"*Luke!*" I rode his face as I came, my fingers entwined in his hair as he lapped me up like I was his last meal.

When Luke kissed me, I could taste my own arousal on his lips.

"Let me make love to you."

As if I was going to deny his plea.

I answered him by removing my nightgown. The bed creaked as he pulled back. When he was hovering on top of me, I wrapped my legs around his waist once more, but this time, he was naked as well.

Nothing stood between us now. No secrets, no resentment, and the need we still had for each other had not gone away.

"Your pussy is so pretty and swollen, begging to be filled with my dick." His voice was dripping with lust.

My needy moan had him holding on to my waist as he filled me with one hard thrust.

"So good," I breathed.

"*God, Summer.*" He pulled out only to thrust back in.

He began to suck on my neck. I could feel his lips by my artery. The way he was devouring me would leave a mark, and that turned me on even more. After a few seconds, he stopped moving and pressed his forehead against mine.

"You have no idea how incredibly lucky I feel to be the one you trust to give your body to." He kissed between my eyes, then down to my nose. "That you give your body so willingly to me." His kiss was slow because now we had all the time in the world. One of his hands moved to where we were connected, and he circled my clit with his thumb. "That I get to please this needy pussy whenever I want."

His hips began to move faster, as did his thumb. His heavy breathing, my pants, and the noises of our bodies connecting were all I could hear.

"You're going to come so fucking hard for me, aren't you, Summer?"

"Luke," I whined, feeling like I was at the edge.

He pressed his mouth to my cheek and smiled against it. I loved that he did that because otherwise, I would never know when he smiled while looking at me.

"If you let me, I'll love you for the rest of my life." It wasn't a statement but a vow.

I moved my face and sought his mouth. I kissed him like he was the air I needed to breathe, the colors that I would never get to see. He was the part of me that allowed me to jump into the unknown wild and free.

When I came, I finally felt like I was flying because this high was freeing and liberating, knowing that I would not fall as long as Luke was there.

WHEN I WOKE LATER THAT DAY, THERE WAS A WARM, furry body pressed to my side. I sat up immediately and hugged Bear. He licked my face as his tail wagged with joy. I knew Luke said Bear was okay, but having him in my arms and touching him made this day even better.

Something else was in the bed beside Bear. I moved my hands and smiled when I felt my cane and his two leashes.

Putting on Bear's service leash, I let him guide me out of the room while I used my cane to feel my new surroundings. When we made it down the stairs, I could hear Luke's voice. He was probably on the phone with Pedro, figuring out the next step for the company.

"I don't care. I just never want to see them again," he spat. "The only reason they're not dead is because my father wouldn't want that."

Conflicted feelings assaulted me. I knew he had to be talking about Cecilia and her daughter. It made me sad because she had been someone I had trusted, and that trust almost got me killed. I felt worse for Luke because this betrayal cut him deeper.

I walked closer to him, and I could smell the menthol from his cigarette. He extended one arm toward me and then enveloped me into his body. I liked that he needed to feel me close.

"Probably not for a while, so just make sure everything is in place and come back."

Once he hung up the phone, he kissed the top of my head.

"How are you feeling?"

"Lighter than I have in years."

"Good," he uttered.

He sat me down in a chair while he fed Bear and made us a sandwich.

"What do you want to do about the company?"

I stopped mid-bite at his question. My brows scrunched in confusion.

"What do you mean?"

"It's your birthright. I was just keeping everything in order because I'd rather it be me than that bastard."

"You want *me* to be the face of a beauty company?"

"Summer," he warned.

"I know nothing about running a company," I told him.

"I can teach you." His voice was gentle and sincere.

I shook my head. "I don't want it. That part of me died a long time ago."

Luke cupped my cheeks, and one of his thumbs traced the edges of my scars. I could hear him clearing his throat. "If you want, we can make consultations with the best plastic surgeons."

"You'd do that for me?" My voice wavered.

I never imagined that I could live without my scars.

"I'd do anything for you. I want you to be happy, and if that makes you happy, I'll make it happen."

I thought about it for a second, and I could feel the heat of his stare on my face. Regardless of whether the scars remained or not, the impact left on me would always remain. I must have taken too long to answer because Luke kissed each side of my eyes.

"You'll be beautiful either way, little dove."

This time, I cupped his face.

"Luke..." I murmured his name with a smile. "I'm on my way to being happy just the way I am."

He gave me a peck on my lips.

"I love you," he told me, and I knew he meant every word of it.

"I love you too."

He smiled against my lips, letting me know he, too, was happy.

We talked about both the important things and the silly things. For now, we both agreed to remain in the city. He would work out something with Eve and get the board and company under control.

It was scary to finally soar without restraints, but it was hauntingly beautiful.

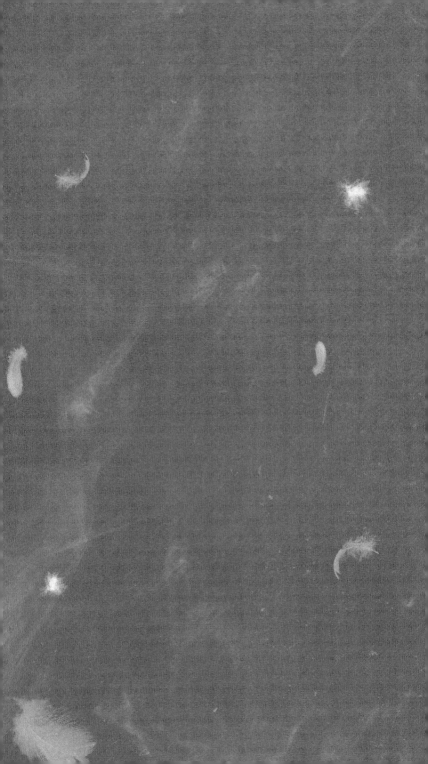

EPILOGUE

A few weeks later

Living in the city was overwhelming—or maybe I had gotten used to my peaceful oasis at the house. Although the penthouse had a balcony, it wasn't the same. I missed the purpose my flowers would bring me. I was glad I still had Bear to keep me company.

My days were spent with Bear. I mostly practiced my braille or listened to audiobooks. My afternoons were spent with Luke as we figured out how to cook together or explored our surroundings, searching for takeout. Neither one of us trusted anyone enough to come to stay with us. Luke didn't trust anyone with my life, perhaps only Pedro, but he preferred to keep to his own.

Living in the city did have some perks. The fact that there were more shops and restaurants. The other day, Luke surprised me by giving me a card in case I ever wanted to wander down with Bear while he was at work. It meant the world to me to know that he knew I could get around when he wasn't here, even if he didn't like me wandering alone. He also gave me cash, and when I tried to refuse, he gave me a pocket money brailler that stamped the bills so I would know their amount.

While Eve tutored me and taught me all things academic and how to use the technology that was available for people like me, Luke taught me to live.

He taught me how to play poker with the braille card deck he bought me. He randomly came home with games designed for me: Chutes and Ladders, dominoes, and a wooden tic-tac-toe set.

I fell even more in love because he played with me just so I could regain a little bit of the life I had lost.

One thing I loved about this apartment was the smart system he had installed. If I wanted a song, all I had to do was ask; same for checking the weather or if I wanted to make a call.

I had finally gone to visit my father and my uncle. It was hard because although I knew I loved my dad with everything I had in me as a little girl, that part of me was gone. As for my uncle, it was hard to reconcile my conflicting feelings. I knew he had not been the one to sell me out, but the level of hate and hurt I had for him had not disappeared completely, but I did love him, and it didn't hurt to admit it anymore.

My mother was another thing. I was happy that her memory was fading. It was for the best. Wherever she'd ended up, I hoped it was all worth it to her.

A ding went through the penthouse, alerting me that the door was open, and I sighed in relief. I hated thinking about my mother, and instead, I smiled.

The first day Luke went back to work, he startled me upon his return. A few days later, he had a security system installed, and he'd added that extra feature for my benefit.

"You're back early!" I exclaimed as I got up from the couch and headed toward the door.

"Meetings are more productive now." His answer was a bit tight-lipped since neither one of us wanted to talk about *him*.

"Want to take Bear on a walk? Maybe we can get some lunch along the way?" I grinned, trying to ease the tension.

"Let me get his things, and we will get going."

With one arm wrapped around Luke and another holding on to Bear's leash, there was no need for my cane.

We were trying to find a new place to get lunch when my heart stopped at the familiar melody drifting from the building we were about to pass.

"It's a dance studio," Luke said right away upon noticing my confusion.

"Can we go in?" I asked.

He led me toward the door. Since Bear was a service dog, there weren't many places he was denied.

As soon as we walked through the doors, the smell inside was one that had once saved me. There must've been something written on my face because Luke whispered in my ear, "You miss dancing, don't you?"

"Not like this," I let him know before he tried to do something about it.

My stuff was at the house somewhere in my old room, and even if he brought it to me, I didn't know if I could use it. Everything there felt tainted.

We walked farther in, and sure enough, I could hear the acts used in *Danza dei Morti*. Had the dance really made that much of an impact in the dancing world?

I heard the soft whoosh of a paper by my ear.

"They're holding auditions for *Dance of the Dead*." He sounded as confused as I felt.

There was no way this was Nico. To the world, he was dead, so whoever was doing this was trying to profit from someone else's work, or they knew he was not dead and were looking to lure him out.

"Let's get out of here." His voice was low and alert, probably coming to the same conclusion as I had.

If whoever was bringing this act from the dead knew the company and what it stood for, then they would recognize me.

"Stay close, Bear," he commanded the dog.

Luke's hand wrapped around my waist protectively, and he began to walk us out when suddenly someone called my name.

I stopped dead in my tracks, but Luke kept walking, dragging me along.

"Summer?"

It was a soft, feminine voice that I couldn't immediately place.

I tugged on Luke's shirt to let him know it was okay to stop. He did so but didn't let me go. I maneuvered my body so I could face whoever was talking to me.

"Ohmigod, it is you!" The woman rushed to me and grabbed my hands—something that Luke didn't like by the way he grunted—and pressed them to her face.

A smile tugged at my lips because there was only one person who did that whenever they greeted me. I could feel wavy hair tickling my knuckles as I touched a face that had changed in the time I had been gone.

"Clarissa," I said her name, and she giggled.

I didn't know her full story, but I did know that she was the youngest out of all of us. She wasn't as fucked-up as the rest, and she had been our joy when the months at sea got rough.

"You look great." She beamed. "Your boyfriend is hot."

"That's good to know. I was positive he had lied about his good looks."

Luke pinched my side, losing some of his tension.

"We should catch up. I don't know anyone yet, and I'm happy I ran into you."

All I could do was nod. I knew Luke wanted to get out of here, so I exchanged numbers with her and figured we could talk another time.

After a few minutes of walking with enough space between us and the dance studio, Luke finally spoke.

"She was part of it, I assume?"

"Yes, the youngest out of all of us."

"Fuck," he whispered.

I turned my face toward him and waited patiently for him to explain.

"I'm going to have to contact Nico and let him know about this. I also don't think she should audition—"

"Clarissa never danced with us," I told him. "Before it all came crashing down, she was the prima ballerina's understudy. I heard them say that Clarissa's talent was sure to surpass Ofelia's one day."

"She's going to get the part, then," Luke murmured, none too pleased about this turn of events.

"So, when they start touring, I'm guessing we won't be seeing them?"

Luke's growl was almost comical.

LUKE

A few weeks later

There was something peaceful about living after weathering your storms. The drive from the city to the manor was long, but I figured Summer needed this. She liked the city, liked the independence she felt out in the streets, but in a way, she still felt caged there.

After a few discussions, we agreed that we shouldn't let anyone win. The manor was once her safe haven, and I was determined to make it so once again. If the problem couldn't be fixed, then we could burn it down and rebuild it from the ashes.

Summer rested her head on my shoulder as we made our way down the driveway. Pedro was driving, and Bear was in the front, happily letting his face out the window. When we arrived, I held her hand as we walked up toward the door.

"Is there anything else you need?"

She seemed to think about it. The stuff from the library had already been moved to the penthouse. She had more clothes now than she did when she arrived here all those months ago. The piano and the swing were picked up last week. Other than that, I didn't think she'd want anything else.

Summer shook her head.

"Do you want to go in one last time?"

Another shake.

I brought her body in front of me and wrapped my arms around her middle, my hands resting on her belly. She wasn't pregnant, and we weren't being careful, but I couldn't help but hope that maybe things would work out for us.

"I love you," I told her as I kissed the top of her head.

She twisted her head sideways so she could face me. Those turquoise eyes always slayed me. They were nothing like the ones her cunt of a mother had. What good did it do for her to have seeing eyes if they were still fucking dead?

"I love you too," she said with a smile.

Pedro nodded as he came back out, letting me know everything was ready. Once he was near us, I could smell the trail of gasoline he was leaving behind.

"Come on, my little dove. We have to move."

Once she and Bear were far enough, I left her with Pedro while I jogged back toward the house, getting close enough so I could light the bitch on fire. This house had saved me and condemned me, and now it was time to burn all those memories and build a new foundation.

Money solved all problems, so I wasn't worried about the repercussions that would come from the police.

The place caught on fire rapidly. The heat from the flames was so fucking close to my face it was making me sweat. I pulled a smoke from my back pocket and took my time making it toward the left wing. Pedro opened the window to the only room in use before walking out.

When I finally made it to my destination, I stood still as I inhaled, letting the burn of the cigarette calm me. Faint, pained screams carried in the hot wind. Instead of enjoying the last piece of my revenge, I felt relieved.

I didn't have the heart to tell Summer her mother was alive and had been residing under the same roof as her for months. For all intents and purposes, Melissa had died on that same day Summer had lost her sight because what was left behind was a shell of the bitch she once had been. Luciano would have succeeded in choking the bitch had Summer not interrupted. With all the chaos, he failed, but the damage done to her brain by the lack of oxygen remained.

I stood there for a few more seconds until the screams stopped.

Finally, no more secrets. Once we rebuilt, it would be a fresh start for both of us. Summer was clutching Bear's leash as she stood close to Pedro. A bigger security team for a while would make her feel safer, I imagined.

"What took you so long?" she asked as my footsteps got near them.

"Just saying goodbye." It wasn't a lie.

I pulled Summer into my arms. I kissed between her eyes first. I did it so she didn't doubt that I found her beautiful, and then I placed a kiss on her lips.

"I'm thinking I'm going to build you a bigger greenhouse, and we can put the piano in your dance room, maybe an indoor pool, and definitely a hot tub," I told her. She seemed pleased by these plans, but then her smile dropped.

"I've been doing good. I hope coming back doesn't trigger any panic attacks," she whispered, and Pedro and I shared a look.

"You'll be fine, my dove." It was a promise.

The reason for those panic attacks was nothing but burnt flesh now.

The first panic attack was due to the fact that the door to the left wing was left open by the cleaning crew. Melissa had wandered off, and even if her brain was not all there, she must have recognized something in Summer. For some reason, the bitch tried choking her. When I walked into the room, I almost killed her. I was positive that Summer would have questioned her attack, but since she couldn't see and her brain was in fight-or-fly mode, the last thing she would conjure up on her own was that someone had tried to kill her. Lying to her about what had happened was easier than

I thought it would be. She believed the lie, and I could live with this because it kept her inner peace intact.

The time I found her curled up by the edge of her bed was because the night before, Cecilia had brought Melissa out for some fresh air in the greenhouse. Summer could probably feel her stare burning into her but didn't know why she felt uneasy.

And the final time had been in the lab right before she was taken. Cecilia had been feeding Melissa when they both heard someone come into the lab. If it wasn't for Pedro walking in, Melissa would have probably killed Summer.

"Thank you, Luke," she said, breaking through my thoughts.

"For what?"

"For teaching me to fly."

And just like that, nothing else mattered.

THANK YOU

For taking the time to read Broken Dove.
My Dm's/ Emails are always open for you guys. If you liked this book and even if you didn't I would appreciate it if you could leave an honest review.

Stay Tuned for **Black Bird** coming soon

You can add to your TBR- https://bit.ly/blackbirdkindle

And Preorder Here- https://mybook.to/blackbirdkindle

ACKNOWLEDGMENTS

Thank you so much for taking the time and picking up another one of my books. It means the world to me that you guys show up release after release.

Becca & Jenny you guys are my rocks! Johhnaka I am sorry for stressing you out lol

Kristen and Sue, you guys are my dream team! Daddy is happy with you guys!

To my Master Bloggers, you guys are awesome; thank you for all the support this wouldn't be possible without all your hard work!

To my ARC team and Coffee Shop, thanks for continuing to be on this journey with me.

To Rumi & Sandra, I am so so sorry I am a massive pain in the ass. I love and appreciate you guys! Thank you for making my babies shine.

Cat, you always slay baby. Thank you for helping me make this book something I can be proud of.

ABOUT THE AUTHOR

Claudia lives in the Chicagoland suburbs, and when she's not busy chasing after her adorable little spawn, she's fighting with the characters in her head. After not being able to keep up with them, she decided enough was enough and wrote her first novel.

Claudia writes both sweet and dark romances that will give you all the feels. Her other talents include binge watching shows on Netflix, obsessing over 2D men, and eating all kinds of chips.

If you want to know more, you can always find her here:

Reader Group: Claudia's Coffee Shop
www.clymaribooks.com

facebook.com/c.lymari

instagram.com/c.lymari

amazon.com/author/clymari

tiktok.com/@c.lymari

goodreads.com/clymaribooks

Printed by Amazon Italia Logistica S.r.l.
Torrazza Piemonte (TO), Italy

51097097R00206